Irem of the Crimson Desert

Farzana Moon

Irem of the Crimson Desert

Copyright © 2010 by Farzana Moon

This is a work of fiction. Any resemblance to actual persons, living or
dead, is purely coincidental.

ISBN 13: 9780984621613
Library of Congress Control Number: 2010912310

Cover design by All Things That Matter Press
Published in 2010 by All Things That Matter Press

Dedicated to Shashi dearest
One of those rarest of friends who love — grandly and unselfishly

Irem indeed is gone with all its rose
And Jamshed's sev'n-ringed cup where no one knows
But still the wine her ancient ruby yields
And still a Garden by the water blows   Omar Khayyam

Fragrant and awesome is the Garden of Irem mentioned in the Quran. Lost to the world, but still existing under the winged shadows of time and timelessness.

Sophia seated by the tranquil stream called Lake Shisha could see mirrored in its depths the entire Garden of Irem. Her thoughts, too, were reflected shuddering inside the sparkling pools of her eyes, rather twinkling over the blue lagoons of waters like stars, bright and capricious. Suddenly, the palm tree under which she sat shook like a rickety ladder, startling her from her abode of reveries.

No, the tree is as solid as this dumb plateau in the wilderness of Aden.

Sophia gathered her silvery skirt around her ankles. One crescent of a smile was frozen over her poppy-red lips like a fresh wound. The fronds of the palm tree suspended midway down the stream with their arms stretched like guardian angels were absorbing her attention. A cold sigh escaped her heart, fogging the waters with a thin film of foam as if an invisible blanket of grief was lowered over the ruins of Oman in this lost city of Ubar.

One gossamer web of a shawl strewn with stars was Sophia's only raiment, woven with secret charms, and draped over her sinuous body in seductive folds, cascading down to her feet in ripples soft and shimmering. Sophia had been sitting by Lake Shisha since eons, her heart longing for her lost lover who had disappeared into some philosophic retreat, abandoning her and both the worlds, corporal and temporal. Centuries upon centuries of wait slashed with countless incantations, and she had been granted a glimpse of her lover, lending her the knife of hope to carve a path of union with her love lost and love unforgotten. Sophia—the goddess of wisdom, spurned by gods for falling in love with a mortal philosopher who had died, but was resurrected by his own eternal desire for love to dissolve all barriers of separation amongst the multitude of lovers and beloveds. A great abyss was surfacing from under the fog of grief from Sophia's eyes. A sparkle and a glimmer, and she gasped, her gaze tracing the seven-ringed cup, sinking and foundering.

> *They say the lion and lizard keep*
> *The courts where Jamshed gloried and drank deep*
> *And Bahram' that great hunter—the wild ass*
> *Stamps o'er his head, but cannot break his sleep* Omar Khayyam

Sophia almost fell into the Lake, visited by Omar Khayyam in her psyche for what seemed to be but a few minutes, or that's what she thought. But her gaze was searching the gold cup diving and swaying frantically amidst the grove of frankincense, above which stood yawning the reflection of Dhofar Mountains, dark and towering. A scream of anguish, washed by the gold of joy was stifled inside Sophia as the hand which held the seven-ringed cup traced a circle of light where Jamshed was visible, seated on his throne with all splendor inside the very heart of Azerbaijan.

"Isn't it the Takhti-Jamshed, and the glorious king holding the cup of immortality no other but Jamshed?" Sophia murmured aloud under some spell of awe, forgetting the wilderness of Aden all around her. It appeared to be rising aloft to greet the night stars in great clusters.

"Yes, fair Goddess, an unfortunate king, holding on to this empty cup!" Jamshed's voice was sad and clear, much like the rippling of songs from a lone cataract. "God's grace and radiance are gone from me, and the elixir of immortality is drained from this cup."

"A king, indeed," Sophia murmured again, lost into the sherry pools of his eyes which danced and sparkled in affinity with the jewels on his throne. His purple robe with gold stars glittered in rhythm with his crown studded with amethysts. And yet, his pallor glowed brighter than the moonlit vistas over the rocks and sand-dunes polished to crystal brilliance.

"A king robbed of his wit and wisdom, and wounded by a cupid's arrow! Eternally damned in his quest to find his beloved in the Garden of Irem which seems lost and obliterated." Jamshed's throne shuddered in the waters much like a ship doomed to sinking, his handsome features washed by waves of pain and despair. "A few glimpses of Irem I have had in between intervals of oblivion and lucidity, and yet all is gone. Lucky chance, my Jam-e-Jam filled with incantations found you! I must write this incantation on the tablet of my heart, lest I forget. Come, Sophia, help me find my beautiful Beloved."

"Alas, O King, centuries lie barren between me and my Beloved, and I haven't found him yet." Sophia lamented to the shuddering vision under her gaze, the periwinkle blue in her eyes sharp and dazzling. "With your seven-ringed cup you are the *master* of the earth and the heavens. Encrusted in there are seven seas and seven planets, and seven heavens. With this Cup you can find anyone, anywhere, no matter how remote and how far yonder, high above and deep under, so why this hopelessness? I should be the one imploring you, O King of the world, to find my lover!"

"A king of the four worlds, alack, and fourth king of the world, no more, no more!" Jamshed swirled his cup between his fingers, his signet-ring of large ruby throbbing like a wound. "Phraortes, Darius and Cyrus ruled before me, yet I ruled the best. Priests, warriors, farmers, and artisans were my four kingdoms within a kingdom. For seven hundred years I ruled with such wisdom and justice that people lived long; sickness became nonexistent, and all were content, living in peace and prosperity. For the sin of my pride, God abandoned me. All the magic is gone from this cup, the luster is—"

A great wave from down under tilted the throne, Jamshed clutching tight his seven-ringed cup to his breast. The waves lapping over the turbulent waters were churning a spray of froth, almost devouring the king and his throne.

"Don't leave me, O King!" Sophia screamed down the whirlwind of waters, roaring and foaming. "Do you remember the incantation which brought us together?"

"Odd numbers of magic and enchantment." Jamshed's voice was muffled, as if placating the angry spirits. "My Jam-e-Jam of magical number seven, yes, my seven-ringed Cup! Nine towers of exquisite splendor, cradling the Garden of Irem. Eleven nights of enchantment, fashioning the palace of Irem, the number of transgression! Thirteen sublime verses from the living, glorious Quran."

Lake Shisha had become an emblem of tranquility in a flash, as if no turbulence had ever churned its waters. Now it was shining clear and solid like a bright mirror. Reflected in its polished depths were pillars of alabaster, looming over a palace studded with onyx. Its façade was trimmed with gold, and encrusted with jewels precious and sparkling. Jamshed seated upon his gorgeous throne with Jam-e-Jam poised before him, seemed to be gazing into the eyes of his own magic-mirror, his features transfigured with joy and wonder.

Sophia was concentrating to pry into his world through his own Jam-e-Jam, and succeeding quite swiftly and astonishingly. Twelve halls with fluted pillars, cradling one Zodiac sign, each in clusters of jewels, were brighter than the entire dome of a firmament housing sun, moon and stars. These stars were no ordinary stars, more dazzling than the large diamonds honed to perfection.

Beneath that luminescent globe stretched quite far and beyond mortal sight, were layers upon layers of mists gossamer, and shimmering.

Some sort of violence was erupting forth from deep within the mists, rainbows swirling and bolts of lightning piercing the heart of Lake Shisha. The fireworks of lightning were revealing a vaulted Garden, its pearly gates swung open, boasting the bliss of Eden with all its beauty of fruits, flowers and orchards. Sophia's gaze was riveted to the sylvan and floral wealth of Eden, her heart jumping right into one azure stream as limpid as beryl, espying upon its banks the loveliest of creatures she had not ever seen before, not even in her imagination. This flower of a girl in silvery gown of stars and crescents appeared to be singing, her fingers moving over the strings of the silver lyre at her breast. One tremor of a scream escaped Sophia's lips as she noticed her lover sleeping at the feet of this young girl, his blue silk robe as vivid as the night sky, and his long, white beard just a spray of moonbeams.

"Ibrahim, my only love and true lover," Sophia's voice was seething down Lake Shisha with the hiss of serpentine lightning. "Wake up, wake up, come back."

"Aleena, sweet Beloved, don't disappear! Show me the way to the Garden of Irem, to be with you!" Jamshed's voice was a lament, loud and excruciating.

Mists upon mists were enveloping the Garden of Irem into thick fogs, blocking out the many-columned Irem, along with the paradise and the beloveds. Incantations from deep under were grazing Sophia's avalanche of agony and despair.

Magical number seven, Jam-e-Jam! Nine exquisite towers guarding the Garden! Eleven nights of enchantment to build the palace of Irem. Thirteen sublime verses of Light. All odd numbers seeking the forty nights of vigil!

Jam-e-Jam was the first object to appear before Sophia's gaze, the beat of her heart catching the rhythm of the incantations she had heard but recently. Her heart was murmuring prayers. Takhti-Jamshed was coming into view, the king still reciting incantations. His own gaze was arrested to the seven-ringed cup clutched between his hands, his knuckles white and glistening. His expression was one of awe and surrender, as if the whole wide world was shoved into his hands, and he had no will to hold it intact. The turbulence in the stream was abated and the trees of Paradise were sprouting everywhere. Golden trees with multicolored trunks were bearing not only fruits, but jewels and jewel-blossoms most exquisite in size and color. The scent of figs, dates, and pears was reaching Sophia, but her senses were already swooning against the heavy scent of musk, ginger and camphor.

"I have found you again, Sophia." Jamshed was watching her through Jam-e-Jam. "That's the scent from Paradise your senses are catching and holding, release it slowly and consciously. Did you see my Aleena? Alas, I can't reach her!"

"And my philosopher, O King, grown so old and bewitched!" Was Sophia's startled lament!

"Did you not see the Garden of Irem?" Jamshed's voice was urgent and strained. "We must never let go of each other and stay in constant communication. That's the only way to break through this enchantment, to visit the Garden again and again."

By the dawn
And ten nights
And the even and the odd
And the night when it departeth
There surely is an oath for thinking man
Dost thou not consider how Thy Lord dealt with the Tribe of Aad
With many-columned Irem
The like of which was not created in the lands
And with the tribe of Thamud who clove the rocks in the valley
And with Pharaoh firm of might

Who all were rebellious to Allah in those lands
And multiplied iniquity therein
Therefore thy Lord poured on them the disaster
of His punishment.   89:1-13

A great tide with cosmic wrath was lowering this Quranic verse, while the waters of Lake Shisha were turning glassy and turbulent. Sophia's gaze was whipping the agitated waves apart to reach down the shore of tranquility. Her gaze itself was searching Takhti-Jamshed as if her heart was stung by the arrow of cupid to love no one but King Jamshed. She was aghast and overwhelmed by this sudden hurricane of passion inside her, demanding a glimpse of the king, and abandoning her old philosopher inside the Garden of Irem. After centuries of anguished search for her lost lover, and now maddeningly and astonishingly her seat of love was shifted toward the young king. The weight of wisdom in her head was crushing her thoughts to smithereens, commanding caution and restraint if she was to succeed in winning the love of this handsome king. The beauty of the girl with the silver lyre was awakening the serpent of jealousy within her, but her gaze was frantically following the glimmer of Jam-e-Jam appearing and disappearing like the flight of a firefly.

"Ah, Sophia, my intellect is rusted, and I can't be united with Aleena until you help me!" Jamshed upon his throne was coming into view, his look wild and woebegone. "I have mastered the incantations which would keep us together. Between the two of us, we would rip apart the veils of illusions. Can you see me, Sophia?"

"Yes, fortunately." Sophia could barely hold her sigh of pain and relief. "My wisdom is on the verge of expiring. How many veils of illusions?"

"Countless, if the hand of magic stays numb!" Jamshed's voice was opiate, his Jam-e-Jam secured in his lap perfectly. "Forty nights of vigil to break just one veil of illusion in forty zillion times four of light years!"

"That Garden was no illusion though, O King!" Sophia began tremulously, her heart longing to embrace the king and his lost kingdom. "Isn't Irem the earthly paradise—the replica of heavenly paradise, promised to the believers in life hereafter, shrouded in the mists of magic and mystery?"

"A desert of illusion, Sophia—this Aden and the lost city of Ubar, which holds you prisoner in its tentacles of spells and enchantments!" Jamshed appeared to study the ruby in his signet-ring. "And yet, dare I expound? Garden of Irem is illusion of this world and the illusion of Paradise in the world hereafter. Hence, a great illusion this tempest of life and death, isn't it obvious? Life aspiring for immortality, and death drumming the beat of mortality, and we lowly mortals loving the eternal dance of magic and mystery, fleeing light, embracing darkness."

Allah is the light of the heavens and the earth
The similitude of His light is a lustrous niche
Wherein is a lamp, the lamp is in a glass
The glass as if it were a glittering star
It is lit by a blessed tree—an olive
Neither of the east nor of the west
Whose oil will well nigh glow forth
Though fire toucheth is not
Light upon light
Allah guides to His light whomsoever He wills
And Allah sets forth parables to men
Allah knows all things full well 24:35

A choir of angels, it seemed, was raining down this revelation. It was pouring beads of mercy—pearly raindrops, braiding Sophia's hair into a coronet of jewels, radiant and reflecting colors of the rainbows. Sophia's heart was on fire, flames of longings inside her sharp and stabbing.

"Did you hear that revelation from the Quran, O King?" Sophia appealed, her thoughts challenging her to drown herself so that she could reach Jamshed, but she knew the futility of such madness. She was trying her best to tie her thoughts into neat, little bundles of discipline, while commanding her heart to wield the oars of patience for many chasms and centuries before she could join him.

"Is he not already consumed by the fire of love for Aleena?" Sophia was thinking, but aloud she said. "Is this an illusion, too, you and me talking? And this Jam-e-Jam of yours, through which you may behold the earth and the heavens, the Prophet and the prophets, illusions all?"

"All illusions! Neither of the east nor of the west, illusions everywhere." Jamshed's gaze was dreamy and poetic. "I was dead and forgotten since centuries when the gold-dust of such revelations was scattered over the sands of Arabia. Yes, illusions grand and quicksilver. Vast and boundless is the ocean of mind where lands and seas merge and coalesce, defining no borders and erecting no boundaries. The compass of time shuddering over the poles of north, south, east and west, is nothing but a splinter of universal imagination, fashioned by mankind to keep their own selves entertained by the gullies of blood inside the desert of contentions."

"Foolish of me to ask, O King, but in this scheme of illusions, how could you be certain that you are still, not *dead*?" Sophia was lost into the sherry pools of king's eyes. "And that those revelations which we heard are nothing but the figments of our own imagination?"

"Many deaths I have known and many lives squandered! But this birth is the child of reality and illusion both, since I have journeyed inside the ether of spirituality where Islam is the first valley of knowledge over the borderless kingdom of God, Allah,

Beloved, all in one!" Jamshed's pallor was accentuated by the moonlit vistas towering over his throne. "Directions have no meaning. East, west, north and south dissolve and disappear into the river of unity. Four poles of the world are minarets of imagination, piercing the heart of the sky. They come crashing down as the circlets of unity, appearing and disappearing within the circle of universal whole. The mirror of cosmic reality reflecting the dance of ego and illusion."

"What is cosmic reality?" Sophia asked, more so to keep the vision of Jamshed arrested inside the waters of Lake Shisha, than to replenish the treasury of her depleted wisdom."

"Cosmic reality itself is the mother of illusion!" Jamshed was looking into his seven-ringed cup, his crown of amethysts ablaze. "Illusion of the world which we see, feel and touch through our senses, and illusion of the paradise which we perceive through the breath of divine presence! When one's divine spirit awakens to the perfume of beauty within and without at all levels of awareness, one begins to see beauty in each speck of universe and in each mystery of the heavens. All attracted toward the pole of reality which we call God in its essence of love and majesty, beyond which nothing exists but light upon light. This light is accentuated by darkness of the universal soul which seems crystallized into a mountain of pain, grief, sorrow, and inside the cycles of birth and death." He seemed oblivious of his own state of being. "And yet again, this darkness, with its chunks of woes, is another illusion against the veil of ignorance. Ignorance is strong and mighty, creating barriers where none exist, sundering apart nations and territories which are kneaded solid into the dough of existence. The long, sinewy hands of ignorance are wrapped around the necks of all mortals, teasing the harps of their perceptions where beauty as the seat of reality disintegrates, carving chunks of tragedies and afflictions which are neither of this world, nor of the world hereafter. The afflictions which we see, feel and touch every moment of our lives are the phantoms of our inner fears and desires which could be easily whisked away, if we could behold the face of beauty as beauty incarnate!" His gaze was restless and searching.

"Are you beholding the face of beauty, O King, or wondering why we suffer?" Sophia's heart, smitten with love, was devising means to arouse king's passion for her alone.

"Suffer, do we?" Jamshed appeared to gaze straight into the eyes of Sophia. "Suppose, we do—suffer death and sickness, and all the maladies perceived as misfortunes. Who are we? Who suffers? Flesh and bones, blood and mish-mash of bloody organs, ballooned with the helium of pride that each one is doing something, not just functioning, but performing their duty. Why, how and for whom? This mish-mash of sinews and ligaments calls itself, Self! Self, seeking Self? Who has seen one's own self, but into one's reflection, and that, too, the physical aspect of oneself. One whole as a circle of unity is the answer to all ills, nurtured by the necessity of shredding and destroying, of dividing and separating. From this heap of disintegration, shrouded by ignorance, one succumbs to the multiplicity of ideas and thoughts, which are as elusive as the act of inhaling and exhaling."

The waters of Lake Shisha were suddenly reflecting a brilliant sun, its glare stinging Sophia's eyes. She could feel the overpowering scent of frankincense, as if it was emanating forth from the very womb of Ubar in Oman, and spiraling up before settling in the city of Azerbaijan. This scent was soothing and intoxicating, and Sophia's heart was brimming with longings, her gaze arresting the sparkling beauty of Takhti-Jamshed. Jamshed, too, seemed drunk by the scented downpour from the gold-platter of a sun's disk. His jeweled throne was catching shafts of light, and rising above the scenic vistas of hills and orchards like a jeweler's dream in colors vibrant and dazzling. Jamshed's gaze was searching a nest upon the branch of an olive tree where a swallow sat upon her eggs most possessively.

Spare O King, my nest, and harm not my babies! Was swallow's frantic appeal, as the Throne began a slow descent!

Jamshed's response was swift to the swallow's appeal. He tilted his throne to one side, thus saving the swallow's nest before landing upon his former oasis amidst a blaze of jewel-lights, dancing and shuddering. The swallow was quick to show her gratitude, leaving her nest in a flash, and offering Jamshed the leg of a locust. She sprinkled upon him from her beak some water, calling it the *water of mercy.*

Nauroz, O King, the first day of New Year you may celebrate with gifts and rejoicings. Thank you for saving my home and the lives of my unborn babies. The swallow sailed past the grove of frankincense, disappearing into the city of olives.

The jewel-dance of gems upon Takhti-Jamshed was catching and holding Jamshed's laughter, his Jam-e-Jam blazing much like the blaze of amethysts in his crown. At the foot of his throne his subjects were gathering, cheering and singing songs of felicitations. But he seemed oblivious to all, gazing into the eyes of Sophia warmly and enigmatically.

On Jamshed as the people's jewels streamed
They cried upon him that the New Year beamed

"You hear not the cries of jubilations from the lips of your subjects, O King?" Sophia ventured, watching the denizens of Azerbaijan disperse and disappear.

"I hear only the songs of love and beauty from the lips of the birds and from the lips of nature!" Jamshed sang ecstatically.

"Is it true, O King, that you are the architect of Nauroz, and the *master* of arts and sciences?" Sophia was awakening from the spell of awe and wonder.

"The solar year and the lunar I have invented, time and rhythm of the seasons." Jamshed boasted ruminatively. "Wine, too, is my sole discovery by proxy. I had preserved some grapes, which fermented over time, wafted forth an aroma most astringent. My physicians told me that this concoction had become poison, but I didn't destroy it with the intention of testing their claim and its efficacy. One of my wives, sweet Lucretia, was suffering a painful malady of the joints and stomach. She drank the entire concoction in an attempt to kill herself, but was only overpowered by sleep, and woke up cured and exuberant. Sweet poison, most precious and—"

All sounds and visions were effaced. The great desert of Ubar was shaking violently as if awakening after the onslaught of a cataclysmic embrace. Lake Shisha was foaming and frothing while the garnet sands were swirling with the dizzying speed of hurricanes. A falling star from the great lake of turbulent sky was diving right into the middle of the country of Oman, its brilliant beams cascading down, and silencing the swirling sands in the city of Ubar, while polishing the palace of Irem to its lost glory of mystery and seduction. Turrets encrusted with mother-of-pearl and domes gilded with gold were towering high above the shimmering mists, beyond which minarets rose aloft. The thousand-pillared Irem emerged chaste like a veiled bride, pure and dreamy.

An astonishing sense of peace had settled over the city of Ubar. Even the Garden of Irem surrounded by sand dunes crimson and glittering, looked serene and welcoming. Lake Shisha was washed by the waters of serenity, its depths tranquil and gleaming. Reflected in there was the lone King upon his Takhti-Jamshed with Jam-e-Jam as his dear companion. Sophia hugging her knees by Lake Shisha, could see him smiling into her eyes, his hands clasped in a knot, revealing one wound of a signet-ring. He seemed so near, and Sophia had the impulse to put her hand in the Lake and touch him, but she knew he was continents away in time and space. Both were endowed afresh with the knowledge of the worlds perished and worlds to come, but understanding very little of the mysteries lurking behind which they could neither touch, nor explore. And yet, they possessed wisdom, knowing deeply and profoundly that they were brought together for a certain purpose which would manifest itself by degrees if their desire for learning was kindled by love and patience. Jamshed's love for Aleena was shining in his eyes, and Sophia's newborn love for Jamshed was concealed inside her heart. Apart from being the queen of wisdom in the chess-game of cosmos, she had to play the part of seeking her lover in order to win the love of a king bewitched by the beauty of Aleena.

Night had fallen over the crimson desert as Sophia sat hugging her knees by Lake Shisha. Her shawl, broidered with silvery stars, was as beautiful as the night sky. She seemed content, simply smiling back into the eyes of Jamshed, but his arm was shooting up with an abrupt gesture, indicating the west, where the flaming disk of a sun was sliding into the heart of the wilderness. Sophia looked and gasped, despite the fact that what she saw was not new. It was but a glimpse of memory, long forgotten, which would return in snippets like the flashing of images on the screen of mind

The flaming torch of sun was polishing a pearly gate, enormous in width and height. Alone and majestic it was, embedded in an octagonal fort, lofty and immense. The façade of this fort above the pearly gate, catching one shaft of light from the dying sun was revealing a handiwork most chaste and exquisite. A pair of hands, beautifully sculpted, appeared to be reaching out. Above those hands was a silver key, horizontally affixed as if guiding and guarding the hands which dared strive for union. A bright star and a gleaming Crescent were suspended right below the hands, more alive and fascinating than the pearly gates. Across from this Crescent shone a Cross, all fiery and bronzed.

"The key to Paradise. Another level of existence for the Garden of Irem!" Jamshed murmured thoughtfully. "Remote, this Garden of Eden, glittering most seductively behind the pearly gates. A dream-jewel, allusive and alluring!"

"Cyclopean sculpted hands, it seems, so very beautiful!" Sophia's gaze was trying to decipher meaning beyond symbols. "Where I have seen this, how and when? Familiar to sight, yet alien to memory. There were times when I could read through every form, even through formlessness."

"From Aden to Eden if you wish to travel, Sophia, you must learn the song of incantation." Jamshed murmured again, his gaze contemplating the gleaming façade. "This silver key is the hand of Yahweh to unlock the door to Paradise. And when that door is unlocked, these hands below would meet in twain. Then the Cross and the Crescent would merge, shedding light of love, peace and harmony." He heaved a sigh, contemplating his cup. "We have to find a way to reach that vaulted Garden. My sweet Aleena, beloved all, how do I—" His longing was shaken by the shuddering of rocks in the distance.

Sophia leapt to her feet as if stung, pulling her starry shawl together, and shivering. The wilderness of Aden was groaning, but the thundering of violence was straight from the heart of Ahkof desert, beyond which huddled the black rocks, remote and menacing. Tides upon tides of sifting sand-ridges were rippling and spinning as far as Sophia could see, her gaze hovering over the Hadramout Mountains. Doom and gloom were dancing in the sky, one colossal mountain heaving and exploding into coffin-like apartments. It was as if the entire graveyard of black rocks was suffering the labor pains of cataclysmic births. Jamshed had closed his eyes, but Sophia's eyes were wide open, unblinking and stinging. One she-camel, big with her young, was raging out of one graveyard of a rock, which itself was split-open and shattering.

MIRACLE OF THE SHE-CAMEL

And to the tribe of Thamud We sent their brother Salih. He said: O my people, serve Allah! Ye have no other God save Him. A wonder from your Lord hath come to you. Lo, this is the camel of Allah, a token unto you; so let her feed in Allah's earth, and touch her not with hurt lest painful torment seize you. Quran 7:73

A sepulchral hush had descended upon the crimson desert after the she-camel was lost into the void of blackness. A night visitor had materialized at the foot of Jamshed's Throne, reciting verses from the Quran, and making obeisance. Sophia had abandoned herself at the edge of Lake Shisha, watching the king and the intruder with a sense of intrigue and curiosity. She seemed oblivious to the splendor of the night, lowering a canopy of stars over Takhti-Jamshed, while she listened intently to the story of the man who had introduced himself to the king as Kilabah. Drunk as she was by the wine of sweetness in Kilabah's intonations, her mind was throwing open a gate of recollection. With a sudden flash of clarity, she knew that she had seen him once inside the palace of the gods and goddesses.

"Have you not heard about the prophet mentioned in the Quran, O King?" Kilabah was saying.

"Why don't you tell me, since my memory fails me?" Jamshed asked indulgently. "I have heard about the prophet Shueyb from the Midian. Also about Noah, and about one of his three sons by the name of Shem. I might have seen the son of Shem called Aram, and vaguely remember seeing Uz the son of Aram. The two sons of Uz by the names of Ad and Hud came to my court as far as I can recall. But tell me whence came this she-camel?" He looked into his Jam-e-Jam, catching and holding Sophia's rapt expression in his own eyes which were already brimming with volumes upon volumes of recollections.

"That she-camel, O King, came from the rocks as you saw her." Kilabah smiled, pumping his thoughts with the bellows of pride and profundity. "Those giant rocks protect the city of Thamud. You didn't see its inhabitants. But centuries ago that city was teeming with people of a tall race steeped in utter ignorance. They fashioned their own idols, and if some alien tribe brought their own collection of idols, they were quick to get angry. Conflicts and disputes were common amongst those people, which were brought before the authority of their prince by the name of Jonda as the final arbiter. Under his rule, a man known as Salih proclaimed himself the prophet of God. That was five centuries before the advent of prophet Muhammad. Salih began urging all people to abandon their idols, and to worship one God alone. This message of Salih was spurned by the people of Thamud, and the matter was brought before the jurisdiction of Prince Jonda. The Prince decided that on the day of the High Festival, all the priests of his kingdom would pray to their gods, and Salih would, too, before his own God. All involved in such prayers would be seeking answers to their dilemmas and whomsoever God could satisfy all with answers, he would be chosen as the High God of the Thamudites. On the appointed day, the priests had the privilege of praying first to their idols. Yet, none of the idols were able to answer, so the priests were upset and disgruntled, not even permitting Salih to pray to his God. Prince Jonda was kind enough to intercede on behalf of Salih, investing him with a challenge that if his God could perform the miracle of bringing forth a she-camel out of the solid rocks, he—Jonda would convince his people to believe in one God. It was easy for Salih, O King, to perform such a miracle, but the people still refused to believe. Salih, in return, warned the people not to harm the she-camel lest God's wrath fall on them. But the people of Thamud were seized with fury and superstition, claiming that this she-camel drank all the water in the city, going about in offering milk to anyone who ventured forth in believing that her supply of milk was inexhaustible. Young Thamudites, heedless of the warnings, were gathering around the miraculous she-camel, and before anyone knew they cut one of her legs, making her lame, then they slashed the tendons of her skin, and finally killed her most brutally. Another miracle was that the young foal out of her womb was delivered unscathed, vanishing quickly down the ridge of the mountains. Salih was mad with grief, prophesying that within three days, God's wrath would fall upon them for the sin of killing the she-camel, and they themselves would perish. No one took this warning seriously, going about their business, sneering and jeering. On the third night, as prophesied, while they slept in their homes, a great calamity visited them, annihilating the entire population with the exception of a few artisans and philosophers who were opposed to the violence of killing the she-camel. Some of the survivors thought that they heard a terrible noise from the heavens before the city was destroyed. But the others conjectured that a volcanic eruption had reduced the city to a black crater of mass graveyard."

"We sent them the flood of Irem, and in exchange for their two gardens gave them two gardens bearing bitter fruit, tamarisk here and a Lote-tree there 34:16."

Sophia heard herself recite this verse from the gold lettering of living Quran.

She could trace her voice diving deep into Lake Shisha, creating ripples around Takhti-Jamshed. Kilabah seemed frightened, shifting his weight from one leg to the other, his gaze pleading.

"Where did that voice come from, O King?" Kilabah's voice died with a perceptible shudder.

"You didn't recognize the voice of the goddess?" Jamshed tilted his Jam-e-Jam for him to look into its panoramic wonders of the worlds.

"Where am I?" Kilabah gasped, looking into the blue lakes of Sophia's eyes with awe and bewilderment. "That's the city of Ubar? I thought I had landed in Ubar."

"You are in Azerbaijan, O besotted Bedouin!" The tinkling of Sophia's laughter went coursing down Lake Shisha, creating more ripples. "I heard your story of the she-camel, but I am more interested in the Garden of Irem and in the tribe of Aad who dared bring the Garden of Eden on earth."

"Oh, that garden of Eden, promised to the believers in heavenly Paradise!" Was Kilabah's befuddled response. "The Garden of Irem lies at your feet, O fair Goddess, but you can't see it. And the glorious verse which you recited has nothing to do with the Garden of Irem you desire to enter. That verse was written about the people of Saba who lived in the middle of the two beautiful gardens. Their Lord told them to enjoy the abundance of those gardens and be grateful. But they despoiled the gardens day after day, returning to the city in the evening for drinking and feasting. For their ungratefulness, their Lord punished them with a flood of the Irem. The city was destroyed, those gardens replaced by two other gardens interspersed with two kinds of trees; the tamarisk bearing bitter fruit, and the Lote-tree laden with the knowledge of God's creation, sublime and sweet-scented." He returned his attention to the King, his look glazed and searching. "Should I ask why I am here? Why the goddess sits by the Lake Shisha? Why the fourth King of the world sits all alone on his Takhti-Jamshed?" His gaze was peering through Jam-e-Jam, beyond Sophia, beyond Jamshed, into worlds vast and borderless. "I better not ask, following the example of Luqman in the court of King Solomon. When Luqman saw King Solomon transmute base metal into gold, he refrained from asking the secret; knowing, that by asking he would not learn."

"Wiser than Luqman you are, Kilabah!" Jamshed laughed. "Maybe wiser than Sophia down there? She has lost interest in your stories and in the absurdity of my pomp and splendor without the pageantry of court and courtesans. Look, how she sits there gazing at the moonless sky, as if divining secrets out of black voids. Alas, I can't even see the voids! Unlike Luqman, though seated on my own throne, I must learn from you about the history of those trees I have not ever seen. Your knowledge is boundless, it is obvious."

"My knowledge is faulty, O King, as of any mortal striving to know all." Kilabah smiled, his look profound and enigmatic. "If you don't know about the tamarisk and Lote-tree, then you might not have heard about the tree of Zaqqum mentioned in the Quran.

Lo, the tree of Zaqqum (the accursed tree), the food of the sinner; like molten brass, it seetheth in their bellies, as the seething of boiling water" 44:43-49.

"Centuries removed from time and distance from the advent of Quran, I was probably trapped in a grave, murdered most brutally by Zohak, the ruler of Arabia, far from my capital, half way across the world?" Jamshed reminisced without bitterness.

"Sins as large as the mountains, and Dark Age descending." Sophia shuddered, still seated by Lake Shisha. Her eyes lowering blue flames of inquisition at the King and the Bedouin, whose eyes were locked together as if gazing into depths deeper than the oceans, entranced and speechless.

"Sophia knows when radiance departed from me, and when my people rebelled?" Jamshed broke the silence, fixing his attention to the Jam-e-Jam in his cupped hands. "But that is of no consequence now. Tell me about Zaqqum, tamarisk and the Lote-tree. That knowledge might carve the way for me to the celestial sands of Irem."

"Zaqqum tree, O King, is a bitter and pungent tree at the bottom of hell." Kilabah began dreamily. "Prophet Muhammad's Night Journey to the heaven also included a visit to hell where he was shown the tree of Zaqqum as a warning to mankind as is obvious in this verse:

Behold! We told thee that thy Lord doth encompass mankind round about: We appointed the Vision which We showed thee but as a trial for men as also the accursed tree in the Quran. We warn them, but it only increases their inordinate transgression 17:60.

Much like Jesus, Prophet Muhammad died to the self, descended to hell, before he was brought back to life on this earth. Tamarisk tree on the other hand is of the earth, could have been the source of Manna mentioned in the Bible, since it produces a small sap sucking insect that turns the toxic sap into a honey-like substance that drops to the ground. People still gather it in Arabia, and sell it in the bazaars. Tamarisk sucks dry the desert springs, but it provides windbreaks, enhancing the life of other vegetation. Abraham was the first one to plant Tamarisk tree in Beersheba, invoking the name of God, as a mark of his ownership of the well he purchased from Abemelekh at the price of seven female sheep." His voice was sucked dry by Sophia's abrupt query.

"Do you know how to reach the secret gate to the lost city of Irem and its Garden?" Sophia's voice was heavy with the burden of a challenge, her gaze holding both men in its flashing intensity. "So well you describe the incidents of the ancient past that I can't help but think that you could lead us straight into the Garden of the seven seas and seven heavens."

"Wish that were true, if I knew half as much?" Kilabah sighed to himself. "About the seven seas, seven planets and seven heavens, I am longing to learn from the King." He was trying to divert Jamshed's attention from Jam-e-Jam, but was not succeeding. "Which Irem do you wish to see, dear Goddess? The Irem of great wickedness on earth, or of the splendid paradise, fabulous and glorious? Both glittering most seductively through the window of mind, but I can't even begin to trace the path, unless guided by him who alone went near the Garden of Abode —" His voice was muted back again, this time by the symphony of voices, sibilant and threatening.

Shuddering over the city of Ubar was a shadow colossal, lapping over the desert sands, and turning Lake Shisha into a droplet of water, round and glistening. The night sky, with the promise of dawn, was slashed with streaks gold and garnet, peering out of the thin fabric of the dark shadow, all fierce and encompassing. Three pairs of eyes, sparkling like the beacons of light during a stormy night, were those of Sophia, Jamshed and Kilabah. All forms were swallowed by darkness with the exception of eyes of the trio, glittering against the rumble of the choir-like accolade.

So did Allah convey the inspiration to His servant what He conveyed
The Prophet's mind and heart in no way falsified that which he saw
Will ye then dispute with him on a second descent
Near the Lote-tree beyond which none may pass
Near it is the Garden of Abode
Behold, the Lote-tree was shrouded in mystery unspeakable
His sight never swerved, nor did it go wrong
For truly did he see of the signs of His Lord the Greatest 53:10-18

An overwhelming scent of musk, ginger and camphor was in the air, raw and seething. Heart of the night was pierced by a giant tree spanning the length of the earth and the heavens. Each branch of this tree was stretched far and wide beyond the scope of mortal sight. Five pointed stars, much larger than several oceans was each leaf in its emerald glory of peace and surrender. From its polished trunk were sprouting four springs. One of clear water meandered by Lake Shisha where Sophia sat straining through darkness, her sight getting accustomed to the downpour of scenes mystical and splendid. The crimson sands were parting, revealing a river of milk, besides which was materializing a river of wine. And another river of pure gold and honey was coming into view parallel to the one of crystal-clear water, pure and sparkling.

We are the inhabitants of the Lote-tree! The secret ones, created from the absolute secret of our Lord.

A myriad of angels haloed by light were appearing upon the leaves of the tree, carrying a staff of light, brilliant and varicolored. A symphony of mystical knowledge was escaping their lips, throbbing with the pulse of life and enchantment.

This Lote-tree carries the knowledge of all of God's creation from the beginning of its sequence in time. Whatever of created is part of it and contained in it. It is the tree of uppermost boundary, for everything ends in it after it begins a new life. God's light reaches all creation from its branches and fragrance from its flowers lend scent and beauty to the entire creation.

Suddenly, the trunk of this tree was ballooned into a globe of light, illuminating the ruins of Ubar with Sophia as the sole witness. She could behold once again the reflection of Takhti-Jamshed. Kilabah appeared to be immersed in conversing with the King, but she couldn't hear any part of their conversation. Before she could seek Jamshed's attention, Kilabah's voice came trickling down her awareness like the sound of music from a distant cataract.

"You can see the face of our beloved Prophet, O King, through your Jam-e-Jam. Just sit still and let your thoughts capture and follow Gabriel and the Prophet." Kilabah's own gaze was riveted to Jam-e-Jam, his voice smooth and mournful like the falling of leaves in the Garden of Eden. "What appears to be the tunnel of light is the trunk of Lote-tree. From the hollow of its secret gate, Buraq has entered ,carrying Gabriel and Prophet Muhammad. They have almost reached the top of the tree, all the generations of the past and present are there, amongst them saints and prophets. If you concentrate upon names you would see Abraham, Moses, Jesus and the rest of the prophets. Can you see Azrail—the angel of death, greeting Prophet Muhammad. The Prophet is asking him how the souls of the dying are released. Azrail is saying: *I send my servant with a branch of sweet-scented tree from Paradise. When my servant holds that branch between the eyebrows of the dying person, the spirit of that person catches a whiff of Paradise, and starts ascending with a great longing. Then I come down on earth and carry the soul of the dying person with utmost tenderness to Paradise, and then deliver it to the Lord of the worlds.* Look Azrail is gone and Buraq is slowing down. *Why are you leaving me, Gabriel*, the Prophet is crying? *I can't go further*, Gabriel is leaving, *if I were to continue with you I would be annihilated by the greatness of the Light.* Buraq is flying higher and higher, leaving all the angels behind. Those golden veils, at the least thousands of them pose no challenge to Buraq. He is swift and adamant, tearing through all veils and stopping suddenly. Prophet is entering the veil of oneness. The Prophet is gone, but his voice, can you hear, O King? *The taste of honey is on my tongue, the breeze of divine mercy over my shoulders, the perfume of love in my heart! Ah, eternity and endlessness!* Listen O King, what rumbling in silence, who is speaking. *My end is my beginning and my beginning is my end.* Prophet's voice again. *Where are you, my heart? Where did the spirit go? Where have I left the secret?* This roaring silence again, O King, can you hear?

O heart, I granted you love and beauty. O spirit I granted you mercy and honor. O spirit, you have Me. Look to your left, look to your right, to your back, in front, above and below, what do you see? The secret of your divine presence, ineffable, indescribable! Allah, God, Beloved! My mercy overpowers my anger —"

Hail our chief, thy scepter away
Rule Irem, Shedad we obey
Thy seal bade spirits by thy thralls
Hail, god of Irem's magic halls

A peal of laughter from the ruby-red lips of dawn ripped open the curtain of night, effacing all but Sophia by Lake Shisha. Or that's what she thought as she looked deep in the crystal-clear waters, thirsting for one glimpse of Jamshed. She didn't know Jamshed was right behind her, alighting from his Takhti-Jamshed. He stole behind her, swiftly and majestically, startling her as she caught his reflection in Lake Shisha, hovering over her shoulders.

"O King!" Sophia leaped to her feet, whirling around to face him, their eyes locked. "How!"

"In one dramatic instant the mystical bull shifted the earth from one horn to the other, and I was uprooted from Azerbaijan, tossed into the mouth of a whirlwind, and then flung into the crater of Oman. Don't know how?" Jamshed sighed, shifting his gaze to Lake Shisha, while spinning his Jam-e-Jam between his palms absently.

"The master of a divining cup, O King, to behold the seven seas, and seven planets and seven heavens, and knowing not how one journeys on the wings of time?" Sophia sang ecstatically, drunk by the nearness of her new-found love.

"Dreams dancing over the drums of time. How would a king know, about anything, in the absence of his beloved imprisoned inside the Garden of Irem?" Jamshed laughed, gazing into his Jam-e-Jam under some spell of utter hopelessness.

"We would work together to secure the release of your beloved." Was Sophia's mock eagerness, her heart sinking at the very thought of beautiful Aleena in the vaulted Garden of Irem. And of my philosopher's, too!" She added as an afterthought, trying to conjure means to win the heart of this King. "It would be helpful if I could look into your divining cup at the seven seas and the planets and the heavens?" She murmured sweetly.

"It would help me, too, against those ruins of Oman in this city of Ubar." Jamshed permitted himself the luxury of a smile. "Come, welcome to my Takhti-Jamshed. We would look together and devise means to reach the Garden of Irem." He retraced his steps, Sophia following, humbled and distraught.

Through the eyes of the divining cup, the desert of Oman was silent as a graveyard, with the exception of brilliant Sun enveloping sands in the gold-dust of sparkle and glitter. Takhti-Jamshed was hosting the king and the goddess, both absorbed in looking at the universe inside the wondrous globe of Jam-e-Jam. Jamshed was naming sites as if convincing his own self of the validity of creation. Sophia sat there rapt and silent, but her heart was suddenly sore and aching. She was excruciatingly aware of the warmth and nearness of the king, overwhelmed by her own painful longing to love and to be loved.

"The seven seas in succession." Jamshed was saying. "There is Arctic and the Antarctic. Over there the Pacific North and South! Atlantic is coming into view, North and South. The Indian ocean all by itself, vast and fathomless! Now, let's see the seven planets up close. There is the Moon, below it Venus. Mercury is enveloped in haze. Can you see the Sun, above it Mars hovering! And Jupiter and Saturn! Might as well show you the seven heavens in the realm of Jewish mysticism. Shamayim is the first heaven guarded by Archangel Gabriel. The second is Raquia controlled by Zachariel and Raphael. Make note of the third one, Shehaqim with its Garden of Eden. If we ever get to the Garden of Irem, it would be the replica of Paradise, ruled by Anahel in heavenly splendor. The fourth one is coming into view called Machonon, cradling the Altar, the Temple and Jerusalem. Can you see Archangel Michael kneeling at the Altar? Mchon is the fifth one under the care of a dark servant of God by the name of Samael. Zachiel over there is the guardian of sixth heaven named Zebul. There, the holiest of the holy, Araboth, the seventh heaven under the leadership of Cassiel. The Throne of Glory resides here, but we can't see. It is guarded by seven archangels. Can you see the Seraphim, Cherubim and the Hayyoth under the silver canopy?"

"Barely! So far, so far." Sophia whispered, the violence of love inside her the drumming of grief and implacability. "I am so lonely. Just the two of us, all alone! Can we—" Her unvoiced appeal and anguish was blown to pieces.

The desert itself seemed to be splitting and groaning. The sands were shifting, and revealing up yonder the cavernous hills. A volcanic shudder was ripping through the heart of the mountains, illuminating one cave the size of Babylon. Sumptuous halls with galleries were towering high. The gurgling of marble fountains could be heard clearly, and the fragrance of baths reaching down to the sandy ruins in Oman. From the grove of gold trees with clusters of fruits, a form was taking shape, none other than Kilabah's.

"You are not alone!" A cry of anguish was lowered from the sun-beams, it seemed. "Oh, wretched me, exiled from the hearth of my love, and that is Chaviva!" Kilabah was raving. "Look, how she wanders stricken with grief and hopelessness. We had pledged our love under the Lote-tree, but fates mocked us, separating us continents apart most mercilessly. She is the virgin child of youth and beauty; longing to be united with me in the palace-garden of Irem, her parents dared build to enjoy the Eden of heaven on earth."

"Chaviva, the frail child of Eve." Jamshed said, his gaze following the young maiden with dark eyes and dark hair. "Come, Chaviva, tell us about the Garden of Irem, and we would help you find your lover."

Chaviva's white wraith of a face was lifted up to the sky, her dark eyes glittering. She seemed oblivious to all, her long hair rippling down her back in silken wavelets. Sophia's gaze was burning through the silvery folds of Chaviva's dress, it was obvious, for the girl turned abruptly, darting a wild look, her gaze unseeing.

"She can't tell you, O King, until she finds the secret gate to the lost Irem." Kilabah's gaze had arrested Chaviva, knowing fully well that she couldn't see him.

"Come down from that wondrous place, Kilabah, wherever that is, and join us in our search for the Garden of Irem." Was Jamshed's half appeal, half command?

"Yes, make haste, Kilabah. Chaviva is waiting for you." Sophia urged, stung by jealousy the way the King looked at the young heathen.

"I can't." Kilabah lamented. "I am imprisoned in this garden of Alhambra. The walls of Granada are closing in, and this city of Spain is gathering fogs as solid as the glaciers of ice. But I would tell you a little about the ancestry of Chaviva, hoping that your wisdom and knowledge would be revived to gain entry into the Garden of Irem. Chaviva is from the tribe of Aad, the name of her grandfather similar to the name of this tribe. Her grandfather Aad was well versed in the art of necromancy. He succeeded in conjuring the spirit of Iblis, commanding him to build him a garden in the likeness of the Garden of Eden. When the garden was completed, and he was on his way to see it, he was overwhelmed by fear and apprehension. Not far from the gate, he mumbled a wrong incantation and was confronted by a legion of beasts, all hideous and ferocious. They would have torn him to pieces, had he neglected to hold out his mystic signet-ring before them to ward off evil. But the shock was great, and he died out of sheer terror. Before dying, he could summon enough strength to entrust his sons with the knowledge of the secret incantations. The names of his sons were Shedad and Shadid, who were not only entrusted with the secret, but commanded to build the Garden of Irem with the help of charms and incantations, so that they could bring Eden to earth to enjoy its beauty and abundance. What happened next, only Chaviva can tell!"

"What could I say to the rivers of Ubar?" Chaviva had begun spinning on her toes. "Imagination is more powerful than dreams, and dreams more powerful than the wand of magic. For the wand of magic cannot work without the light of imagination, and light of imagination cannot shine without the sparks of dreams. Garden of Irem! Such is the Paradise promised to the Believers. Eyes of non-believers have seen it on earth, this earthly paradise. But the eyes of the believers wander restlessly to catch a glimpse of this heavenly paradise. Here it is, the Garden of Irem! Here! I can see!" She had fallen in one white heap, the ruins of Oman awakening to the command of vivification.

SECRET GATE TO LOST IREM

The ruins of Oman against the wind-carved sand-hills of Ubar seemed alive, burnished by sunset most awesome and heliotrope. Lake Shisha was hosting the King and the Bedouin and Sophia. Splashed by the colors of the dusk, they looked more like the ghosts of the past than the living, seeking creatures of myth born to the universal truth of mystery and conjecture. Jamshed was more alive than any king doomed to suffer the follies of his own youth and misfortunes of the world, his heart slashed by longings insane and terrible. Kilabah — the Bedouin, too, was suffering the tortures of the damned for a gulf of separation from Chaviva, his flushed cheeks gathering blotches of purple. Sophia's pallor was enhanced by the glittering blue oceans in her eyes which concealed her great love for the king whom she could not claim as her own, not until he lost hope of being united with Aleena.

Aleena was within reach of the king's gaze and thoughts, reflected deep down the mirror of Lake Shisha. Much like a beautiful blossom inside the Garden of Irem, she was oblivious to her surroundings, immersed deliciously in evoking doleful notes from her silver lyre. Lying sprawled beside her could be seen Ibrahim, in utter abandon to his senses of sight and hearing, his bushy eyebrows as silvery as his long beard. His blue robe of Chinese silk was shimmering like a distant stream against the tranquil landscape. Chaviva was standing above the grove of frankincense, her back toward Aleena and Ibrahim. Her arms were stretched before her as if hugging thin air, her gaze wild and searching.

A panorama of mountains was rising before her sight, overlooking the silhouettes of towers and pillars. Some sort of light was emanating from deep within the foot of the mountains, casting fantastic shadows. Haze and light were trembling in the distance, revealing doors and windows. One giant sheet of gold embedded with clusters of jewels was highlighted in between the middle of the mountains, as if engulfed in the fire of rubies; emerald flames licking the dark shadows.

"From the beautiful palace of Granada into the ruins of Oman, and then straight into the sand-hills of Ubar, I am tossed." Kilabah lamented suddenly. "Fated to see my beloved hurled by sand-dunes into the sylvan deeps of Irem, where neither the King, nor the Goddess can help me reach?" His gaze appeared to be swinging from Chaviva to Aleena, carrying in its orbs the flames of agony.

"The king is getting closer to Aleena day by day. By the whispering winds of incantations, or by the invisible hands of providence!" Jamshed sighed into the calm waters of Lake Shisha. "From Azerbaijan into the ruins of Ubar in Oman I have landed, meeting the goddess, and arresting Irem in Lake Shisha without the help of Jam-e-Jam. Next, my throne would carry me to the feet of my beloved. Kilabah, you, too, would be united with Chaviva. And Sophia with Ibrahim."

"Ah, is that the secret gate to Irem?" Sophia cried.

Her jealous heart was heeding not the king, intent on discovering the mystery of Irem, so that she could exhume Aleena—the Gothic princess, reducing her to a handful of dust with her own spells of fiery incantations. Before her searching gaze, the sheet of gold was turning to the golden gate, bursting forth into a jeweler's dream of exquisite handiwork kindled into red and green flames from the very hearts of rubies and emeralds.

"No, the secret gate to Irem is dark as death!" Kilabah exclaimed enigmatically. It's called Rab al Khali, meaning door to the void, the secret gate to death. No one has ever come back alive after crossing that gate. Chaviva, alone, is blessed with divine sight to see that gate, and knows not to approach Irem through it, but by another."

"She is already in the Garden of Irem, isn't she?" Jamshed demurred aloud, as if talking with his own self. "That's where I found my Aleena the first time through my Jam-e-Jam."

"This is the Irem of the Old Ones, O King; a fraction of what the real Irem looks like." Kilabah darted a suspicious look at Sophia as if divining her thoughts. "If you saw the real one of the dreadful and the fabulous, you would be drawn to it like one moth to a flame. Chaviva was carried over there I am sure, but—"

An awful cry from somewhere ripped through the sky, skirling down the mirrored deeps in Lake Shisha. Chaviva was bending down to touch a mound of dust-gold to her left, her marble-like profile sad and glistening.

"So, that's where my grandfather lies buried in this land of Uz, bearing the name of Job, generations after generations." Chaviva's voice was a tremor long and ubiquitous.

Chaviva was not even aware that she was being watched by Aleena, who had abandoned her silver lyre in her lap, her liquid-gold eyes thoughtful and shining. Ibrahim, beside her, was awakening, the hazel gleam in his own eyes devouring Aleena, as well as kissing the hem of her gown of stars and crescents. Jamshed's fingers were circling around Jam-e-Jam, his lips moving as if kneading prayers inside the beads of a rosary. Down in the mirrored depths of Lake Shisha, rocks were jutting out from the top of the mountains, polished and omnipotent. Sophia was averting her gaze, watching the sand-dunes sliding closer to Takhti-Jamshed. Kilabah was stricken dumb by the unveiling of a grand city, bathed in the light of jewels which sparkled and glittered against the shafts of sunlight.

An arched portal of magnificent size was guarding the city of marble and gold. Chaviva was becoming aware of the city of enchantment. It was unfolding before her sight, but she had turned her back on it, her arms stretched out in an act of greeting and welcoming someone only she could see.

"Uncle Shadid!" Chaviva's cry of dread and astonishment was choked inside her, her arms falling limp to her sides.

"Come not close, dear child, or you would be caught into the everlasting void of life and death, spinning around the globe of unity while avoiding the chasm of annihilation." Voice of the invisible Shadid was rising high, ricocheting back like the clanging of bells. "You have succeeded in pulling me out of my peaceful abode, yet I am not that displeased. I am commanded to follow your parents into the Garden of Irem as they did eons ago, and explaining their intent so that your spirit is comforted. But first I need to cast a spell of silence over the Gothic princess and the clever philosopher. Up there someone is longing to be with you, all feverish and besotted. A couple of others beside him, equally besotted, and they, too, must be charmed into silence lest they disrupt my concentration." He made a circle in the air with his arms.

Chaviva gasped at the vision alighting before her eyes, that of her parents as she had seen them when she was barely a child of seven. Almeena, her mother, looked just the same as she remembered her, but her father Shedad looked older, rather shrunken and preoccupied. Both were riding their dromedaries, both silent, their faces shining with awe and astonishment. An amused and mysterious smile was curling upon the lips of Aleena, her gold eyes speaking volumes, though she, herself, was under the spell of silence. Ibrahim was watching only Aleena, now seated at her feet, the look in his eyes tender and contemplative. He, too, was under the spell of silence. Sophia, Jamshed and Kilabah were under the same spell, seated at the edge of Lake Shisha, turned to statues of curiosity, vigilant and attentive.

Make room, Chaviva, and follow your parents to know the mystery of Irem palaces and gardens. The handiwork of genii or angels, you may explore at your own discretion.

Shedid's voice was commanding the attention of all who sat witnessing the replay of Shedad and Almeena's journey into the Garden of Irem. They alighted near a magnificent portal, tying their dromedaries to the gold handles before proceeding toward the vista of enchantment. Behind the portals were two lofty gates of such exquisite design, encrusted with so many jewels that they appeared to be mocking the luster of the constellations above and beyond.

We think that Paradise and Calvarie
Christ's Cross and Adam's tree
Stood in one place
Look, Lord, and find both Adams in me
As the first Adam's sweat surrounds my face
May the last Adam's blood my soul embrace

Shedad sang with a great gusto, wiping the beads of sweat off his brow while leading Almeena through the gates aflame with the fire of jewels. Beyond the gates was a forest, revealing the sylvan peace of paradise with flowering trees and orchards laden with fruits luscious and abundant. In the middle of the forest was a dazzling scenery that of a garden—a jewel-garden, resplendent with flowers and foliage the color of sunsets and rainbows. Almeena was shielding her eyes as if blinded by the collage of colors, vibrant and throbbing. Shedad was enchanted, holding his head high, and admiring the limpid lakes, smooth and serpentine. Chaviva had regressed back into her childhood it seemed, wide-eyed and spellbound. Her gaze was slipping past her parents over to the crystal pools scattered there like mirrors, embossed with lichens in shades of jade and emerald. Shedad's pace was slackened, distracted by the sudden warble of birds with plumage bright and silken.

The Garden of Irem was expanding, perfumed and voluptuous. The vines in full bloom were twining around the trunks of the trees, their branches overhead embracing amorously. Clusters upon clusters of roses entwined with bougainvillea were shooting high and spilling low in wanton surrender to the ardor and exuberance of this garden. Chaviva and her uncle were a part of this enchanting garden now, dazed and intoxicated. Reaching closer to the mirror-like pools, they were freshly stricken with awe at the pearly fish of such exquisite form and delicacy that the waters appeared to be changing colors, and attaining the hues of aurora and mother-of-pearl.

Shedad and Almeena were silent also, but their mute gestures had tongues of praise, their eyes speaking volumes while holding and beholding the marvels of this paradise with fear and longing. As if compelled by ravenous hunger, they began to eat figs, pears and cherries. Also ravishing the grapevines of their ruby-red grapes, and then devouring dates in great quantities, their hungers fiery and unslaked! Their need for gluttony was overwhelming, and they would have kept on eating, had not a voice, much like the peal of thunder, had come crashing upon them amidst their spree of overindulgence.

Master of the potent seal, O mighty Shedad! Look at the palace of Irem before you, constructed in eleven nights at your command.

Many columned Irem was rising before their sight like a beautiful dream, silent, majestic and awe-inspiring. Pillars of alabaster were round and high, supporting gold domes, encrusted with jewels, sparkling under the sun in every hue of the rainbows. An enormous colonnade edged by trees was strewn with pearls and rubies, its radiance reaching up to the golden trees laden with blossoms of jasper and emerald. Chaviva dared not move, standing there transfixed. Shadid stood apart from everyone, wearied and distraught. He was turned to the statue of immobility. Only his gaze was wild and restless, as if he was afraid that this dream-palace would vanish soon, leaving him alone in the desert of imponderables.

The Garden of Irem, only partially discovered by Shedad and Almeena ,was left behind, but visible to Aleena and Ibrahim in its entirety by the sheer potency of magic, controlled by both, secretly and separately. Unseen by the foursome group of Shedad's family, the princess and the philosopher could witness even the expression of awe and fear upon the faces of Shedad and Almeena, smiling to themselves most deliciously and deprecatingly. Another threesome group, who could see all four approaching the Garden of Irem, was Sophia, Jamshed and Kilabah. They could hear each rustle, each voice in this Garden, even beyond the gates of the Irem Palace.

"Look, Almeena, the genii obeyed me precisely, replacing gravel with jewels all the way to the palace!" Shedad exclaimed, turning to his heels, and urging his wife to keep pace with him. "Even the façade of the palace with its fluted pillars, set with onyx and trimmed with gold surpass my creative genius."

"An evil omen lurks here somewhere, I fear." Almeena murmured low. "You have forgotten to build here an altar for God Who created the heavens and the earth, the stars and the spirits and the seven worlds. Don't you remember our ancestor Noah, how God's just wrath destroyed his people and your uncle Hud who proclaimed the truth of God, but no one—"

"Be quiet and be comforted, Almeena." Shedad interrupted boisterously. "Your husband Shedad is God, dear wife. Didn't you hear Iblis himself proclaim me God! My palace would be a temple for the tribe of Aad, and my throne their altar. Soon the stars would bow before me, and kings of the world would flock to the city of Irem, paying me homage and receiving scepters from my grace. I would be the god of my people, and you their goddess."

"If I be their goddess, I must acquaint myself with this creation, our palace and our garden!" Almeena retorted, bewitched by the pearly gates of the palace under carved arches and vaulted ceiling, imitating heavens with stars sparkling like diamonds.

"Can't you see the great spirits welcoming us, dear wife, in our own palace of gold and jewels? And this banquet on the table fit only for the gods?" Shedad led her gallantly toward the banquet hall in the middle of the palace.

The dishes of gold and goblets studded with gems were inviting them to the table of delights where dishes of viands, fruits and sweets of most delectable aroma welcomed their indulgence. And indulge they did, tasting each and every dish most ravenously, but their hungers remained unslaked. They had to literally tear themselves away from the table of sumptuous feast, succeeding in disciplining their thoughts and appetites in favor of exploring the palace and its priceless treasures.

Twelve bejeweled halls bearing Zodiac signs, one constellation each, had the appearance of anxious brides, longing to be adored and worshiped. The first hall, with its golden Ram, surrounded by the fire of rubies on the rotunda looked spectacular. Its marble floor was catching the reflection of vines carved on the walls, lending itself the appearance of a floating garden. Almeena was leaving this hall, her curiosity goading her to explore more, but noticing a stream under the green archway; she lifted her skirt up and took off her sandals with the intention of crossing. A peal of laughter escaped her lips as she became aware that what she had mistaken for a stream was actually another marble floor, absorbing liquid-green from the archway and reflecting its murals of gem-like trees and vegetation. Shedad was right behind her, joining his wife in mirth, but their laughter was suddenly truncated.

Both husband and wife stopped in their tracks, confronted by a Rukta coiled up on one imperial davenport at the door of the hall studded with emeralds. Almeena stood there numb with fright, while Shedad's gaze was witnessing the baring of Rukta's fangs with utter fascination. If that was not terrifying enough for poor Almeena, a pair of fiery eyes that of a lion were peering out from behind the davenport. Snatching Almeena's hand into his own, Shedad commenced walking, godlike in all affectation as if he was the sole master of this palace and its creatures. He was dragging Almeena along with him, neither heeding the roars of wild animals, nor sweet melodies from behind the velvety draped windows of many halls yet to be explored.

An imposing staircase across from the Zodiac magnificence was luring their attention toward its winding mystery. Shedad was still holding Almeena's hand while descending the marble steps, his haughtiness replaced by caution, if not by apprehension. Shadid was left quite behind, lost in the sudden haze of mists, luminescent and enveloping. Chaviva was becoming a part of the mists gossamer and pervading, her heart light and restful as if feeling peace and coolness of the night. At the landing of the staircase was emerging forth another city beyond the eight lofty gates, embowered with roses the size of sun-disks, and reflecting the color of sunsets. The fragrance of roses was sweet and overwhelming as Shedad and Almeena passed through one gate, marveling yet at another garden. It was paved with bricks of gold and silver, its golden trees bearing real fruit. Flanked by terraces and balconies studded with precious gems, this miraculous garden appeared to float over a crystal barrier. Beneath this crystal barrier could be seen fish of variegated shapes so exquisite and delicate that they appeared to be chiseled out of light, all prismatic.

Shedad and Almeena were lost in the labyrinthine wonder of this garden. So were Chaviva and Shadid, slashing the mists with their eyes alone, compelled by some powers absurd and fabulous to follow the royal couple. Fountains could be heard gurgling in the distance—falling over the marble slabs in silvery ripples, flushed golden by the haze in sunshine. Beyond the fountains were undulating hillocks, interspersed with cataracts, cascading down into rivulets smooth and quicksilver. They were approaching close to one hillock, discovering a path carved in between, spiraling up and leading toward a grand staircase. Guided by instinct and curiosity, they began mounting the steps, hand-in-hand, almost blinded by the light of a golden dome, colossal and blazing.

At the landing of the stairway was an arch as if fashioned out of beaten gold, reflecting all the colors of a rainbow. It was inviting them toward the throne hall illumined by Zodiac signs in heavenly splendor! In the middle of the hall was a great throne, supported by four real tigers with distended paws, their eyes gleaming and challenging. Almeena clung to Shedad in absolute fright, shifting her attention to the canopy of gold over the throne. It was stitched with rubies and diamonds, evoking the illusion of ice and fire, dazzling and shimmering. Shedad counted mentally nine steps to the throne, approaching steadily with the courage of an aspiring god, leaving Almeena at the foot of the throne. She stood there in awe, bewitched and frightened.

Shedad lowered himself upon his throne and was instantly mantled in the radiance of exaltation. His head was haloed by a magnificent crown and a royal scepter materialized in his hand. A symphony of music was lowered down from the heavens in honor of his coronation. The luminaries above the canopy began to move in their heavenly orbs and Shedad could behold all like all-seeing god his dominion in its entirety. The palace, the courts and the gardens, the lakes, the fountains, the pavilions and the colonnades, all singing!

Who on earth is mightier than me!

Shedad, in his mind, was already communing with his tribe that he is their god. With this grand thought in his head, he leapt suddenly to his feet. In a flash, the music stopped, royal scepter vanished from his hand. His head was divested of the crown, and gone were the halo and the radiance. Silence was deafening, and primal haze was descending. Only the fiery eyes of the tigers were bright and menacing. Shedad inched his way toward his wife, more stunned than befuddled.

Allah promiseth to the believers, men and women, gardens underneath which rivers flow, wherein they will abide—blessed dwellings in the gardens of Eden. And—greater (far) acceptance from Allah. That is the supreme triumph. 9:72

An awful cry was heard in the distance and the Garden of Irem was plunged in complete darkness. Jamshed was pacing by Lake Shisha, restless and exhilarated, recalling with great precision how the Garden of Irem was destroyed. He had no need to look into the depths of Lake Shisha to know how Shedad had returned to the tribe of Aad to bring his people back to the gates of doom, for he could see it happening in his head exactly the way it happened five hundred and fifty years before the birth of Prophet Muhammad. Sophia and Kilabah were still lured to the reflection of the Garden of Irem enveloped by haze and mists in Lake Shisha, but Jamshed was divining omens from the mansions of stars in the sky. Yet, his thoughts were running a commentary over the fate of Shedad and his family.

"Radiance is gone from Shedad." Jamshed thought aloud. "When radiance departed from me, even the glory of my dominions was diminished. I was hounded all the way from Azerbaijan to Zahak where I was brutally murdered, and darkness fell over—"

A raging wind pierced by thunderbolts went coursing down the desert with a high speed, muffling all sounds but the sound of thundering. It lasted but for a few moments, disrupting only the thoughts of Jamshed. Sophia looked up, the light in her eyes matching the sparkle of stars, cold and glittering. Kilabah also looked up as if divining omens from the sky which was turning cobalt and capricious.

"You have abandoned your seven-ringed cup here at the Lake, O King, and are not interested in looking after your golden goddess with silvery gown?" Sophia teased, her eyes shining with laughter and mockery.

"Ah, the cup, I have neglected it only twice during the past seven hundred years of my existence!" Jamshed permitted his own self the luxury of laughter. "And that, too, during the dramatic event of mystical bull when he shifts the earth from one horn to the other? That's precisely what happened just now in the blink of an eye. As to my beautiful goddess, I can't get to her until this catastrophe is over."

"What catastrophe?" Kilabah leaped to his feet. "I don't want to lose my Chaviva this second time around."

"You will find Chaviva after you lose her, and you have already lost her, can't you see?" Jamshed began his commentary while pacing. "Chaviva in only seven years old, she was two when her parents left for the Garden of Irem. They think they stayed in the Garden for five days, but it was five years. If you can see, you would notice how Shedad and Almeena have changed, looking bloodless and cadaverous. They have brought the whole tribe of Aad to occupy the city of Irem—"

The rumbling of a dreadful earthquake swallowed Jamshed's voice. A fatal wind swirling crimson sands came from nowhere, lifting Sophia off her feet and tossing her over the edge of Takhti-Jamshed. Kilabah appeared to be dancing amidst a whirlwind of sand, his feet unsteady and his arms groping for anchor. Jamshed was trying to retrieve his Jam-e-Jam, both he and his cup whipped by the raging winds. Down below at the gate of enchantment was a great pandemonium. The tribe of Aad was scorched and buffeted by swirling sands, perishing along with the city of Irem with its palaces and gardens. A large crater of a furnace was sucked deeper into earth, its mouth closed by red sands, attaining the color of blood freshly split.

Take warning o proud
And in length o' life vain
I am Shedad, son of Aad
Of the forts Castellain
Lord of pillars and power
Lord of tried might and main
Whom all earth's sons obeyed
For my mischief and bane
And who held east and west
In mine awfulest reign
He preached me salvation
Whom God did assain
But we crossed him and asked
Can no refuge be tak'en
When a cry on us cried
From through the horizon plain
And we fell on the field
Like the harvested grain
And the fixt day await
We, in earth bosoms lain

"Did you hear what I heard?" Sophia's voice penetrated the stillness which had fallen swiftly after the storm abrupt and devastating.

The storm had ended. Irem was no more, the palaces and gardens were vanished as if those wonders never existed. The desert of Ubar was silent, too, where Kilabah sat by Lake Shisha, plunged in deep mourning. Jamshed was sitting opposite Sophia on Takhti-Jamshed. He was totally absorbed in watching through his Jam-e-Jam the creation and destruction of worlds and galaxies.

"Do you see what I see?" Jamshed's voice appeared to hover over Lake Shisha. His gaze was fixed on Jam-e-Jam, his lips moving involuntarily. "Shedad, Almeena, Chaviva, the entire tribe of Aad, all gone, all gone. No trace of any life. Must find a way to reach Aleena?"

"How would you find her, O King, if Irem is no more?" Sophia's blue eyes were reflecting both pain and glee. "You have to catch genii by their throat to rebuild that city of wonder and enchantment."

"Some say Irem was built by giants, and others conjecture that it was built by the tribe of Aad, but it was here on earth before any mortal was born," Jamshed said aloud, not taking his eyes off Jam-e-Jam. "And though swallowed by earthquake, Irem would protect her secrets from the profane, revealing them to the knowing."

"I have seen, yet understood little." Kilabah moaned, disrupting the placid depths of Lake Shisha with his tears. "Irem was an earthly paradise to the initiated. Towers rising high, the great octagonal fort, alas, no more! And I could see places there of power and hidden knowledge."

"There are many levels of existence for Irem." Jamshed was saying as if spellbound. "Many levels of reality! Irem of the old ones still exists in some form. This great desert is not an empty quarter connected to the great void, but it contains all, the palaces and the gardens. I got it!" He lifted his eyes, his face radiant and glowing. "I know the secret to reach Ibrahim, and he is the architect who built Irem. Aleena, beloved, I am coming!"

"A poor Bedouin meeting a king, an architect and a goddess, and no chance of finding Chaviva!" Kilabah lumbered to his feet, swaying.

"Ibrahim is no architect, but an astrologer and a wizard of lies, I am beginning to understand!" Sophia laughed hysterically.

"And yet I have the key to Paradise!" Jamshed's laughter was strident and ricocheting. "Signet-ring is my talisman, and my Jam-e-Jam the stairway to heaven."

LUMINARIES OF THE EARTH

The subterranean abode was awakening to the saddest of tunes from the silvery lyre of Aleena. This tune was reaching the wilderness of Aden in Ubar, carrying along with it a subtle scent from the Garden of Irem. Jamshed could inhale that scent in his sleep, which was becoming heavy, startling him to wakefulness over his Takhti-Jamshed. Sophia, sleeping beside him, was enveloped in some aura of bliss and sweet surrender. The lone lover seated at the edge of the Lake Shisha was Kilabah, fogging the clear waters with sighs cold and bitter.

Hath not the fame of those before them reach them — the folk of Noah, Aad, Thamud, the folk of Abraham, the dwellers of Midian and the disasters which befell them? Their messengers from Allah came to them with proofs of Allah's sovereignty, so Allah surely wronged them not, but they did wrong themselves. 9:70

One thunder of a revelation rang loud in the wilderness of Aden, jolting Sophia out of her sweet reveries. She pulled her starry shawl together and sat up, blinking hazily and in disbelief. Her blue eyes sparkled, meeting and holding Jamshed's gaze in wonder and abeyance. Jamshed tore his vision away from Sophia, bending double to claim his Jam-e-Jam, the look in his eyes distant and troubled.

"Who dares awaken me from my sweet slumber?" One echo of admonition from Ibrahim's lips went skirling up Lake Shisha, sending Kilabah whirling away as if whipped by gusts violent and relentless.

Jamshed sat transfixed looking into his Jam-e-Jam. Sophia had shifted close to him, sharing the scene of distress down the valley of Irem under some spell of awe and exhilaration. Kilabah was drifting toward them, unsteady and terrified. Jam-e-Jam had become the window of the trio to view the subterranean Garden of Irem in its entire splendor. Ibrahim was pacing in circles, agitated and distraught, his white beard against his blue robe suspended like a witch's broom. He appeared to be murmuring incantations, oblivious to the presence of Aleena by the bower of roses, her face wreathed in a quicksilver smile, most charming and mysterious.

"Ibrahim, we need to communicate. Help us to reach you." Jamshed's plea echoed through the void of his Jam-e-Jam.

"Ah, the voice is familiar, that of my king and master, King Habuz." Ibrahim contemplated aloud. "I can't see you. I can sense more than one? Are you close to Lake Shisha? That's the only medium through which one can reach me if one is determined?" A subtle richness of warmth and magic in his voice was enveloping the trio of lovers under a spell of hope and euphoria.

Lake Shisha, like a great window into the heart of the subterranean world, was lending the spellbound trio a wide view of the Garden of Irem. Ibrahim had stopped pacing, while Aleena had strolled away, hugging her silver lyre to her breast. Jamshed was stricken afresh with the arrows of cupid, his gaze following Aleena with intensity both tender and heartrending. Kilabah was turned to a portrait of grief, his gaze searching the sparkling depths of Lake Shisha for any trace of finding Chaviva. Ibrahim's gaze had settled Sophia inside the waters of Lake Shisha, and against the ardor in his eyes she was crumbling like a rag of misery.

"Ah, my Beloved! You have abandoned your old philosopher and chosen a new lover, I presume?" Ibrahim caught and held Sophia's gaze most endearingly.

"I have been faithful, my venerable Lord!" Sophia lied, permitting herself the luxury of guile and cunning. "You are the one courting a beloved young and disdainful, it is obvious." She shifted her gaze to Aleena, her lips parting in a velvety smile.

"You mean the Gothic Princess, sweet Sophia!" Ibrahim laughed, his laughter vibrant and youthful! "We are prisoners of fate! I am as much her prisoner as she is mine. She keeps me drugged under the spell of her music, and the power of my magic doesn't allow her to leave this Garden of Irem."

"Woe is me, where can I find my Chaviva?" Kilabah lamented, suddenly in a state of grief and hopelessness. "God must be punishing me, all the bounties of God are denied to me, including his love. My beloved gone! All perished; my folks, my dreams, my orchards, and the most precious of all, my dear Chaviva. Why do I keep thinking, I have done more good than ill?" His eyes were brimming with tears.

"God is Rahman as mentioned in the Quran, meaning generous and gracious, O young heathen!" Ibrahim admonished with a sudden flare for drama. "In conformity with the teachings of Quran, bounties are not bestowed on men as a result of any good they do. They are given to them as a grace from God. God initiates good and gives it gratuitously, and does not wait until people take the initiative of doing something good and only then reward them for it."

"Pity that Chaviva is gone, yet the Irem stays." Jamshed murmured to himself.

"Alas, that the earth has swallowed up Irem indeed, as far as the Irem of the crimson desert is concerned!" Ibrahim's tone was dreamy and nostalgic. "No more caravans of frankincense pass through the city of Irem. Many have called it the town of wickedness, but no one dares comprehend the fabulous. What you see now, though under the earth, is the replica of Irem which I built in the great city of Granada for the King. You do sound like King Habuz. Are you not the same king, trying to trick me into releasing Aleena?" He intoned suspiciously. "Who are you?" His bushy eyebrows were arching up like a pair of pyramids.

"Jamshed, that's my name." Jamshed could barely murmur.

Ibrahim snatching the pause with a cheerful exclamation! "Ah, Shah Jam! I should have known. No wonder you can view the whole world, and reach the invisible heavens if you wished. The inventor of arts and sciences, and the architect of solar calendar! The living legend of splendor and opulence!"

"And murdered most brutally by Zohak!" Jamshed exclaimed bitterly. "The tragedy of my death didn't reach you perhaps."

"I know too well, Shah Jam, but the same Zohak, in turn, suffered a terrible death, if that is any consolation to you?" Ibrahim's gaze was wandering from Sophia to Kilabah before returning to Jamshed. "Zohak was chained up inside Mount Doemavand, exposed to the agony of a living death."

"Agony of living!" Kilabah moaned. "Where can I find my Chaviva?"

"You can, but first you have to tell me who you are?" Ibrahim's philosophic gaze was settling on Kilabah.

"I am that wretch of a madman who fell in love with Chaviva!" Kilabah groaned. "Kilabah is my name, a Bedouin and a simpleton."

"Even a simpleton, if in love, could be passed as the greatest of sages." Ibrahim responded profoundly. "I would help you find your ladylove if you could join me in this paradise away from Paradise. Shah Jam could help you. He knows all the incantations."

"If my incantations work, we can all come, can't we?" Jamshed sang amidst a surge of fresh hope and longing.

"Not possible, not as yet." Ibrahim stroked his conical beard. "Not until Kilabah is joined with Chaviva."

"Why, my dear Lord?" Sophia chirped belligerently. "All these years I have been longing to be with you, my only love." She infused the warmth of false love in her beguiling tones. "It is obvious now, that you don't want to be with me?"

"You have lost the light of the One, dear Sophia, and your wisdom is frayed." Ibrahim began half tenderly, hall impatiently.

"Yet you remain charming and irresistible as ever. Of course I want to be with you, but you can't come till Kilabah goes through the twelve halls of Irem in the ritual-quest of finding his ladylove."

"I must admit, Ibrahim, I am longing to be united with Aleena. Not in the least tricking you into releasing her, but begging to be admitted to her presence." Jamshed shoved his own cause down Lake Shisha before Sophia or Kilabah could speak.

Aleena was retreating her steps toward the bower of roses. Upon reaching there she looked up, the liquid-gold in her eyes emanating shafts of sunlight. A thin smile curved upon her lips into a crescent wound as she smoothed her gown into silvery ripples. Ibrahim, in his act of stirring, appeared to hold Aleena inside the pools of his eyes, his gaze slipping from the silver lyre on her breast to the rippling of stars and crescents on her gown. Abruptly, he tore his gaze away from Aleena, returning his attention to Jamshed, his hazel eyes burning.

"You can't enter the replica of the Garden of Irem, Shah Jam, you cannot! Ibrahim's look was piercing, his voice quivering with emotion. "Chaviva is love and she is already here. Kilabah is innocence, and he would find her. Sophia is wisdom, and she would bring Aleena to you. No king of the world is permitted entry into this Garden of Irem."

"Aleena doesn't remember me, it seems?" Jamshed demurred aloud, his gaze holding her captive. "Why so quiet and reserved, Beloved, don't you remember me?" His look was puzzled, his heart leaping out to her.

"A memory vague and beautiful!" Aleena murmured dreamily, the mysterious smile upon her lips fading. "Since the loss of my parents and of their kingdom, I remember but very little." She fondled the strings of her silver lyre with the intention of playing.

"No, dear Aleena, please!" Ibrahim reached her side with great swiftness. "Spare me the spell of your sweet music just this once, otherwise I would fall asleep. I need to release you from my spell, too, and be released from yours. But in order to do that, we must work together, striving toward dissolving the fogs of magic and incantation. Be a silent witness, please, as I initiate the process of unlocking the secret doors of space and time."

"I would kiss the door and the floor, and the ether and void too, if I could find my Chaviva!" Kilabah's heart was voicing this madness; it was obvious, his dark eyes following the graceful retreat of Aleena.

"To begin with, young Bedouin, you need to plead with Shah Jam to practice his incantations on you," Ibrahim suggested, his eyes flashing a challenge at Jamshed.

"Not so quick, O venerable philosopher!" Jamshed quipped profoundly. "I need to know the truth of your assertions. Why do you say this is the replica of Garden of Irem? And if you are the architect, why did you build it in Spain?"

"A long story, even the prologue of it, if you have patience!" Ibrahim began reluctantly. "The Irem of the old ones was sucked into earth by God's wrath, but this Irem of Granada I built, and I am the one who caused it to sink under earth. "I built it in Spain because I happened to be under the patronage of the king of Spain, King Habuz."

"So you have not seen the real Irem since it was destroyed by God's wrath?" Jamshed exclaimed suddenly. "How could you build a replica if you could not see the original?"

"I have." Ibrahim appeared to be thinking aloud. "I was young then, tending my father's camels in the desert of Aden. One of the camels strayed, and I went after it searching for days. One afternoon, wearied and exhausted by wandering, I fell asleep under a palm tree by the side of an ancient wall. Upon awakening, I noticed a tall gate. Without thinking, I opened it, and discovered a city of pillars with wide streets and great houses. Not a soul lived in that city, and I wandered aimlessly, coming upon a palace with awe-inspiring façade and a garden furnished with fishponds and fountains. Abundance of flowers with exquisite color and fragrance were delightful, and orchards bearing fruit of each size and variety tempting. The silence and beauty of that place was frightening, so I hastened to leave. Once outside the gates, I was tempted to have a last glimpse of the beautiful city with its palaces and gardens. Alas, when I turned back to look, there was nothing but the stark nakedness of the crimson desert."

"So you were the one I saw in the Garden of Irem, eluding me from hall to hall, and I could never find you," Kilabah exclaimed abruptly, his look fiery and reminiscent. "I too had lost my camel, and came upon the Garden of Irem. It vanished from my sight, too, when I turned back to have a second look. None of my folks would believe me when I told them."

"Now you can boast of a witness inside the Garden of Irem, Ibrahim!" Jamshed chuckled. "Still, you can't replicate the Garden of Irem by having a glimpse of it once."

"Twice, Shah Jam! And the second time I visited I stayed for several days." Ibrahim retorted, his eyes shooting stars of memories.

"How well I remember, my Lord! You promised you would take me there?" Sophia laughed, more so by the befuddled expression of Jamshed than by the rush of pleasant memories. "I didn't believe you then, but I still remember the fabulous story you told me. How you got hold of the book of knowledge from the bosom of a mummy inside the very heart of the pyramids of Egypt. And I still don't believe you." Laughter died upon her lips, her heart aching to be with Jamshed alone and together.

"That book, my dear Sophia, whether you believe or not, was given to Adam after his fall, and was handed down from generation to generation to King Solomon. By studying that book, he was able to build the temple of Jerusalem. How it came into the hands of the architect of the pyramids, only the God of the Hebrews knows."

"With the aid of that book alone you built the Garden of Irem?" Jamshed found his voice, the signet-ring on his index finger throbbing like a ruby-red wound.

"That book would be worthless if one was not skilled in squeezing wisdom and understanding out of parables," Ibrahim intoned enigmatically. "Understanding comes through grace and knowledge. I was recipient of both, since my father Ayub was last of the companions of the Prophet."

"You never told me that, my Lord, though I knew you possessed the secret knowledge of youth and immortality!" Sophia's eyes were flashing accusations.

"Alas, that I discovered the secret of immortality when I were old and wrinkled!" A wrinkled smile washed Ibrahim's features with a touch of sadness. "Be assured, dear Sophia, I possess not the knowledge of the fountain of youth."

"Yet, my philosopher friend, you have arrested youth in all its essence of charm and loveliness, and that no doubt is my captive Aleena." Jamshed tossed his own arrow of accusation. "I will get to that later. But first, would you kindly satisfy my curiosity as to how you amassed so much wealth to build this replica of the Garden of Irem?"

"Such a question from the king of Azerbaijan! I wonder if you already know." Ibrahim's eyes were lit by the ocean of profundity. "Just like you, I possess the knowledge of spells and magic. When I occupied the real Garden of Irem, all the genii who watch over the lost treasures of this world became obedient to my will. The same genii helped me build this Garden of Irem in Spain as you see it now."

"Partially, since I am blinded afresh by my love for Aleena." One furnace of a sigh escaped Jamshed's lips.

"The cure for this, Shah Jam, if you care to see the sacred road to Beloved, is to make the events rolling by your incantations. The inception of your journey on this sacred road begins with your success in sending Kilabah to the Garden of Irem. He would be the one guiding you, and I would be guided by him."

"Then let it begin!" Jamshed fanned another furnace of a sigh, closing his eyes. "My seven-ringed cup of magical magnificence! Nine towers of exquisite splendor. Eleven nights of enchantment! Thirteen sublime verses from the Sura of Dawn from the glorious Quran," Jamshed intoned passionately.

A sudden convergence of mists enveloped Lake Shisha. Mists white and gossamer, whipped into rags by the sudden onslaught of thunder and lightning. Bolts of lightning zoomed from the sky in a fury, serpentine and dazzling. Earth and heavens were turned into ocean of light, lowering a meteor of tunes most dulcet and enchanting. Nothing seemed to exist but the islands of light, reflecting words most sublime. Something within the heart of the universe was ripped open, illumined and throbbing. It was the lamp of unity, swaying ecstatically, its light shuddering and falling into a cataract of songs. The rosary of revelation was spinning and dancing.

Allah is the light of the heavens and the earth
The similitude of His light is as a lustrous niche
Wherein is the lamp, the lamp is in a glass
The glass as if it were a glittering star
It is lit by a blessed tree—an olive
Neither of the east nor of the west
Whose oil will well nigh glow forth
Though fire toucheth it not
Light upon light
Allah guides to His light whomsoever He wills
Allah sets forth parables to men
Allah know all things full well 24:35

VISTA OF ENCHANTMENT

Allah promiseth to the believers, men and women, gardens underneath which rivers flow wherein they will abide—blessed dwellings in the Garden of Eden. And greater far, acceptance from Allah! That is the supreme triumph. 9:72

An awful cry from nowhere whipped the garnet sands to swirling circles as Jamshed clutched Sophia to him, staying anchored to the edge of Lake Shisha. Both were watching in horror the zooming speed of Kilabah's body which was being sucked into the tunnel of water toward the subterranean abode of Irem.

"Forty nights of vigil to break another veil of illusion in forty zillion times four of light years." Jamshed's incantation was a catapult of fear and command hurled at the heavens and the earth, surging and shuddering.

"Rab al Khali." Sophia was repeating her own litany of a prayer-incantation.

"Ah, Sophia's fear and anguish of losing her own life!" Ibrahim mocked from the magnificent depths of Irem, welcoming Kilabah into his arms and laughing. "Rab al Khali means a secret gate to the void, and great entry into the city of old ones." He expounded, distracted by the sudden appearance of Aleena.

She had materialized down the shining steps of the ruby palace as the very incarnation of Venus. Her whole being was transformed as if she had dispelled her sadness by the sheer light of her inner love and radiance. She was smiling, the silver lyre over her breast as vibrant as her gown of stars and crescents. Her liquid-gold eyes were spilling warmth of welcome, holding both men prisoner in her sparkling intensity.

"Sophia up there is still wondering, perhaps, how she lost the light of the One and why she fears death?" Aleena shook loose her raven locks from the coronet of pearls. "Not even knowing that her fear and anguish created—accidentally, should I say, the matter and soul through the elements of air, fire, earth and water?"

"I know, O Gothic queen of ignorance!" Sophia's razor sharp exclamation carved serpentine ridges in the subterranean hole of Zodiac splendor, claiming the attention of Ibrahim and Kilabah. "I created much more, dividing humans in three categories. The ones who bond with matter stay with the principle of evil, and who bond with soul are saved from evil. The third in the category are the few rare ones who achieve knowledge through the light of gnosis and are absorbed in the light of grace."

"And Gnostics believe, Sophia, you are the holy spirit of Trinity." Jamshed's hysterical mirth attracted not only the attention of the goddess, but of the inhabitants of the subterranean world, too.

Amongst them, Chaviva appearing on the balcony of the ruby palace like a pearl of the orient, her small white face smooth and glowing! Her silvery gown was accentuating her eyes, dark and sparkling. She appeared to be caught inside the bonfire of rubies from palace gates to lofty domes, all rosy and bulbous.

"Sophia would cast all of us down into the abyss if we are not careful!" One tinkling of a warning escaped Chaviva's lips, all eyes turning to her as moths to a flame.

Kilabah swung around; ready to fly to his beloved, but Ibrahim restrained him with an astonishing grip of steel with his arm. Aleena merely smiled, condoning Kilabah's agonized cry of *Chaviva*, her own eyes locked with Chaviva with a light of understanding.

"You would destroy your beloved, Kilabah, if you dared but stir!" Ibrahim's touch and warning chilled Kilabah in his act of moving. "You have to follow my orders strictly, as I command.

Chaviva doesn't even know that you exist. She can't see you. You have to follow her through the twelve halls of Zodiac, learning the art of life and living before you could be united with her."

"Your success, Kilabah, opens the gates of hope for me. You must obey the philosopher." Jamshed lowered his own string of warning, his eyes riveted to Aleena, hungry and devouring.

"I am the next one to enter the Garden of Irem, and the only one who can dissolve the mists of enchantment." Sophia's eyes appeared to shoot arrows of hatred laced with the venom of jealousy at Aleena.

"Of course, your plight and distress, Sophia, would be no different than those goddesses, half mortal, half divine!" Aleena's face was lifted up, haloed by a smile, both sarcastic and challenging. "Such goddesses are molded alive into the crystal-time of myths where illusion becomes the shadow of reality." Her smile was widening, as if drawing a veil over her arrogance. "Persephone's descent into Hades three months every year, is that still true? Did Eve ever live? Was Mary really the receptacle of Virgin Birth? Eurydice rescued by valorous Orpheus from the Underworld? Was Helen of Troy ever abducted and then rescued? Or Andromeda ever rescued by Perseus? Cinderella, also Sleeping Beauty living happily Ever after! God Rama's wife Sita, was she ever abducted, and then rescued by her husband?"

"No doubt, they all lived and suffered, O Princess vain and arrogant!"Chaviva's exclamation went swirling up from subterranean depths to earthly heights. "You should have started with Church as the bride of Christ. It lived even before Christ and it still lives after Christ. I don't hear all, and I can't see all, but the treasure-trove of my memory is fresh forever. I have the wisdom and patience of Penelope, though I would not welcome the return of Odysseus."

"I would rather shut myself in Pandora's box than wait for any faithless man-god!" Sophia's mirth went tinkling down Lake

Shisha. It was enveloping all in some mist of enchantment which neither came from the desert of Ubar, nor was a part of the Garden of Irem.

"Seven deadly sins of the world are more delightful than all the evils in Pandora's box!" Ibrahim was free from the spell of this enchantment, so were Sophia and Jamshed by Lake Shisha.

"Nothing deadly about sins, or sinful about evils, if number seven is a part of their attributes by the virtue of its being a sacred number!" Jamshed's mystical smile was chilled by Sophia's open derision.

"Is that number seven your sweet Aleena studying at the Gate of the Garden of Irem?" Sophia's very eyes appeared to be gloating over her skill in casting the spell of enchantment. She scoffed and smirked, but her heart was longing to win the love of Jamshed.

"No, that's the key to Paradise. Surely, a fake one, my beloved Aleena knows." Jamshed, ignorant of Sophia's passion, was utterly absorbed in admiring Aleena's beauty as if she was sculpted alive out of pearly dawns. "This is not the same as that silver antique key. The key which could unlock successive doors that bar our entry down the corridors of space and time to the border where no man or woman has dared cross since Shedad's thousand-pillared Irem under the sand-dunes of crimson desert." His gaze was reaching down to Ibrahim for answers. "This is the keystone of the arch vainly grasping for something which is not there?"

"Shah Jam of seven-ringed cup is right of course!" Ibrahim's laughter ricocheted through space and water, breaking the spell of enchantment. "Shedad's palace and garden were built within a span of three hundred and forty years, while I built this one in eleven nights. Number eleven is the number of transgression, remember?"

"How can one forget if one has visited the Golgothan Rock of Jerusalem?" Jamshed smiled wryly. "Eleven is the first act of transgression over ten — the number of God's commandments. Iblis is the one who accomplished this task for you in just eleven nights, I am sure."

"Genii worked for me, Shah Jam, creatures made out of fire even before the creation of Adam." Ibrahim let his gaze roam from Aleena, still under the spell of half enchantment, to Chaviva, to Kilabah. "Those airy creatures are subject to mortal wants like eating, drinking and propagating. And just like us are corruptible and perishable. When their wickedness provoked Allah's anger, He ordered Iblis to cast them into the desert and keep them secluded. I have learnt to keep them imprisoned under my spell, and they obey me absolutely."

"Take my seven-ringed cup, Ibrahim, and let me come into your enchanted Garden of Irem," Jamshed proposed, longing to be with Aleena.

"Even for your Takhti-Jamshed, Shah Jam, I cannot allow you to come until Kilabah is joined with Chaviva. Most probably, it seems like, never. Chaviva's love must be resurrected out of the enchantment of life and death before we can achieve peace and paradise on earth and in space. We will begin with number seven to commence the purging of constellations. Observe how Chaviva leads us through the Hall of Aries. Become a part of her awe and bewilderment. Learn through the tongue of perceptions, for words would never convey to you what you want to know."

Allah is the light of the heavens and the earth

A symphony of sounds was creating visions grand and dazzling. The façade of the pearly gate guarding the palace of Irem was shrouded in haze golden and crimson. A familiar pair of hands, beautifully sculpted, was coming into view. Above them was the silver key washed by moonlit brilliance. Right beneath the key was a bright star embedded into a Crescent, facing horizontally, one Cross bronzed and sparkling. The pearly gate was sliding open, revealing the first miracle of Zodiac splendor. A jeweled Ram guarding over the Hall of Rubies appeared to glow with the fire of magic and mystery. Chaviva, wearing the color of Mars, sailed into the Hall of Rubies as if enveloped in flames.

"My God why hast Thou forsaken me! Can you hear the last seven words of Christ?" Chaviva drifted toward the shining Cross emblazoned with the silhouette of Christ, accentuating wounds against the light of teardrop rubies.

"Not only do I hear the sweet voice, but see the beloved face, holier than holy in utter surrender to suffering." Kilabah drifted after Chaviva as if intoxicated by awe and wonder.

Both the lover and the beloved appeared to move in a dreamlike trance, seemingly communicating with each other, yet mantled in mists of oblivion and bewilderment.

"Seven Hebrew names of God to sprinkle blessings!" Ibrahim, too, had become a part of the dream-mists, his voice strange and reverent. "El, Elohim, Adonai, Yhwh-Jehovah, Ehyenh-Asher-Ehyer, Shaddai and Zebaot."

"Four and three!" Aleena studied her bejeweled hands, four rings blazing on her right hand and three on the left. "Number seven, the lucky and mystic number of the Pythagoreans." Her small white face was shining like a luminary amidst the misty dreams of her own making. "Seven sacred planets of the Egyptians. Moon, Mercury, Venus, Sun, Mars, Jupiter and Saturn!"

"No luck for Nebuchadnezzar!" Jamshed's voice spluttered forth in a volley of mirth. "Incarcerated in the body of a beast for seven years!" He was enjoying his own sense of liberty and euphoria, obviously not imprisoned inside the fogs of enchantment.

"Samson believed in lucky number seven." Sophia awakening from the fogs of enchantment, breathed softly. "His wedding feast lasting for seven days. Not so lucky when he told his bride the answer to the riddle on seventh day, and she cut seven locks of his hair to deprive him of his strength." Her gaze was tracing Jamshed's own down the subterranean deeps where Aleena and

Ibrahim were caught in abeyance under the spell of fresh enchantment.

Chaviva and Kilabah were drawn into their own world of rapt wonder, communicating in the dream-world of magic and mystery. Both were drifting together under some spell of awe and wild abandon, not even knowing that their thoughts were strewn together into words, spiraling across the borders of time and space toward the very core of creation. Ruby red wounds of Christ were replaced by the pearly splendor of the voids, creating and recreating sounds, charms and symphonies.

"Seven days of creation. Seven days in a week. Seven graces. Seven deadly sins! Seven divisions of the Lord's Prayer!" Chaviva's voice was carrying a brushstroke of miracles. Each shifting scene was painted vividly in a dazzling array of colors against the artwork of fluted arches and pillars edged with pearls, within which shone rubies, much like the play of fire and ice.

"Seven stages in the life of man, climactic years are seven and nine with their multiples by odd numbers. And the seventh son of a seventh son is born with formidable magical and healing powers and clairvoyance." Kilabah's voice was attaining the quality of a distant cataract, his spellbound gaze following Chaviva.

To swear the Hebrew verb, literally meaning, coming under the influence of seven things; thus seven ewe lambs figure in the oath between Abraham and Abimelech at Beersheba. The Arabian oath in which seven stones are smeared with blood!

Chaviva's restless spirit in that Hall of Rubies was suspended over the bridge of purification, its light cascading down over the shoulders of Kilabah. His gaze was darting past the lights toward the bulbous domes encrusted with pearls and rubies, glowing and shimmering in the distance. He was standing still, as if straining to catch the least of sounds, but by the stillness of his expression, it was obvious that he could neither hear a word, nor catch a glimpse of Chaviva. Her eyes were flashing, lit by the fire of rubies all around, and spilling profundities. Beliefs, ancient and profound, were escaping her ruby-red lips in a string of words both clear and melodious.

"Seventh year is the Hebrews sabbatical, and seven times seven becomes the year of jubilee. Three Jewish feasts last seven days each, and seven weeks separate the first and second feast." Chaviva was watching a swing of light being suspended from the bulbous domes. Claiming it swiftly, she began swinging, letting the cataract of her thoughts sparkle and meander down the Zodiac splendor."

"Levitical purifications lasted seven days. Even Balaam had seven altars, and sacrificed on them seven rams and seven bullocks. Namaan was commanded to dip seven times in Jordan, it is written. Elijah, we are told, sent his servant seven times to look out for rain. Pharaoh in his dream saw seven years in each of his wives. Seven priests with seven trumpets marched around Jericho once every day." Kilabah's thoughts, not his lips were lowering this platter of knowledge.

Suddenly, a symphony of trumpets shook the subterranean deeps, splitting loose the mosaic of rubies and diamonds overhead. The swing of light was sucked back into the shining void. Chaviva was tossed headlong into a balcony ablaze with rubies as big as the walnuts. Kilabah had found a stairway of light, his feet involuntarily guiding him toward his beloved. Aleena was lured toward a ruby throne; its velvety canopy ballooned like a parachute as it descended on the marble floor, radiating the aura of mystery and challenge. More mysterious than any sound or scenery was Ibrahim's conical beard, sweeping his shoulders right and left under some spell of fever and denial. Prayerful litany from the lips of Jamshed was tearing apart the fogs inside the Hall of Rubies in affinity with the claps of thunder.

Ten times seven Israelites went to Egypt, exile lasting the same number of years under the guidance of ten times seven elders.

A tinkling of mirth from Sophia's lips was colliding with the claps of thunder, and lowering its own incantations.

Apocalypse! Seven churches of Asia! Seven stars, seven trumpets, seven candlesticks, seven spirits before the throne of God. Seven horns, seven vials, seven plagues! Seven-headed monster and the lamb with seven eyes! Seven heavens, the seventh of pure light ruled by Abraham!

An avalanche of fogs was whipping up a storm. The Hall of Rubies had begun to spin upon its axis, reflecting seven heavens. Seven seas, too, were coming into view like the mirrors cracked and glittering. From where Aleena sat on her ruby throne, she had the vantage of watching seven seas and the seven heavens, concurrently and simultaneously. Ibrahim was keen on arresting the glitter of Arctic and Antarctic. North and South Pacific were luring Kilabah's attention, while Chaviva was fascinated by the placid deeps of the North and South Atlantic. Takhti-Jamshed could be seen sailing over the waters of the Indian Ocean, hosting the king and the goddess.

Sophia's expression was rapt and prayerful, while Jamshed, beside her, looked vulnerable and bewildered. By the virtue of his honed perception, Jamshed could see the parade of the first seven kings in succession. Aleena, too, had the power and perception; in fact, the procession of the kings was right at the foot of her throne. She was identifying aloud the name of each king, as if holding dear the book of remembrance.

Romulus; Numa Pompilius; Tulius Hostilius; Ancus Martius; Tarquinius Priscus; Servius Tullius and Tarquinius Superbus.

"I feel like one of the seven champions of Christendom, cursed by God and the whole host of demons," Jamshed whispered to Sophia, as if the angels above were testing his patience. "The seven champions of old, I mean, George of England, imprisoned for seven years by Almidor the king of Morocco. St. Denys of France turned into a horse for seven years by some evil spell. St. James of Spain was smitten by the love of a Jewess so profoundly that he became dumb for seven whole years. St. Andrew of Scotland was more of a magician than a saint, helping six ladies out of the prison of enchantment, who were turned into swans, serving seven years of swan-hood. The tragic end of St. Patrick of Ireland was inside a prison cell where he dug his own grave for seven years with his nails. St. David of Wales was fortunate, though he slept for seven years in the enchanted garden of Ormandine, but was redeemed by St. George. St. Anthony of Italy was imprisoned in black castle under the enchantment of deep sleep. He would have stayed there till eternity if St. George's three sons had not come to his rescue, dissolving the spell of the seven lamps by the water from the enchanted fountain."

"No demons have the power to cast a spell over you, King Jamshed." Sophia laughed; her laughter bitter and joyless. "Perchance, by good fortune, if you were caught under some spell by my beauty, I would have the power to release you from that spell with my prowess of lighting the lamps of life, truth, power, beauty, memory, sacrifice and obedience."

"By the lamps of the splendid heavens, Sophia, you sound as if you are in love with me?" Jamshed's strident mirth shook the sky and the earth. Even the subterranean depths were churning a storm, jolting its occupants to awakening. "My knowledge concerning women and goddesses is shallow. Yet I would barter away my knowledge of music, rhetoric, literature, arithmetic, geometry and astronomy for one ounce of wisdom in understanding the heart of the women. Are you in love with me?"

"I thought you would never guess!" Sophia teased sadly and earnestly. "The heart of a woman is not complex, but the heart of a goddess? You would have to contemplate the heights of Mount Everest, and dive deep down the Victoria Falls. To look into the heart of the Grand Canyon and to embrace the beauty of the Great Barrier Reef! To look into the eyes of the Northern Lights and to feel the peace and warmth of paradise! It would be simple if one could feel the pulse of Brazil under the canopy of the Harbor at Rio de Janciro."

"If I could only believe—" Jamshed was caught in the eye of a hurricane, it seemed, spinning at the speed of light. Yet swiftly and astonishingly a beam of light from subterranean deeps was bringing the royal throne to a standstill, and lowering it gently into the wilderness of Aden. The same beam of light was unleashing a litany of voices, above them a voice most deep and commanding, of no other than that of Ibrahim.

Shah Jam, fall not into the error of dreams and enchantments. Behold the Hall of Emeralds, and pray to the sages true and ancient. They might pave your way to the Garden of Irem. Seven sages: Solon of Athens. Thales of Melitus. Pittacus of Mitylene. Cleobulus of Rhodes. Chilon of Sparta. Bias of Priene. Perionder of Corinth.

The earth and the heavens were shaking like cymbals, but Takhti-Jamshed by Lake Shisha was solid and immovable. Jamshed was trying to catch each sound, each inflection, his gaze pensive and profound. Sophia's gaze was piercing the waters of Lake Shisha. It was reaching the scene of turmoil down the subterranean deeps, and holding in abeyance the trauma of the future tragedies. Aleena was teasing the strings of her silver lyre, yet evoking the tunes most pensive and heartrending. Chaviva on the balcony of the Hall of Rubies was watching Kilabah pace in circles, looking demented and possessed.

Through my seven senses, beloved Chaviva, I can feel and taste the scent of your being. Kilabah was thinking aloud, oblivious to his own act of pacing or speaking. *Feeling and animation are in my brain. Taste, sight, speech, hearing and smelling are swollen with the promise of your homecoming, yet I see not.*

A great volley of laughter from somewhere spluttered forth, against which Chaviva's voice fell and rose in great tremors.

Look into the light of your inner holiness, Kilabah, and find your way under the influence of seven planets. Fire animates. Earth gives the sense of feeling. Water gives speech. Air gives taste. Mist lends sight. Flowers bestow hearing. South wind carries the scent of home.

The crimson sands in the wilderness of Aden and the Hall of Rubies in the Garden of Irem were bursting into a conflagration. The tongues of the licking flames were revealing and devouring the coliseum of Rome. Consuming also the catacombs of Alexandria in Egypt. The Great Wall of China was rising and shuddering. The gleaming Stonehenge in the distance and the leaning Tower of Pisa were drawing closer. The porcelain Tower of Nanking was dissolving in the mists. And the mosque of Hagia Sophia was rising aloft with its marble minarets, cutting through the heart of the sky.

Garden of Irem number one amongst the seven Wonders of the World.

Beams upon beams of light were enveloping, encompassing.

MANSION OF STARS

Allah is the light of the heavens and the earth
The similitude of His light is as a lustrous niche

A canopy of stars lowered over the Garden of Irem was accentuating the palace and Zodiac halls splashed with jewels. A great Bull, ablaze with emeralds, was embedded over the façade of the Zodiac hall next to the Hall of Rubies. Kilabah, standing under the mehrab, was blinking disbelief and astonishment. From where he stood he could see the jeweled balcony housing Ibrahim with Aleena and Chaviva on either side. Sophia and Jamshed, in the wilderness of Aden by Lake Shisha, were witnessing the same scene through the tunnel of water, turned telescopic green from the subterranean sparkle of jewels and luminaries.

"Beloved, Chaviva," Groaned Kilabah in an act of taking a step over the marble floor! It was shining like a limpid pool, absorbing waves and colors from multifaceted gems and symbols.

"Don't move, Kilabah, lest you lose your beloved forever!" Ibrahim warned. The large emerald on his forefinger was a dazzling mirage of planets and continents as he traced a circle in the air!

"What Ibrahim means, dear Kilabah, is that you need to purify your soul from the fire of jealousy in order to proceed further, so that you could finally join me in the twelfth hall of Zodiac?" Chaviva consoled enigmatically.

"Purification aside, Kilabah, your journey would be swift if you could chisel your love to the perfection of a diamond." A diaphanous smile lit up Aleena's features as she shifted her attention to Chaviva.

Ibrahim was smiling indulgently, his gaze reaching up to Sophia and Jamshed as if challenging their wits to practice arguments.

"Love would be my talisman against envy or jealousy, more brilliant than a diamond burning to cinders, when I leap through heavens to reach my beloved, my paradise!" Kilabah dreamily replied.

"Paradise itself has eight mighty gates, and you would be burning more than your envy or jealousy, naming flesh of your flesh to reach the highest paradise," Jamshed quipped abruptly, his gaze riveted to Aleena.

"Seven heavens for sure, but paradise is only one! Shah Jam of Azerbaijan should know that much?" Sophia murmured rather bitterly.

"My dear Sophia!" Jamshed indulged caustically. "You would quench the fires of your own jealousy if you could contemplate the sanctity of number eight. Of course, any pious fool knows the difference between heaven and paradise. This wretched world is the first level of heavens out of seven."

"Neither piety nor foolishness can withstand the light of my wisdom, yet I must claim the fair share of ignorance since I don't know the difference between heaven and paradise!" Sophia laughed without taking her gaze away from the subterranean splendor.

"A subtle difference, my goddess, how could you possibly know?" Jamshed squinted disbelief, casting a sidelong glance at her. "Heaven is seven heavens. Paradise, as you profess to know, is *one* inside the core of the seventh heaven."

"I was stuck in the second heaven!" Kilabah cried suddenly. The fire of emeralds around him, lending his features the glow and warmth of bonfire! "I can vividly recall Moses standing there conversing with angel Nuriel on his way to Paradise. I couldn't go further, my ascent barred by angels Raphael and Zachariel," He sighed, his features washed by pallor suddenly.

"Don't be sad, Kilabah!" Aleena smiled, moved by a sudden impulse of kindness. "Nothing much of interest lies beyond second heaven. The third one is drab with its Garden of Eden and a tree of life. Angels up there can whip up some kind of holy food called manna, which is tasteless. Creatures of Eden are prone to make a pilgrimage to hell on the north side quite often and most religiously."

"North side of Eden didn't attract me in the least when I was there." Chaviva's dark eyes were encompassing heavens. "I hurried on to the fourth heaven. Exploring it to my heart's content; the Altar, the Temple and the heavenly Jerusalem."

"Fortunate for you, dear child, for fourth heaven is guarded by Archangel Michael," Ibrahim indulged thoughtfully. "Avoid the fifth one guarded by angel Samael—the evil one, the dark servant of God."

Behold I am Zachiel, the guardian of sixth heaven. I am here to warn you if you dare profane the name of seventh heaven with false boasts. No one has reached there but the prophets and the Elect of the Elects.

A veil of stars was lowered over the Garden of Irem, starry mists churning and spiraling up to the very mouth of Lake Shisha.

Behind the veil if you can see sits the angel Cassiel, guarding the gate of the seventh heaven. The Throne of Glory you cannot see, attended by seven Archangels. This is paradise, the home of the Seraphim, the Cherubim and the Hayyoth.

A symphony of warnings from the lips of the angels was the only sound to be heard and disseminated. All forms were concealed by mists gray and gossamer. Suddenly, the mists were slashed by flames, their green tongues licking clean the Garden of Irem till it shone like a jewel bright and polished. Arrayed in subterranean wealth of jewels, Aleena and Chaviva were sparkling from head to toe, their demeanor as of the houris of Paradise. Even

Ibrahim was transformed from old philosopher to majestic-looking Khidr, donned in green silks of love and purity. Kilabah had turned to a statue of awe, his white robe absorbing the glow of emeralds, and his dark eyes riveted to Chaviva.

"I believe I have to play the role of Khidr, assisting the lovers on the path to unity, rapture, and annihilation!" Ibrahim lifted his arms up. The shimmering green in his robe shooting beams of light up to the wilderness of Aden.

Jamshed was journeying through his Jam-e-Jam, witnessing the changing of seasons, worlds and continents in the hour-glass of time and timelessness. An amused smile was hovering over the ridges of his lips as he sat gazing at the newly discovered scene of subterranean transformation. Astonished at first, then utterly bewildered, he had become a prisoner of his own Jam-e-Jam, oblivious of Sophia by Lake Shisha. She was rather bewitched by this new jewel of a Garden of Irem, her senses suspended, dazzled!

"Khidr is of the world!" One grimace of an exclamation escaped Kilabah's lips. "In paradise, no one needs Khidr, and this is paradise indeed!" He appeared to be raving than speaking, his gaze now restless. "This paradise is surrounded by eight gateways, and bricks of silver and gold dividing eight gardens. And the seats encrusted with jewels the likes of which I have never seen on earth! The Lote tree down yonder, and my beloved Chaviva! Am I not in paradise already?"

"Ah, the auspicious number eight and its mystery!" Ibrahim stroked his white beard which was absorbing colors from the jewels decking the Zodiac Halls. "This is not paradise, but the replica of palace and a garden which none of us have the privilege to see, with the exception of the saints and the prophets."

"This is no palace, but the Temple of Solomon!" Sophia's features were lit up with awe, her voice a hymnal of reverence. "Look, it's almost dark, a moonless night! How the Temple shines like a brilliant lamp of polished gold and encrusted with so many jewels that it could be passed as a mountain of light. And the miraculous garden! How the trees are glittering like gold, and shimmering with real fruit of the paradise, the pomegranates."

"Only a goddess can witness the miracles of the past!" Jamshed darted a quick look at Sophia, abandoning the glorious vistas encased in his Jam-e-Jam. "A goddess, who didn't know the difference between heavens and Paradise! Hopefully, now you know the sanctity of number eight."

"No sanctity in numbers, Shah Jam, none!" Ibrahim protested abruptly. "A burden too great for someone to carry, if one begins to match numbers with the holy waters of Ganges!"

"Ganges is the paradisiacal river of the earth!" Jamshed began exigently, his eyes lit up with laughter. "I don't see Ganges in your mythical garden of changing forms and shifting realities. You sure are rambling, Ibrahim. Surely, eight is a holy number. Are you not aware of the Christian Belief that Jesus rose to heaven on the eighth day of Passion?"

"And don't you see the Ganges of the Christians here?" Ibrahim mocked. "This octagon shaped pool of water is for the baptismal rites of children. Though I don't believe in this mumbo-jumbo!" He laughed.

"Breathe the scent of the heavens, my Lord, and look!" Sophia challenged. "What fantastic scene is unfolding before your very eyes? Prophet Muhammad is ascending the Throne of the Beloved. And I think this is the eighth day of Ramadan. I believe you would be a staunch believer amongst the believing by the time this night is over, my *master* of illusions!"

Seven hells right beneath the eighth heaven were churning the fury of the damned and the tormented. The subterranean Garden appeared to be consumed by volcano of a bonfire as large as the sky. This sheet of volcanic bonfire was slashed by pale flames, swirling and dissolving into circles of light, radiant and shimmering. Infinite and boundless were those circles of light, polishing the fiery sky into a mirror bright till it shone like one luminescent disk of unity. From the very center of that disk was emerging forth Gabriel, appareled in light; his head crowned by stars all white and sparkling. His wings were flashing a rainbow of colors, and his gold robe studded with gems was reflecting the beauty of fiery sunsets.

Indeed he saw Him another time
By the Lote tree of the Boundary
Nigh which is the Garden of Refuge
Where there covered the Lote tree which covered
His eyes swerved not, nor swept astray
Indeed, he saw one of the greatest sights of his Lord   53: 13-18

Starry realms beyond, catching the refrain of this verse, were cleaving the circle in twain, the upper half illuminating the ascent of the Prophet, and the lower half revealing the subterranean garden of enchantment. Ibrahim was lulled to sleep under the bower of roses where Aleena sat teasing the strings of her lyre, evoking the tunes most sweet and intoxicating. Leaning over the parapet of emeralds, Chaviva was framed inside the window of her balcony like a figurine carved in alabaster, the expression on her face one of awe and disbelief. Kilabah was a prisoner of his own awe and astonishment, his gaze riveted to the golden mare with glittering wings.

Her name is Buraq, Muhammad. Our heavenly mount to carry us on our Night Journey to the Lord of Power!

Gabriel's voice was breaking the concentration of Kilabah; the mare's eyes the color of jacinths, fierce and dazzling. The wilderness of Aden above, with its pearly dawn, was cradling Sophia and Jamshed in an amorous embrace. In fact, both had fallen asleep under some spell of love-intoxicating oblivion and surrender, and now were startled to awakening by the downpour of trumpets, and by the dancing of moonbeams into a fountain of light from the braided hair of Buraq, already close to the summit of Mount Sinai.

"Look, Ibrahim, Prophet is landing on Mount Sinai where Jehovah gave tablets of stone to Moses!" Sophia's exclamation went skirling down Lake Shisha, but Ibrahim was not heeding.

"In my dream I made love to you, dear Sophia!" Jamshed murmured dreamily. His gaze resting on Aleena seated beside Ibrahim, before tracing the journey of the Prophet to Bethlehem.

"No doubt, the Prophet is praying at the same spot where Jesus was born!" Sophia didn't even hear what Jamshed had said, her eyes following the Prophet reverently.

"Against the light of this holy journey, Sophia, your voice can't reach the subterranean Irem." Jamshed sighed to himself, his gaze singeing the pale beauty of Aleena. "So hold off your excitement."

"Don't you see? Can't you convince Ibrahim later?" Sophia continued without losing her concentration in witnessing this holy rite of a journey. "Jesus, Moses and the Prophet, praying together in the Temple of Jerusalem!"

Glory be to Him Who carried His servant by night from the sacred temple of Mecca to the Temple that is remote, whose precinct We have blessed, that We might show him our signs. For He is the Hearer and the Seer. 17:1

The wilderness of Aden and subterranean Irem were polished by a mountain of light against the thunderous downpour of holy verses. The Night Journey of the Prophet was unfolding like a dream long lost, ethereal and beautiful. Outside the Temple, anchored on Jacob's stone was a silver ladder spiraling up and beyond ether, toward the white globe of a sky, remote and shrinking.

Prophet Muhammad was mounting the steps of this ladder as if floating effortlessly over waves upon waves of light, rising higher and higher toward realms unfathomable. Suddenly, a vault of dazzling brilliance was ripped open from above, snatching Prophet from the last rung of the ladder, and carrying him straight into the first heaven of pure silver, lit by a canopy of stars.

Adam was greeting the Prophet with extended arms before throwing open the gates of the second heaven. Noah, Jesus and John the Baptist in the second heaven were offering warm welcome to the Prophet. In a flash, the Prophet was whisked into the third heaven — the abode of David and Joseph, Gabriel was expounding. An abrupt bolt of lightning was tearing open the heart of the fourth heaven where Enoch was seen rushing forth to embrace the Prophet. Another bolt of lightning and the Prophet was caught into the welcoming embrace of Aaron in the fifth heaven. The sixth heaven was fluttering open its wings with a choir of angels.

O Allah. Who has united fire and snow; unite all Thy faithful servants in obedience to Thy Law.

The song and the glory of the sixth heaven were swallowed by one shining vault of seventh heaven. A Lote tree of magnificent height was shooting dazzling colors of light upon light. The Prophet was invited into the House of Adoration, its walls embellished with rubies and jacinths. The scent of Paradise was in the air, infusing even the wilderness of Aden and the subterranean Irem with its perfume, sweet and intoxicating, while the Prophet stood facing the Beloved only two bow shots away from His Throne. The face of the Lord/Beloved was veiled in twenty thousand veils, and still radiating the light of fifty thousand suns, it seemed, clustered inside the heart of a single day.

There is no God but Allah, and Muhammad is His Messenger.

The Prophet's very soul was singing under the spell of ecstasy and exaltation.

O Muhammad, salute thy Creator.

Shafts upon shafts of light were obliterating everything with the exception that the Prophet was seen blinking away light inside the home of his cousin, Umm Hani.

Dear Umm Hani, last night I went to Jerusalem and prayed at the Temple. Journeyed through the seven heavens and expired at the Throne of my Beloved. Now I am back, you won't believe me —

I do, Muhammad, I do —

The crackling of dawn was like circling of firecrackers from lands invisible, wiping clean the mists of cosmic wonder. The wilderness of Aden was turned into an island of pulchritude against the backdrop of sunrise. Jamshed was absorbed in looking into his Jam-e-Jam, his expression one of awe and bewilderment. Sophia, seated not far from him ,was utterly absorbed in her own world of deep contemplation, Lake Shisha her mirror and mirage. The object of her stark admiration was the Garden of Irem. It was now sparkling like a jewel, reflecting only its charm of magic and serenity.

"I believe I have seen the Dome and the Rock of Jerusalem." Ibrahim was smiling into the dreamy eyes of Aleena, her silver lyre abandoned at her feet. "Now I understand the meaning of *niche* in the Quranic verse. Dome is the niche, within which sits the lamp."

"It seems you didn't see the Prophet?" Aleena's eyes were flashing all of a sudden, polished by disbelief and sadness.

"Ibrahim would deny seeing God even if God Himself confronted him face-to-face!" Chaviva laughed before Ibrahim could respond.

Ibrahim was consumed by the dazzling beauty of the balcony studded with emeralds; barely discerning the tremulous form of Chaviva in silvery dress. Instead, he was becoming aware of Kilabah robed in the light of the meadows, standing still and rapt under the balcony of emeralds. He appeared oblivious of all but Chaviva, his gaze burning and devouring.

"God is dead. I killed him with my own hands." Ibrahim returned his attention to Aleena, an evil smile playing upon his lips.

"You didn't bury him, did you?" Aleena mocked, her gaze shifting to Chaviva. "For there she stands alive and radiant. Look how Kilabah is aflame with the fire of jealousy even of the silvery dress of Chaviva which hugs her body."

"God is He, not she; if there is a God!" Challenged Ibrahim, his eyes gleaming with love and amusement!

"God is here and everywhere without any form or gender!" Aleena bent low to claim her silvery lyre. "God is love, lover and beloved."

From the hand of delicate faced beloved
Whose breath is like Jesus
Drink down the wine and give up the tale
Of Aad and Thamud — Maghrebi

A sudden clapping of thunder as abrupt as the night sky was lowering a canopy of stars. Aden and Eden of the nether worlds were lit up by a myriad of stars, twinkling much like the brilliance of firecrackers. Kilabah was lifted off his feet and tossed into a bonfire of emeralds, his heart dissolving the rust of jealousy amidst throes of agony. The earth and the heavens were pregnant with the pain of love, carving rivulets of light for the purification of the universal soul. Islands of clouds, swollen with light and dusted with gold were sailing amidst the sparkle-crackle of stars and galaxies. Kilabah was escaping the bonfire of emeralds, his face ashen and his lips trembling.

The way to wisdom is through Sophia, but only the love of Chaviva would break this enchantment. And yet, Aleena's beauty is the light which sustains Irem, and yet again Ibrahim is the one to deliver us from—

Kilabah was stricken with terror and hopelessness as the Garden of Irem began to slip from under his feet, drifting away like a dream severed from the rock of reality.

Allah is the light of the heavens and the earth
The similitude of His light is a lustrous niche
Wherein is the lamp, the lamp is in a glass

Some remote, primal cry of torment was ripping the night to shreds. The stars were flying and the earth and the heavens chasing each other with the dizzying speed of light.

What is a niche? It is the inner soul which carries a lamp. This lamp is a true believer itself as the receptacle of purity and knowledge which is reflected in a glass—spiritual heart named glass.

A mantle of Sakina was lowered, even the stars falling asleep. And galaxies cradling the earth and the heavens!

LAMP IN A GLASS

Hath not the history of those before you reached you! The folks of Noah and the tribes of Aad and Thamud and those after them? None save Allah knows them — 14:9

A crater of fire suspended over the horizon was lowering its glow over the wilderness of Aden. But this glow was diffused when reaching the Garden of Irem, rather changed to the glittering of oceans and attaining the color of aquamarine. The Garden of Irem was perched over a mountain, below which was a cavern, revealing a flight of narrow staircase. Above the mouth of the cavern was a giant water-skin, it seemed, jutting out of the belly of the mountain. Chaviva, bathed in the light of aquamarine, was wandering aimlessly, unaware of the cavern beneath this Garden of Irem. Kilabah was wandering, but in the opposite direction in the grove of jeweled trees. At the farthest end of this grove could be seen Aleena, seated under the tree of rubies and diamonds. She was evoking the saddest of tunes on her silver lyre, the colors of jewels dancing over her head, as if weaving and braiding her dark hair. Ibrahim could not be found in the Garden of Irem. Alone and distraught, he was exploring the beautiful cavern which he, himself, had conjured with his prowess at incantations.

"There, I found your old lover, Sophia!" Jamshed exclaimed. He was looking into his Jam-e-Jam, though seated beside Lake Shisha. "Isn't that the Rock of Jerusalem? He is standing right under that. It looks like a giant water-skin"

"I have lost interest in him." Sophia murmured; her expression pale and wearied. She was hugging her star-studded shawl, her gaze ripping apart the waters of Lake Shisha. "Rock of Jerusalem, perhaps, but that's no water-skin. More like the Twins against the ruling planet of Mercury."

"Now I understand, this is the Rock of Jerusalem!" Jamshed murmured back without taking his gaze away from Jam-e-Jam. "And eleven steps down the staircase are crudely carved as I suspected."

"Why eleven?" Sophia's blue eyes were brighter than the starry nights, her poppy-red lips parting seductively.

"Because eleven is the first act of transgression over ten—the number of God's commandments. I said that before, didn't I?" Was Jamshed's response!

"Dear Sophia, pay no heed to Shah Jam, his knowledge is quite shallow." Ibrahim looked up, his bushy eyebrows arched and his beard swaying. "I heard you both earlier, and I can still hear you and see you both. You, dear Sophia, discredit me with your thoughtless opinions. I am a lover, yes, but not old. And you have no interest in me, but are jealous. I would elucidate on that later, but right now I am in a mood to humor you both. Do you see this chain, Shah Jam, hanging from the ceiling? It's the same chain Solomon used to hang the keys of his Temple. And this, indeed, is water-skin, dear Sophia, Shah Jam's conjecture is correct. It is also called the Well of Souls. If you look carefully, Sophia, the Twins are carved on the façade of the aquamarine palace."

"The fogs of your intellect, dear lover and philosopher, are corrupting your sight," Sophia mocked, her blue eyes flashing. "What you have conjured you cannot perceive. Do you know where you are standing?"

"Of course, wise goddess." A merry gleam touched Ibrahim's eyes as he stroked his white beard. "Since Shah Jam is smiling, ask him, he knows better."

"Be careful, O venerable sorcerer!" Jamshed laughed. "You have left Aleena alone in the Garden of Irem. I might join her, or try to rescue her from your spells by the power of my own incantations?"

"That cannot be." Ibrahim's features were washed by philosophic sadness. "She is tied to me with the invisible thread of fate, and you have no power to challenge fates. Might as well satisfy the curiosity of Sophia as to my present abode, real or conjured."

"Aside from your skepticism, Ibrahim, the unhewn Rock upon which you are standing marks the location of Prophet's Night Journey," Jamshed began genially. "That miraculous Night Journey, when the Prophet traveled in one night from Mecca to Jerusalem. He then ascended from this Rock into heaven within two *bow-lengths* of the very Throne of God."

"Skepticism included, isn't this the same spot where caliph Umar prayed after the conquest of Byzantine?" Ibrahim smiled wryly. "And his successor, Abd-Al-Malik ibn Marwar, ordered the construction of a shrine, and this cave is right under it. This is the prayer room of the conquerors."

"Believe it not, my Lord! The glass railing behind you holds the pulpit brought to Jerusalem from Syria after the victory of Saladin over the Crusaders." Sophia tossed this comment with a dint of hauteur.

"For me, seeing is not believing, dear child, if believing precedes not imagination!" Ibrahim raised his arms, the folds of his blue robe shuddering back in unkempt folds. "My secrets are hidden from you, my prophetess, and one of them is in this cave. Behind this glass railing is a wall with marble mehrab which you cannot see, so it doesn't exist for you."

"My secrets remain concealed with God, my Lord, while yours are revealed by the very hands of the devil!" Was Sophia's blistering response!

"Devil must be my guide for I see that mehrab clearly! It looks much like a prayer niche!" Jamshed laughed gustily. "This niche prompts me to recite:

Allah is the light of the heavens and the earth

The similitude of His light is as a lustrous niche.

"Niche is inner soul, as you already know that!" Ibrahim struck his staff over the Rock. The heavy curtain of darkness descending quickly and abruptly!

A thick mantle of clouds was stretched from horizon to horizon. So solid and absolute was this curtain of blackness that all breath of life appeared to be sucked out of existence. And yet from this vacuum of nonexistence was churning forth one gossamer veil of silver lining. The wilderness of Aden was coming alive along with the ruins of the lost city of Ubar. Sophia and Jamshed were stunned by this sudden transformation. Behind them, Lake Shisha was tranquil and glittering.

Behold Al Emal, once it was the city of lofty towers, now it lies in ruins. This is the lost city of Ubar, destroyed by the wrath of the Almighty against the tribes of Aad and Thamud. Look behind over that hole of a lake and discover the grave of a man called Job. But if you are not interested in the skeleton of the man from the land of Uz, retreat further and you would find the grove of frankincense. Its resin is still as precious as gold and more valuable than the jewels in the garden of Irem. More jewels than the sand-dunes of Sahara are ready to be unearthed at the foot of the Dhofar Mountains —

Sophia and Jamshed couldn't hear more, since the sand-dunes began to shift and undulate with the sound and fury of hurricanes.

Lake Shisha appeared to be somersaulting. It was chasing the hurricanes till chaos and violence was appeased, and the ruins effaced under the dusting of scarlet sands. Jamshed's knuckles had turned white against the pressure of his fingers clutching Jam-e-Jam, lest it be blown away by gusts. Sophia looked calm as if the violence of hurricanes had not even grazed her awareness. She was brushing away scarlet sands from the edge of Lake Shisha, its gold waters polished to mirror brightness. Her attention was caught by the beauty of subterranean stillness with all its aura of magic and mystery. Jamshed was drawn toward Sophia by the stark sadness of her profile while she sat there looking deep into the waters of Lake Shisha. Relinquishing his Jam-e-Jam in favor of Lake Shisha, Jamshed followed Sophia's gaze down to the Garden of Irem.

Amidst the glitter of Zodiac splendor, the Aquamarine Palace stood tall and imposing. Not that is was grander than the Palace of Rubies or the Hall of Emeralds, but by the sheer virtue of its privilege in hosting the Gothic Princess, no other than Aleena the beautiful. She was lounging on a velvety couch of the same hue as the Aquamarine Palace. From the balcony where she sat teasing the strings of her silver lyre, she could see Ibrahim below on the marble terrace. Beneath the gleaming terraces lay sleeping the Garden of Irem. Right below the terrace, where Ibrahim stood contemplating, was a low bridge of opaline brilliance. At either end of the bridge were open pavilions of lapis lazuli, hosting Chaviva and Kilabah, the lovers separated by one hump of a bridge embellished with mother-of-pearl.

"You have imprisoned us, Ibrahim, in this tinsel-dream of subterranean ugliness, now I understand." Kilabah's dark eyes were shooting hot coals of accusations at Ibrahim. "You have your Gothic Princess, why can't you let Chaviva join me and set us free?" His nostrils were flaring with anger, making his ruddy complexion alive and vibrant.

"Let it be clear, Kilabah, I am holding no one prisoner. I, too, am a prisoner of forces beyond control!" Ibrahim's hazel eyes were smoldering with anger and chagrin. "And yet I have powers, more enhanced than my imagination, and yet again these powers seem limited—rather inefficient if applied outside of my own interests. As to your false blame and your longing to be united with Chaviva, you need to remove the soot of ignorance from your spirit. In other words, to awaken your spirit, you need to cultivate your love for beauty till you see nothing but beauty. This is but one fraction of a rite of passage on the road to be united with your beloved. So far, you have earned only two points, conquering your awe and bewilderment in the Hall of Aries, and purifying your soul from the fire of jealousy in the Hall of Taurus. Now you will awaken your spirit in the Hall of Gemini, and then nine more rites of passage inside the labyrinth of Zodiac magnificence before you can claim Chaviva as your beloved."

"Chaviva is pure, sublime love, so in essence the beloved of everyone!" A delicious peal of laughter escaped Aleena's lips as she adjusted the coronet of pearls over her dainty head. "So Kilabah might not even get a chance to be united with his beloved?"

"Why I am suffering thus, I don't know?" Chaviva lamented abruptly, her small white face lifted up to Kilabah.

Kilabah stood there mute under some burden of hopeless, helpless pain, and in a state of utter desolation. Chaviva's dark eyes were turning to Ibrahim, but his own gaze was shifting to Aleena, profound and piercing.

"And who, my dear princess, would lend a chance to Kilabah to be united with his beloved?" Ibrahim asked indulgently, his gaze pleading, devouring.

"The *master* of the *path*!" Aleena smiled, caressing the stars and crescents on her silvery gown.

"And who, if I may request, is the master of the path?" Was Ibrahim's amused indulgence.

"Khidr, my Lord! The only one, guiding the lovers on the path toward unity, ecstasy and annihilation!" Aleena mocked, curling the silken strand of her hair around her finger.

"Ah, Khidr, my love, the green knight of the Scriptures!" Ibrahim laughed; the hazel gleam in his eyes polished by the luster of his laughter both inward and outward. "Khidr has no concept of unity since he wanders alone on the path to nowhere. How could he lead young lovers on the brink of ecstasy and annihilation since he himself has not tasted the sweetness of such states, noble and ineffable?"

"Defame not Khidr, O Ibrahim, with lies and far-fetched nonsense!" Jamshed's voice slicing through the waters of Lake Shisha was pounding the awareness of Ibrahim. "Even at this precise moment, Khidr is awakening the spirit of Kilabah. Look, how the poor lover is writhing in agony of a longing!"

I know when death had separated us
I consoled myself with the thought of the beloved Prophet
I said: all of us go on this way one day
Who does not die today, he will die tomorrow
Be happy, o my soul, because your Lord is waiting for you
And the beloved one is calling you

"Ah, Shah Jam, what do I hear? Your voice, and then an invocation!" Ibrahim waved his arms in sheer desperation. "I can't see you. Are you trying to imitate the angels? I don't believe I am saying this. That invocation again, death calling the beloved to beloved! It has nothing to do with Kilabah, his beloved is right here, and she has gone daft with grief."

O God my Creator, in your infinity I stand amazed
In your ocean of unity do I drown submerged
O God, at times you closet me in familiar intimacy
At times, you leave me without, veiled and strange
Hidden in your sovereign Majesty
Give me to drink the wine of Your love
For only drunk from it I am able to say
My Lord, let me see You

"King of Azerbaijan is with me, my philosopher friend!" Sophia's voice was reaching the subterranean refuge, followed by a tinkling of mirth. "No invocations are escaping his sealed lips. The voices you hear are of the angels straight from the heavens."

"Sophia—the wise, cultivating ignorance!" A volley of mirth escaped Ibrahim's lips. "What heavens, my dear, I own the seven heavens and the—" His boast was whipped to silence by the sudden downpour of rain, silvery and sibilant.

The Garden of Irem was enveloped in sizzling mists, as if sheets upon sheets of liquid beads were being lowered in a succession of gusts amidst the fury of thunder and lightning. The fireworks were striking the wilderness of Aden, too, the sands shifting and undulating. Takhti-Jamshed was the only solid ground for Sophia and Jamshed; Jam-e-Jam their mirror and guide to avoid or deflect the fury of the heavens. A great lull was in store in the wake of this storm, but the subterranean Irem was turned into an ocean, its waves raging, and its lights dazzling.

Aquamarine Palace, along with other Zodiac Halls of jewels and crystals, was half submerged in water. Rain was still lashing and pelting, but it had lost its fury, shuddering more like the tinsel confetti than the disjointed strings of beads buffeted by winds. Kilabah in his pavilion of lapis lazuli was gazing at Chaviva, his face radiant—transformed. Chaviva was standing across from him at the farthest end of the pavilion, smiling back at him, her features livid, yet her eyes glittering. Kilabah's right hand was clutching his breast as if he was guarding something precious—rather delicate in its essence of purity and purification.

"I can see the light of spirit in your eyes, Kilabah," Chaviva demurred reverently. "Is the awakening of spirit painful?"

"Like the lancing of a wound to scrape off all cankers foul and malignant!" Kilabah smiled, all blood drained from his face which had turned as white as his Bedouin robe of cotton. "I can actually breathe through my heart now, through my physical and spiritual heart. The wound is still raw and painful, but I feel wonderful. Loving worlds within this world! And you more than ever, my precious; and the pain which brings me closer to you every moment!"

"Does it, I mean, bring us closer?" Chaviva sighed; brushing her dark hair with her fingers absently. "Why I am here I don't know. I know I have longed for you all my life when remembering you didn't desert me. But now that I have found you, it is painful to be separated. Is this real, dear Kilabah? Look around, this chilly drizzle and the waters rising and swelling, much higher than Noah's Flood."

"Much more real than my fall in the wilderness of Aden!" Kilabah's dark eyes were sweeping over the landscape somnambulantly! "Doesn't it look rather beautiful? The reflection of lights from jewels and crystals in the water! The halls and the palaces! The swirling of waves and the ripple-dance of silvery shadows! Another Garden of Irem below the waters, beautiful and fascinating!"

"Dreamy." Chaviva's dark eyes were restless. "Has Ibrahim left us? I have rather grown fond of the old philosopher. His love for Aleena! Never knew anyone who could love so besottedly! Exception of course." Her eyes were gathering gleams of mischief.

"Beyond being besotted, I am madly, insanely and ineffably in love, you know that, always!" Kilabah quipped, letting his gaze wander again. "Yes, where is the smitten lover? Indeed, look! The master of magic and incantation has brought his old cave here along with Alhambra palace on top of it. His Noah's ark with Aleena, his luxurious retreat!"

A wonder itself was this spacious cave within a cavern, hewn out of solid rock under the very foundations of Alhambra palace. It was erected on top of the sloping hill overlooking the jeweled trees in the Garden of Irem. The walls of this cave were decorated with silks from Damascus. Its rocky floor was furnished with carpets, their floral motifs unmistakably from Ispahan. A great bath displaying bottles of oriental perfumes was installed in one corner. Not far from this oriental luxury was a velvety davenport, upon which sat Aleena lolling against a pillow of brocade. Ibrahim was seated cross-legged on a gold ottoman with cushions of satin and damask. His posture was prayer-like, hands joined palms upward, eyes closed and his bushy eyebrows relaxed.

"Delight me with a song on your silver lyre, Aleena. Or should I summon my dancing girls?" Ibrahim opened his eyes, stroking his white beard.

"Your dancing girls, my Lord, are ashes by now, scattered haphazardly over the continents of time." Aleena's liquid gold eyes were shooting disdain. "Why are you keeping me prisoner here, and for how long?" Aleena sighed, her white fingers tangled in her black curls moving much like the black and ivory keys of piano.

"I am your prisoner, dear heart!" Ibrahim cajoled. "You are my love, and when you learn to love me, you would find freedom."

"I love only God, and can love no other," Aleena murmured.

"God, my child, doesn't need love from any form of His creation. He is love. Don't delude yourself by loving an illusion." Ibrahim closed his eyes, his lips moving in silent prayer. "Do you find the Garden of Irem dull?" His lips were sealed shut, and those words appeared to be snatched from a vacuum.

"Somehow it feels like home. Besides, I am getting fond of the king of Azerbaijan up there," Aleena reflected aloud, her look dreamy.

"He loves you!" One groan of a confession escaped Ibrahim's lips.

"So you are afraid, Master astrologer, and jealous!" Aleena exclaimed with unusual burst of animation. "No wonder, you conjure up all these absurdities and cosmic upheavals to keep Shah Jam away from me."

"No, my prophetess!" Ibrahim thundered a protest, his eyes shot open. "If I were afraid, I could command a gnat to kill the king. But since I have drunk deep from the cup of immortality, I am trying to discover the meaning of life and death."

"Which part of the life or death you don't understand, my venerable Lord?" Aleena's eyes were gathering rills of laughter and mockery.

"The art of living in death, and of dying in life if youth can ever grasp this concept, my dear!" Ibrahim smiled enigmatically.

"Youth doesn't pose any hindrance in understanding this concept, my Lord." Aleena appeared to be in a rare mood of ideation. "Any child of faith understands it, since the Prophet talked about it, and tried his best to unveil the meaning beyond words, if we were to heed?"

"Prophet!" Ibrahim stalled with an imperious wave of his arm before Aleena could continue. "You mean you actually believe—" His utterance was disrupted by the deafening sound of a trumpet.

He is the one who sends blessings on you, together with His angels, in order to bring you out from darkness into light. 33:43

A choir of angels had descended from the heavens, it seemed, beams upon beams of light illuminating the cave to naked effulgence. This light was accentuating a variety of silver and crystal lamps exquisitely unique and ornate. More voices were rising in a crescendo, penetrating the ancient cave, and sailing above them was Jamshed's mirth and raillery.

"And listen to this, old philosopher friend! I couldn't say it was not written." Jamshed's mirth was muffled and drowning.

O Muhammad! I have ordered the angels of my heavens, those created and those yet uncreated, to send blessings on you and my creation unceasingly, with my own praise. I am your Lord Who said: My mercy has taken over my anger. And all my angels I have created for you human beings. So take this angelic message, Muhammad, to My creation on earth.

Rain was no more, white mists were arising from above and beneath, and the sumptuous cave was obliterated. Night silence had fallen over the Garden of Irem, before the sight of Chaviva and Kilabah the great flood was transformed into fountains and fishponds. The Garden was scented with the fragrance of roses, blooming in great clusters. Jeweled trees and orchards bearing fruit were peering out of earth.

The gateway to the paradise of Irem was barred shut by pearly gates. To the right, over the façade, was a lone Star cradled by a Crescent, and to the left a silver Cross. A pair of magic hands was shooting forth from in between the Cross and the Crescent, trying to grasp the silver key most craftily embedded atop in the sparkling gravel of crystal and chrysolite.

"The magic hands would grasp the magic key, dissolving the enchantment over the Garden of Irem. It would be freed from the spell of darkness, shining forth in all its glory of gleaming pulchritude." Sophia's voice down the tunnel of Lake Shisha was but a whisper from the lips of the gentle wind.

A GLITTERING STAR

Indeed when the spectator has attentively examined My Beauty, he will find reality to exceed the most extravagant conception of his fancy.

Abu Abd Allah Ibn Zamak

Chaviva stood, reading this inscription on the wall in the Hall of Two Sisters. Aleena, beside her, looked pensive and thoughtful. Ibrahim was their guide in this palace of Alhambra which he had conjured up for the sole pleasure of the ladies in full view of the Garden of Irem. Kilabah was instructed to stay within the boundary of Zodiac colonnade, permitted to enter only the Moonstone Palace, displaying a jeweled Crab over the top of the front doors with the inlay of moonstones.

"This part of Alhambra is called Nasrid Palace, built by Muhammad V in fourteenth century," Ibrahim was saying with the élan of a tour guide, drifting toward the three archways exquisitely carved. "This chamber is called the Hall of Two Sisters. The vegetal and geometric patterns on the wall are framed by Arabic calligraphy."

"These designs, it seems, are glaring at the dome of a ceiling, flanked by ugly, little windows," Aleena scoffed, more so to distract Chaviva from reading inscriptions than to annoy Ibrahim.

"Ah, my charming connoisseur!" Ibrahim exclaimed, hugging his blue robe as if to ward off chills. "The dome which inspires your contempt is a muqarnas dome of exquisite intricacy, lit by celestory windows which you deem ugly."

"Monuments tall and empty don't interest me, but I do take delight in gardens, even if wild and unkempt. Especially, if wild and unkempt!" Aleena said without looking at Ibrahim, whose gaze was following Chaviva.

"How beautiful this mehrab, so ornate and welcoming!" Chaviva had reached a middle door leading to another chamber.

"You are standing at the threshold of Mexuar Oratory, a prayer niche or a reception room for the Nasrid kings!" Ibrahim flaunted his knowledge. "If you were to look through its double windows, you would almost miss the expanse of Darro River, for right across from it sprawls the stunning view of the city of Granada." He sauntered close to another door toward his right. "We must see the garden before dusk is replaced by darkness. This fragrant garden of the Moorish pride lays secluded behind the five arched gateway, tranquil and alluring."

Indeed, Alhambra garden was unfolding its charm like a beautiful dream as Aleena and Chaviva wandered along before drifting apart, quiet and contemplative. Seemingly, they were choosing their own course of exploration, but unconsciously, they were following Ibrahim, lured by the aura of his silence on the verge of oblivion and effacement.

Arched trellises splashed with creepers were flaring and undulating into a labyrinth of lush green chambers. A succession of stairways flanked by boxwood hedges of various sizes was expanding onto porticoes with flowerbeds, brimming with color and fragrance. Terraces and fountains and topiaries and pavilions appeared to breathe and welcome the pilgrims of awe and adoration. Five arched gateway was coming into view once again, the great pool of its foundation reflecting the grand architecture of Alhambra.

Aleena's dainty feet shod in slippers of ruby velvet were coming to an abrupt halt by the central pool. Chaviva had joined her, their eyes riveted to the reflection of Aden in calm waters. Seated on Takhti-Jamshed, the king was absorbed in contemplating his Jam-e-Jam. In full regalia of his purple robe with gold stars, and a crown studded with amethysts, he looked royal and imperious. The large ruby on his signet ring was blazing and he suddenly looked at it suspiciously before shifting his attention to the wilderness, his gaze restless and searching. The object of his search was Sophia, standing by Lake Shisha, her back toward him. She looked more like a silhouette than the goddess in a silvery skirt, her shawl studded with stars.

"After a succession of trial incantations, I have bridged the gap between Aden and Irem." Ibrahim stole behind the ladies, witnessing the success of his endeavors with a wide grin. "Now the king and the goddess don't have to depend upon one hole in Lake Shisha to communicate with us. All they have to do is to tilt Jam-e-Jam in any direction they want, and they can view any section of the entire Garden of Irem. Our voices would be closer than before, and we would be able to catch the slightest of sounds."

"I was wondering when this spell of silence would dissolve." Jamshed chuckled, his sherry gold eyes spilling wine of mirth and disbelief. "So you have brought paradise of Spain in the Garden of Irem with your wicked prowess at sorcery, Ibrahim." His voice was choking amidst convulsions of laughter. "Your own paradise, of course, and two houris beside you, my Aleena and Kilabah's Chaviva! You are having a time of your life, I am sure." He shifted his gaze to Sophia who had just lowered herself beside him.

"This impudence of yours would cost you exile in continents remote and God-forsaken, Shah Jam, if you don't watch your tongue." Ibrahim flashed a stern reproof, his gaze wandering from Aleena to Chaviva as they abandoned themselves at the edge of the central pool, the eyes of both widening in rapt wonder.

"Exiled from paradise to paradise, my prudent Lord of the invisible Irem!" Sophia interceded jovially. "What do you plan to do with the palace of Alhambra and its paradisiacal gardens?"

"What I had planned to do in the first place in the Garden of Irem!" Ibrahim stroked his white beard caressingly. "To pass away my dull hours with sweet melodies from the silver lyre of Aleena, and to find the nuggets of truth!"

"Relatively speaking, old Ibrahim, no one can discover any nuggets of truth, or the absolute truth, leave alone its shadowy existence, slippery and meaningless," Chaviva challenged exigently before anyone else could speak.

"Truth, my child, is in knowing who one is," Ibrahim began as if he had not even noticed her impudence. "A few rare mortals have discovered it, taking it along with them into their graves where it can't be traced. Drinking from the cup of immortality as I have is not enough to find truth. So far I have scaled the first rung of its reality. As I have come to know, truth is one disk of a coin with life and death inscribed on either side. Both linked together, yet never meeting in twain. I have barely begun studying both sides of the coin as to where life begins before reaching some vague destination and where does death go in its journey toward new beginning?" He was thinking aloud, it had become obvious. "In essence where does the pain in living come from? Where does the gulf of sin reside? Is the presence of grief necessary?"

Jamshed had ceased to heed, tilting his Jam-e-Jam to explore the other realms of the Garden of Irem. Sophia was finding diversion in the glory of the desert sunset, as if slashing the lovely streaks with the brush of her own sadness.

"Paradoxically, guilt sits in the wagon of the past." Aleena was as much absorbed in admiring the reflection of desert sunset as Sophia, her thoughts expanding involuntarily. "Yes, guilt cosseted by the luxury of pain, while the pain-loving chariot of future soars past the centuries. Drunk with the wine of fear! Whirling! Exhilarated! Heeding not the cries of the soul which rests inside the lotus of truth! *What is truth*? Ego screams with noble fright. A gentle murmur of a song whispers. *Truth is love. And love is beauty. The knowledge of God within and without! Love eternal and love everlasting!*"

"How many paradises are needed to find truth—to the road to freedom?" Chaviva lamented abruptly.

"As many as—" Ibrahim's response was cut short by Kilabah's equally loud lament.

"That's my Chaviva, so unhappy. I can't endure her unhappiness!" Kilabah stood raving over the balcony of Moonstone Palace. "Ibrahim, where are you? Permit me to come out of this accursed palace, and I would tell you about the only paradise worthy of finding truth."

"Moonstone Palace is not your prison, Kilabah. You are free to come out and roam around the Garden of Irem," Ibrahim thundered, his eyes glinting rage and impatience. "When you come out, follow the ruby eyes of the Crab which would point to your right as you turn. Two terraces apart you would see the five-arched gateway. You would see us by the central pool. Stay across from us, you would know the boundary of your freedom, do not try to come near us. Be assured you would be able to converse with us to your heart's content."

Leaving behind the Moonstone Palace, Kilabah was swift as an arrow to seek the sanctuary of the central pool. Roses as large as sun-disks were making him drunk with their opiate fragrance. He could see a tapestry of larkspurs blooming in a collage of colors to his right, but he was intent on focusing his attention ahead, noticing Ibrahim standing across from him on the other side of the central pool. So vibrant and dazzling was the beauty of flowers all around that he had completely missed the presence of Aleena and Chaviva seated by the central pool. His gaze was lured deep down the pale-gold waters of the pool, calm and mirror-bright.

"What do I see, Lake Shisha? My friends of the crimson desert? The king and the goddess?" Kilabah gasped for breath. The delicate nostrils of his Grecian nose were expanding and twitching.

"Yes, your friends indeed! You deserted us!" Jamshed laughed. "Delight us with your view of one paradise which might dissolve the need and greed of Ibrahim to acquire more paradises. This need of his is equivalent to the ones who possess rare jewels, but are cursed forever with the hunger of possessing more and more."

"I have no need, Shah Jam!" Ibrahim grinned maliciously. "I own the Garden of Irem. And this, the jewel-garden of the worlds with such abundance of treasures that even if someone took away cartloads of jewels, it would never suffer the pangs of any dearth. And yet I am anxious to hear the tale of one paradise from the lips of Kilabah."

"All this magic and mystery and this wondrous garden of Alhambra," Kilabah murmured, becoming aware of his beloved seated there beside Aleena. "You probably know this tale already, Ibrahim. You don't need to hear it from me." He tore his gaze away from his beloved Chaviva. "As it is, I am overwhelmed by these cataclysmic events, longing only to be with Chaviva. You know everything."

"I am immortal, but not young, and I tend to forget," Ibrahim sadly confessed. "I wish I had found the elixir of youth, and had not tasted even one draught from the cup of immortality." His gaze brimming with the ardor of love was turning to Aleena.

"Aleena's reservoir of knowledge is vast and deep. Maybe she would—" Kilabah's request was truncated by the sudden tinkling of mirth from the lips of Aleena.

"No!" Protested Aleena with unusual vehemence; her hands reaching out for her silver lyre! "I only know how to keep my Lord opiate under the spell of these melodies. They make him sleepy; otherwise, he stays awake most of the time."

"I wish he did sleep most of the time!" Jamshed's bundle of hilarity was causing ripples in the central pool. "That way we might accomplish great tasks without the burden of his spells and incantations."

"King of Azerbaijan! Would you do the kindness of introducing a new paradise?" Kilabah pleaded.

"Any paradise, new or old, is my paradise where my Aleena is, no other exists." Jamshed's furnace of a sigh carved more ripples in the central pool.

"Goddess, could you please—" Was Kilabah's half plea, half prayer!

"No, Kilabah, my paradise is right here," Sophia muffled the truth of her statement with a tinkling of mirth both sad and hollow.

"Yes, Kilabah, you better validate your earlier comment now before you find yourself imprisoned inside the Moonstone Palace," Ibrahim commanded.

"I guess I better." Kilabah sank down into a puddle over the grass at the edge of the central pool. "But do stop me if the tale sounds familiar."

"I would, even if your tale is dull or trite." Ibrahim lowered himself cautiously by the pool, planting his staff straight in the wet earth. "Now please proceed."

"Well, this is the tale of Alexander's paradise, rather, his journey in quest of finding *meaning* in life," Kilabah began reminiscently. "During one of his expeditions, Alexander halted at the banks of a river called Ganges. He was told that the source of this river comes from the joy in paradise, which surely could be found within the natural course of its flow by a man of understanding. Curious by nature and adventurous by temperament, Alexander, along with his men, sailed upstream for a month, buffeted by heavy winds or tides in search of the paradise. Finally, his crew espied a wall miles long along the riverbank. For almost three days they kept sailing until they spotted a crevice in the wall. Embarking on the land and deeming himself the conqueror of this island, Alexander sent a squad of men in a skiff, demanding tribute from the inhabitants of this remote place. The leader of the city—an old man, unperturbed by the unjust demands of those strange men, offered them a gemstone the size and shape of a human eye as tribute. Saying that this gift is the most priceless tribute anyone can ever give. Adding that this gemstone has the efficacy of dissolving the rust of greed or ambition!" He paused, but finding everyone attentive, resumed quickly. "Soon Alexander returned to Susa. He invited wise men and scholars to his court, seeking their advice as to the nature and symbolism of this gemstone. One old Jewish scholar by the name of Papas studied this stone before putting it to test. First he weighed this stone against a pound of gold, adding more and more, still the stone outweighed the gold. Then he sprinkled dust over the stone, and it became lighter than a feather. *You are lucky to escape that paradise alive, O King*, the old man exclaimed. *This stone represents your eye, heavy with greed and ambition. Covered with the dust of death it weighs nothing. This is that wonder-stone—a gift from the paradise of your sacred journey. You indeed have traced the water of life which is Ganges. And you have received the gift of understanding which is this wonder-stone, reminding you that the highest virtue in life is the three-pronged vessel of love, peace and unity.* Through the medium of this understanding, Alexander beheld the light of wisdom. Ascribing his conquests to God and retiring to the life of love and repose."

"A paradise without houris, and without gardens! A paradise not worth exploring!" Ibrahim croaked disdain. "No wonder I didn't know about it. As to Alexander, I say he is a fool and a simpleton indeed! Ascribing his conquests to God, though he himself toiled through seasons inclement and lands inhospitable to become the master of many kingdoms."

"A sage and a prophet worthy to be revered by the virtue and purity of his heart in knowing that everything comes from God, since everything belongs to Him." Kilabah's dark eyes were burning with the light of inspiration. "We are only the vessels of His will and grace, whatever He wishes to bestow on whomsoever."

"Your spiritual heart is truly awakened now, dear Kilabah, I know!" Chaviva sang ecstatically. "From awe to the purging of jealousy, to the endearing of spirit, and then to the station of spiritual heart, illumined and illuminating."

"Ibrahim would get credit for all that, of course." Jamshed chortled from above. "Satisfy my curiosity, my philosopher friend, if you will? Do you know the meaning of houris?"

"No words can describe the beauty and sweetness of such celestial creatures, O besotted King!" Ibrahim began with a false sense of euphoria. "How can meaning be ascribed to beauty and sweetness? It is there only to be tasted and experienced."

"That means you don't know, O genius of a philosopher, much less knowing the meaning of paradise!" Jamshed was donning the mask of caprice and indulgence. "Houri comes from the Arabic word hur — meaning astonishment, so no houris awaiting! Despite your ocean of spells and incantations in accumulating gardens of delight, you remain alienated from the realms of paradise. Alexander's paradise is similar to the Talmudic paradise in Judaic Tradition. With your flare for conjuring, you still lack the prowess of choice and priority. If you wish I can summon a succession of heavens in your Garden of Irem, for I believe my powers in that arena are still intact? I would be doing myself a favor so that you could hasten your journey toward the rungs of truth, granting me the supreme privilege of being with Aleena."

"Why not? To test your boast, go ahead, Shah Jam, practice your skill." Ibrahim let his gaze stray and wander. He appeared to be gathering all, Aleena and Chaviva, the bemused Kilabah, beaming Jamshed and listless Sophia inside the vaults of his soul, bright and turbulent.

Allah promiseth to the believers, men and women gardens, underneath which rivers flow, wherein they abide — blessed dwellings in the Garden of Eden, and greater far acceptance from Allah that is the supreme triumph. 9:72-73

A rumbling of thunder and the Garden of Irem itself appeared to groan from the bottom of its foundations. The hills around Alhambra palace were crumbling to dust. From the smooth heap of dust was arising a limpid pool, around which were carved four waterways. A gibbous moon was suspended low, accentuating the narrow streams in four quarters, while highlighting the trees which were sprouting alongside the waterways in quick succession. The earth had begun to shake and the wind picking up speed. Ibrahim, being the light in weight, was the first one to be blown away as if willfully snatched and then tossed closer to the central pool of four waterways.

"What is this?" Ibrahim croaked with indignation, glaring at nothingness.

"A paradise promised to the believers!" Jamshed's voice boomed from above. "Don't you see the rivers of milk, wine, water and clarified honey? And trees laden with fruits, ripe and tempting."

"Is this that paradise?" Ibrahim waved his staff in thin air. "I can do better than that with one stroke of my staff. Turning the water channels of Alhambra garden into rivers of wine, and fountains spilling milk, and honey dripping from the sap of the fruit trees."

"If only you could lay your hands on the wand of Moses, Ibrahim!" Jamshed's chuckle of a response was trickling down into the very center of the central pool. "Your own worthless wand would fall limp before the decree of divine law."

Allah is the light of the heavens and the earth
The similitude of His light is as a lustrous niche
Wherein is the lamp, the lamp is in a glass
The glass as if it were a glittering star

A sudden shower of burning stars was obliterating the Alhambra palace along with its mock paradise and its gardens. Ibrahim was left in darkness, stunned and baffled. Aleena and Chaviva were carried to the Garden of Irem, perched precariously over the tails of the falling stars. Kilabah, aware only of the ripple-dance of stars on the horizon, was startled to find himself transported to the balcony of Moonstone Palace. The Garden of Irem was awakening to life, more jeweled trees of ruby and pearl shooting up and swooping down in cascading brilliance.

The brilliance of those jeweled trees was almost dimmed as a huge tree shot up in their midst in dazzling colors of the rainbows. It was filled with light, its roots spiraling above the ground like sparkling fountains, and its branches seething down under the earth, illumined and illuminating. The leaves of this tree were made of round, flawless pearls designed in the likeness of the ears of the elephants, absorbing light and glowing most divinely. The ruby fruit of this tree, in the shape of pitchers, was spilling a nameless fragrance, sweet and intoxicating. Each ruby-pitcher like fruit was balanced on a bed of thorns, looking like icicles, sharp and glittering. The tree itself was growing rapidly, sailing high and sprawling wide. So immense it had grown in size that it looked like a giant globe of pearls and rubies, concealing the entire Garden of Irem—rather lending shade and protecting the Garden from the cosmic churning of storms and hurricanes! One glimmer of a storm was reaching the Garden of Irem, but it was not of cosmic calamity. In fact, it was not a storm, but the sing-song voice of the goddess chiseling its way through the rotunda of jewels into the Garden of Irem.

"I have not ever seen a Jujube tree in all its glory until now!" Sophia's voice was urgent and tremulous. "This indeed is the Lote tree of the uppermost limit. It marks the end of knowledge, the limit of *being* before the *absolute*. Beyond it lays the highest mystery of divine essence."

"So divine essence always veils the truth!" Ibrahim lamented aloud.

The Lote tree suddenly vanished, its glory replaced by the sudden bursting of fresh blooms on the bushes of rose and larkspur. "But I must tear and rend each veil till I find the kernel of truth. I thought I had started my quest in the Garden of Irem, and now I don't even know where to begin?" Ibrahim's gaze was bouncing off the vibrant colors of roses before settling on Aleena and Chaviva who appeared distant and ethereal.

"The journey to unknown begins in the spiritual heart of the seeker over paths most mystical and terrifying." Aleena's voice was unusually tender and consoling. "Darkness and roaring silence lurk at every step where terror may be swallowed by the light of understanding, and truth may spiral against the bolts of lightning, leaving the seeker aghast and bewildered. But the journey continues, for the seeker at this point has glimpsed one spark of beauty, so precious, that the eyes of heart blinded by tears of ecstasy dare not rest till they hold and behold the mystery of light in all its essence of beauty and rapture. At this juncture the seeker must crawl over and beyond the confines of revelations to touch, taste and cherish the holy scent of blessed truth."

"The blessed truth is that I have a mind to kill the whole horde of humanity to see if the hell would contain the entire creation, or if the myth of paradise would be dissolved into the mirage of absurdities?" Ibrahim's anger was stark and blistering.

The breath of sanity was sucked out of his lungs, it seemed, as he stood welcoming the bolts of lightning. They seemed to be licking the heavens and the earth with their tongues hungry and vengeful.

Do you want to enter paradise? To walk the path of truth you need the grace of God. We all face death in the end. But on the way to life or extinction be careful never to hurt the heart of a living creature.

The Garden of Irem was entering the soul of Leo.

SEAT OF GLORY

It is lit by a blessed tree—an olive.

An ocean of roaring silence was palpitating since Jewish
Paradise had landed into the very heart of the Garden of Irem.
Zodiac colonnade this bright afternoon was attaining the sheen of
pewter against the stark gaze of the sun, hot and searing. In front of
the Palace of Peridot, Kilabah stood gazing at the lifelike statue of a
Lion, emblazoned above the eaves, its ruby eyes fiery and
glowering. His only companion in this Garden of Irem was
Ibrahim, facing the Seat of Glory—the Jewish Paradise most
solemnly.

The old philosopher had chosen a boulder as his own seat of
contemplation right across from the twelve gates of the Jewish
Paradise. With his eyes closed, he was concentrating on the
mystical number twelve, matching the Zodiac signs as luminaries.

In order to improve his skills at spells and necromancy, he had
requested Jamshed to implant the Jewish Paradise in his Garden of
Irem. Now that Jamshed had conjured up this paradise, Ibrahim
had become suspicious of the king, fearing that he might be able to
abduct Aleena, since he had succeeded in rejuvenating his prowess
at incantation. Not only had he become suspicious of Jamshed, but
was also afraid of losing his own skill at spells and incantations.
Overwhelmed by such fears, he had sent Aleena and Chaviva to a
concealed palace of his own conjuring, more so to test his mettle
than to succumb to more fears and suspicions. He was sure of one
thing, that he would never allow Jamshed to come to the Garden of
Irem. So the king of Azerbaijan was virtually a prisoner in the
wilderness of Aden, his only contact with the subterranean
paradise his Jam-e-Jam. Sophia, too, was a prisoner in the

wilderness of Aden, of her moods and thoughts, privileged to stay in touch with the Garden of Irem through Lake Shisha.

"Why did you take Chaviva away from the Garden of Irem?" Kilabah swung around, his eyes shooting coals of accusations at Ibrahim.

A giant tree had sprouted forth close to Ibrahim where he sat on his boulder. His eyes were still closed, his expression one of deep repose as if he was lodged within in some paradise remote and soothing.

"So that you could learn the art of accepting pain!" Ibrahim opened his eyes slowly, studying the contour of each leaf overhead rather than meeting Kilabah's burning gaze.

"I am not in pain." Kilabah's own gaze was lured toward the great wall with twelve gates.

A wave of utter desolation swept over Kilabah's features, his heart constricting by a pang of some loss precious and nameless. His soul was humbled by the unfolding of rare beauty of this wall. It appeared to be hewn out of both gold and crystal with the glow of jasper, which could not be concealed even from under the inlay of gems in dazzling array of cuts and colors.

"I mean the pain of separation." Ibrahim arched his bushy eyebrows, watching Kilabah's slow approach with great concentration.

"That's not pain. That's the agony of the body and soul," Kilabah muttered hopelessly.

"Now you are getting wise!" Ibrahim permitted himself the luxury of a thin smile. "This is the fifth of your trials in your journey toward your beloved, the acceptance of pain and surrender to beauty.

"Surrender comes easy; acceptance is the most difficult of tasks." Kilabah's grief was finding diversion in admiring the most exquisite of symmetrical trees. "It's like forgiving, but not forgetting, the forgiveness of the most wretched kind. What kind of tree it is?" He asked abruptly.

"This is the replica of tree of life. The real one is inside the Jewish Paradise," Ibrahim explained reluctantly. "Didn't you notice the Jewish Paradise behind this wall?"

"That's no paradise, but a city!" Kilabah exclaimed, rapt and humbled by the beauty of this wall once again.

"Yes, new Jerusalem and the assuaging of all grief as the rabbis expound," Was Ibrahim's low, enigmatic response! "Or Jerusalem adorned as a bride for her husband, theologians would make us believe."

"What do you believe in?" Kilabah asked desperately.

"I believe in the magic of life, trying to discover the mystery of death." Ibrahim's eyes were filled with sadness unfathomable. "Come sit with me under this tree." He indicated a polished boulder across from him. "This is a sacred tree. Its branches are the branching of universal thoughts. Whoever sits under it, his thoughts flow toward virtue and goodness, loving all, accepting all! The leaves of this tree are velvety soft, lending shade and comfort to the weary in body and soul."

"Would it lend enough comfort to your wearied body and soul so that you could refrain from upsetting the balance of the cosmos with your need for paradise upon paradise?" Kilabah lowered himself down over the boulder slowly and thoughtfully. His gaze was caressing the velvety sheen of the leaves. "Why do you need this Jewish Paradise in the Garden of Irem?" His dark eyes were turning to the old philosopher, dreamy and searching.

"No comfort for the immortal soul burdened with the quest for youth and truth." Ibrahim combed his long beard with his fingers. "Yet, with the aid of this paradise, I long to be initiated into the secrets of Merkabah mysticism, so that I could have a better understanding of the path leading toward truth!"

"How do you know that Merkabah mysticism would guide you toward that path?" Kilabah was feeling opiate, yet goaded by his curiosity to prod.

"My knowledge might be rusty, Kilabah, but I know this much—that Merkabah mysticism offers insight into the nature of man, of the world and of ecosystem." Ibrahim rambled vaguely. He was trying his best to harness his thoughts.

"I have no knowledge of such things." Kilabah appeared to bemoan his ignorance. "I always thought Merkabah was some sort of throne or a chariot. Chariot of God if I am not mistaken! It was Enoch who saw such a chariot."

"After Enoch, Ezekiel saw the same chariot, both expressing their impression on a level much different from one another,." Ibrahim began reminiscently. "That's biblical Merkabah you are recalling. But Jewish Merkabah is mysterious. Thus, two branches of Merkabah mysticism replete with symbolism make the throne-chariot alive with its own entity of power and prescience. Its four wheels, designed individually, represent base elements of the world. One wheel depicts the lion representing fire, the other an ox representing earth. Another wheel depicts the image of man signifying water, and the fourth one with eagle representing air. Four angels are the guardians of those wheels, while the man on the throne represents God. He can only drive the chariot when four angels connect their wings. It means that God would not be revealed to us by us looking at all four elements as separate and independent entities. However, if we looked at the way that fire, wind, earth and water, with all their opposing qualities still coexist in harmony, we get a tiny glimpse of reality that a higher power called God must be guiding those elements how to act."

"Is that chariot visible in the Jewish Paradise that you have conjured?" Kilabah's eyes were gathering glints of fear as if he didn't want to know the answer.

"I didn't conjure it. The king of Azerbaijan made it possible since he is still the master of such skills." Ibrahim lumbered to his feet laboriously. "I am sure everything is intact in this paradise. Let's find out." He proceeded toward the wall, beckoning Kilabah to follow.

An island of white clouds had veiled the face of the Sun as Ibrahim and Kilabah stood facing the wall of gold-crystal. They were both awed by the twelve majestic gates, each gate decked with precious stones of different kind to complement each Zodiac sign. Starting from left to end in line of the bejeweled gates; rubies, emeralds, aquamarines, moonstone, peridots, sapphires, opals, topaz, turquoise, garnet, amethyst and bloodstone presented a rainbow of colors, all fiery and dazzling. Ibrahim, followed by Kilabah, was entering through the gate encrusted with peridot. They thought they were holding open a sea of glass reflecting soft meadows, polished by sunshine. The gate behind them closed softly, but what confronted them took their breath away, for that was not what they had expected.

The panoramic view before their sight was that of seven glorious mountains with undulating valleys. Groves of figs and olives were laden with fruit ripe for picking. Date trees and orchards of pomegranates were gleaming like the jewels rare and precious. Grapevines were visible, too, overlooking the fields of wheat and barley. Clusters of grapes, much like the red and green marbles, were suddenly incandescent, as if catching shafts of sunlight and bursting into flames.

Mists silvery and gossamer were shooting forth from the firmament, enveloping the mountains, and then effacing them as if they were freshly painted landscape by the brushstrokes of some artist divine. Simultaneously, a tree of colossal girth and height was replacing the vistas swept clean of groves and orchards. Left intact were the marble like grapes, defiant and deriding the impudence of cosmic caprice which dared not touch their glassy hearts filled with the nectar of life and sweetness.

"This tree is a continent by itself," Kilabah murmured, gazing at the swift bursting forth of white blossoms with awe and dread.

"What it is?"

"This is the tree of life, unlike the one which appeared in the Garden of Irem." Jamshed's voice followed by a volley of mirth was penetrating the Jewish Paradise yet to be discovered.

"Why are you laughing like a heathen, Shah Jam, and disturbing the aura of peace and holiness here?" Ibrahim demanded, his gaze riveted to the perfectly rounded fruits from the very core of white blossoms which were no more.

"A heathen, calling a man of God, heathen?" Jamshed quipped mirthfully. "I am laughing because instead of studying the details of Jewish Paradise, you are missing them completely. Old age is catching up with you finally, and the first thing to go is your sight. You didn't even see the large pearls at each gate chiseled with the name of each tribe, comprising twelve tribes of Israel. How would you learn the secrets of Merkabah mysticism if the obvious escapes you?"

"If you stop meddling, king of Azerbaijan, I could learn more than you could ever imagine!" Was Ibrahim's inflamed response! "But I fear you are tricking me with your antics of old, experimenting with your incantations. Now tell me, is this really the tree of life or some fantastic fabrication from the well of your stale imagination? What kind of fruit is this?"

"Pity that you can't even recognize the Tree of Life with its characteristics of twelve kinds of fruit, yielding each kind every month of the year? Look, how its branches reaching—"

A firework of lightning followed by a loud thunder had swallowed all sounds with the exception of its own sound and fury. The firmament itself was carving a cataract, snaking through ether and breaking into beads of shower. Kilabah and Ibrahim

110

could feel the sprinkling of cool water on their feet, but their eyes were turning to the heavens where a pair of hands holding a silver vessel, was validating the cause of this singing, murmuring cataract. The bolts of lightning were multiplying and becoming serpentine. The entire cosmos was lit up in a collage of colors, blinding and dazzling.

I Enoch, the son of Seth and the grandson of Adam have earned the privilege of walking with God.

A voice both prayerful and sonorous was braiding a circle of peace inside the ocean of light.

Nothing was left of the trees or the mountains. A marble palace was floating closer in full view of Kilabah and Ibrahim. They had found refuge against the wall, their looks glazed and their bodies sagging to the ground in consecutive heaps. Ibrahim sat clutching his knees and drawing his blue robe together. Kilabah's white robe had made a full circle around him much like a tent on the verge of collapsing. The eyes of both men were riveted to the double doors of the palace thrown suddenly open. One wraith of a man shivering in his woolen cloak was seen inside the bare room of all marble. Shuddering still, he was lurching toward a door to his right. He had divested himself of his cloak, suddenly tossing it away and muttering:

Strange, that part of the room was cold as ice, and over here it is hot as a furnace.

The man was rushing out of another door and vanishing.

"Adam had sixty-three children, and died at the age of nine hundred and thirty, so this child of his is a little daft of course!" Sophia's sing-song voice trickling down the subterranean deeps was jolting Kilabah and Ibrahim out of their shock and stupor.

"I thought you couldn't penetrate this realm of the Jewish Paradise, my love and my heedless child." Ibrahim infused a little tenderness in his tone seething with anger. "Tell your king to cut short the semantics of this journey and show us the real paradise."

The real paradise was coming into view with claps of thunder and renewed flashes of lightning. The wraith of a man now recognized as Enoch had appeared at the doors again, entering another chamber of marble and stumbling toward a Throne.

A pure Throne of crystal and wheels more brilliant than a thousand splendid suns! How can I look at your Glorious Face when rivers of fire under Your Throne are consuming me alive!

Enoch was kneeling, weeping and melting in his own tears, it seemed.

An island of clouds pregnant with the holiness of divine munificence was bursting open into crystal showers by the bolts of lightning. The Garden of Irem was canopied by flashes of lightning, creating a mosaic of gray clouds edged with a fringe of gold. Enoch had vanished, his seat of pilgrimage occupied by another imposing figure no other than his contemporary, Ezekiel. He, too, was kneeling before a crystal Throne, rather springing back with his hands on his knees, then returning to the posture of touching his forehead to the ground in a succession of prostrations.

Ezekiel was caught under some spell of ritual purification, oblivious to the awesome grandeur of the Throne. The wheels of this Throne had spokes, their rims crowned with brilliant eyes, watchful and restless. Guarding the wheels were creatures with four faces each: that of an ox, a lion, an eagle and eight pairs of eyes on each wheel, vigilant and encompassing. A firmament with glittering stars was lowered over the Throne upon which sat a Majestic Being donned in veils upon veils of light, gossamer and shimmering.

Glory of the Lord I dare not behold.

Ezekiel was prostrating at the foot of the Throne. The Throne itself was immersed in an ineffable glow of fire, amber and luminous. The creatures at the wheels of the Throne were transformed to angels, singing and rejoicing. Heavenly music was in the air, angels spreading their wings and erecting one splendid web of a throne beneath the Throne. The Throne was bobbing up and down with each flapping of the angels' wings in perfect synchronicity.

Watch how the opposing forces interact in harmony. This is perfect Merkabah, striving toward unity. And knowing the will of God despite the conflicting forces which aim to merge together to fulfill a higher purpose designed by God.

Divine visions were flashing and divine sounds slashing the firmament with serpentine bolts of lightning. From the midnight blue bowl of a sky, with stars as bright as diamonds, were lowering mists golden and gossamer. Chaviva was appearing suddenly at the door of this mystic chamber, robed in shimmering mists, more radiant than the ones enveloping the Throne. She appeared to be sleepwalking, her dark eyes glittering.

"Is this Merkabah mysticism? What does it mean? How can one understand?" Ibrahim was heaving himself up, brushing straight the blue puddle of his silk robe. The hazel glint in his eyes was cutting through bright mists and seeking the attention of Chaviva.

"A Jewish mysticism at its zenith!" Chaviva's voice sounded remote, her gaze unseeing. "It's an epiphany, teaching us the possibility of making a sacred journey to the Throne of God, and becoming the vessel of divine powers to bestow upon the world."

"Is this paradise?" Kilabah was stumbling to his feet. "Chaviva! Beloved."

"Any garden dearly tended with flowers vibrant and scented is Paradise!" Chaviva was lost inside the mists golden and shuddering.

"How do I make this journey? Where should I go?" Ibrahim lamented, his arms reaching out to gather the very fabric of mists, it seemed.

"Seek not out the things that are too hard for you." Aleena's gold eyes were peering through mists, suffused with the color of daffodils and sunshine. "Neither search the things which are above your strength, nor venture into realms sublime and forbidden. You are commanded to observe reverence and obedience. Secret and sacred are not to be revealed—"

Aleena too was lost in the mists, her voice becoming a part of the cosmos and her eyes shielded by a myriad of veils, all exquisitely luminous. The Throne was rising, cutting through the mists and aiming toward a mountain decked with flowers the color of rainbows.

This is the mystical day of Shavuot called matchmaker where Moses brought the bride of Jewish pilgrims to Mount Sinai to be wedded to the bridegroom—G-d, and the marriage contract was Torah given to Moses as commandments. In honor of Shavuot Jews still stay up all night to learn Torah.

"More so to atone than to honor!" Ibrahim exclaimed abruptly, followed by a volley of mirth on the verge to hysteria. "The reason Jews read Torah all night is to atone for their sins of neglect or indulgence. The night before Torah was promised to be given to Moses, Israelites slept early to be well rested for the auspicious morning. But they overslept and Moses had to wake them up because God was already waiting on the mountaintop. To rectify that blunder, as the story goes, the Jews stay up all night to recite Torah."

The mists were whirling and suddenly dissipating. Ibrahim was gasping for breath for the air was heavy with the scent of a nameless perfume, sweet and overpowering. Kilabah, on the contrary, was inhaling deeply as if intoxicated by the very breath of the scented air, craving for more and more with wild abandon. The Throne was dissolved in golden mists and the chamber was filled with beacons of light, flaring and dazzling. From the very fabric of brightness was emerging forth a procession of oxen, their horns gilded and adorned with garlands of fresh flowers. They were loaded with baskets braided with gold and silver. Those baskets were laden with a variety of fresh harvests; wheat and barley, figs, dates and olives, grapes and pomegranates.

The season of grain harvest is Shavuot, the season of gladness. Seven weeks of harvest, lending number seven the aura of mystery and sanctity. Seven-week counting of Omer on Passover when Jewish people were freed from their enslavement to Pharaoh! On Shavuot they were given the Torah and became a nation committed to serving God.

Sounds of music sprinkled with praise and blessings were trickling down the marble palace. Ibrahim looked dazed, watching the mists disappear and disintegrate. His eyes were tracing Kilabah's gaze where it was transfixed to Chaviva astride one ox. She was scattering the gold of wheat to the four winds. The palace itself was shuddering to extinction. Golden mists were no more. Ibrahim and Kilabah were left in the Garden of Irem, spent and stricken. They were looking at the Palace of Peridot. A garland of peace and serendipity was weaving its way over and around the bejeweled avenue of Zodiac splendor. Somewhere in the distance, Aleena's silver lyre was evoking the saddest of melodies. From the tunnel of Lake Shisha, Sophia's sing-song voice was just a whisper in the wind.

I am standing upon the seashore
A ship at my side spreads her white sails
To the morning breeze and stars for the blue ocean
She is an object of beauty and strength
And I stand and watch her until at length she
Hangs like a speck of white cloud just where
The sea and sky come down to mingle with each other
Then someone at my side says: there, she is gone!
Gone where? Gone from my sight—that's all
She is just as large in mast and lull and spar as
She was when she left my side, and just as able to
Bear her load of living freight to the place of destination

Her diminished size is in me, not in her, and just at
The moment when someone says: there, she is gone
There are other eyes watching her coming and other
Voices ready to take up the glad shout:
There she comes
And this is Dying   *Anonymous*

THE YEAR OF GLADIOLUS

Allah is the light of the heavens and the earth
The similitude of His light is as a lustrous niche
Wherein is the lamp, the lamp is in a glass
The glass as if it were a glittering star
It is lit by a blessed tree—an olive
Neither of the east nor of the west

Four poles of the world were joined at the top like one dot of a continent in the entire scheme of the cosmos. Under the canopy of this continent east and west were merging, while north and south converging, releasing a bonfire of sparks, golden and smoldering. From Aden to Eden, the earth and the heaven were caught in a shower of gold, creating a haze so thick that neither the wilderness of Aden, nor the Garden of Irem could support the weight of impending storm with the threat of violence.

A storm was surely imminent, startling Sophia and Jamshed as they watched a creature hurtling through space, its body buffeted by jagged rocks before shooting straight through Lake Shisha down to the crevice of the Garden of Irem. Amidst haze and fury, cutting through the colonnade of Zodiac splendor, the Hall of Sapphires was sparkling like a multifaceted jewel. Its façade was hosting a Virgin of chased silver with a coronet of asters in her hair of pearly brilliance. The haze was splintering and crackling open the heart of the Garden of Irem, where the familiar form of the creature traveling with the speed of lightning was crashing into the bosom of the silvery Virgin. Bouncing back on his feet, this amazing creature was falling down over the marble pavement of the Zodiac Avenue like an acrobat made of rubber.

"Are you not the god Hephaestus—the architect of palaces? You built those palaces for gods on the Mount Olympus?" Kilabah asked with utmost calm. He was watching this landing from the balcony of the Hall of Sapphires. His heart, after emerging fresh from the rite of purification, now were all loving, all accepting, all embracing.

"Yes, I am that wretch!" Hephaestus limped to his feet, his body caked with wounds. "The victim of my father's wrath, the great Zeus!"

"How came you here?" Ibrahim watched him with implicit contempt. He was turning his back on the Elysian Paradise he had conjured too hastily.

"Alas, I am a part of that Paradise which you brought here!" Hephaestus groaned, his gaze reaching out to the Elysian Fields beyond Ibrahim. "Can't you see the white ears of grain swollen to ripeness? And the rivers of milk, and the rivers of nectar and the rivers of yellow honey my father let flow from the sap of the green Holm-oak?"

"This is no paradise, but a replica of the garden of a Persian king Cyrus!" Jamshed's laughter boomed through the tunnel of Lake Shisha. It seemed to clear away all traces of haze, as if licking clean the Garden of Irem from the mercurial wrath of the heavens.

"The voice is familiar." Hephaestus murmured. He stood, gathering his tattered robe around him which glistened as crimson as the wounds over his arms and legs. "Who are you? Where are you? How do you know?" His tongue was licking clean his lips of blood and bruises. He could see Ibrahim leaning on his staff, quiet and contemplative.

Kilabah had sealed his lips, witnessing the entire scene with a dint of amusement and self-surrender. Across from the valley of the rivers of milk, nectar and honey was seated Aleena, her silver lyre abandoned at the bed of flowers faultlessly manicured. She appeared to be contemplating the fluted buds which were swiftly and astonishingly turning into flowers, all vivid and colorful. One sliver of a shining river was marking the boundary of the Elysian Fields where Chaviva could be seen promenading amidst the grove of ash trees, hosting at their hearths asters and poppies.

"Shah Jam from the wilderness of Aden speaks!" Sophia's tinkling of mirth was pouring balm to the silent woes of the suffering god. "He knows because he is fourth in line from the progeny of the great kings. King Jamshed is the contemporary of King Cyrus."

"Gods don't bleed!" Ibrahim muttered; his gaze feverish and piercing. "Wounded and bedraggled as you are, how could you be a god?"

"Gods do bleed inside their hearts of blood and flesh! They make other gods bleed, too, in rivulets of vengeance!" Hephaestus exclaimed bitterly. "I am the son of god Zeus and goddess Hera. Often, I became the victim of their quarrels and arguments. Once I dared speak in defense of my mother, incurring the anger of my father and he pushed me out of the heavens. All day long I kept falling till I crashed on the isle of Lemnos, paralyzed with fear and bleeding profusely. You are making me relive that pain since I am caught in that bubble of time and space when I suffered that crippling fall. But now I have landed here in the Garden of Irem, is that it? God, how mortals replicate the handiwork of gods! I would die a million deaths if I were to chisel the Elysian Paradise out of Mount Olympus and bring it to earth."

"And yet gods do not die!" Aleena's voice seemed to sail over the breath of music as she teased the strings of her silvery lyre.

"Who speaks?" Hephaestus moaned, his features washed by convulsions of pain.

"Beautiful beloved she is." Ibrahim murmured evasively, his eyes glued to Hephaestus.

"Beautiful. A mortal goddess indeed!" Hephaestus' eyes were lit up with admiration, pain banished from his expression.

"Mortals lived like gods in an age when even gods lived in harmony." Chaviva emerged forth from the Hall of Sapphires like a silvery wraith, her dark eyes glittering. "And mortals didn't die either; they just passed away as if overcome by sleep."

"Another goddess!" Hephaestus stood there rapt, transfixed.

"Another time and another age when mortals were privileged to enjoy childhood for at least one hundred long years! After which they reached adolescence, but died quickly and painfully before reaching full maturity." Sophia's sing-song voice alighted with the whisper of a distant cataract.

"More goddesses! Didn't I hear that voice before?" Hephaestus was jolted out of his mute pain and reveries, his look wild and searching. "Why I am here? Why is Elysian Paradise transported into this Garden of Irem?"

"I am to blame for all this," Ibrahim began genially. "I brought your Elysian Paradise here to renew my contact with incantations I have forgotten. A whole host of them! One to obtain freedom for my own self from the spell of Aleena's silver lyre, and another one so that she, too, could be free from the spell of my keeping her prisoner. Also, if Chaviva could be joined with Kilabah, the spell of enchantment could be dissolved in this Garden of Irem. Several more to admit King Jamshed into the Garden of Irem, and for Sophia — well, I am heaping mounds of confusion over your shoulders." He struck the ground with his staff in an effort to discipline his thoughts. "I am trying to discover the secrets of the gods through Kilabah by subjecting him to the rites of initiation. Those rites would lend him the gift of union with his beloved, and me the treasures of youth and wisdom to share with the world. So far, he has gone through the valleys of awe and bewilderment, has extinguished the fires of jealousy, has dispelled the fogs of intellect, awakening to the light of his spiritual heart. He has learned the virtue of acceptance to pain and surrender to the power of beauty, and now is on his way through the tunnels of thoughts to melt the thorns of doubt in realms ethereal and limitless. There were times when, through the art of astrology, I could fathom the secrets of the gods, but now that talent is gone from me and I want to re-acquaint myself with that knowledge."

"A secret once told or discovered ceases to be a secret anymore!" Hephaestus exclaimed with a touch of profundity. "Nothing secret about gods, they live the same way as mortals do on earth. Cruel, loving, vengeful and quarrelsome! The only difference between mortals here and immortals on Mount Olympus is that by the virtue of their immortality, they have endless time for arguments and that they are ageless, while mortals have limited amount of time for such luxuries, and they grow old and are subject to death."

"Strange, what kind of arguments?" Kilabah's voice was shuddering on the verge of explosion, his heart arresting Chaviva, yet his gaze keeping Hephaestus prisoner.

"About feuds and rivalries amongst mortals!" Hephaestus responded with sudden vehemence. "While gods fashion the destinies of the mortals on earth, they themselves never share any part of the earthly tragedies. If it was for my father alone, he would shatter the Olympus to smithereens, but other gods interfere, making him desist from such outrage."

"Why do gods love to wield the destiny of mankind?" Chaviva's dark eyes were stabbing the very soul of Hephaestus.

"For their amusement of course! To watch the mankind struggle through life, then die, much like the fate of an ant on the face of this earth." Hephaestus was smiling, as if beginning to enjoy this senseless discourse of the mortals.

"Don't you represent the archetype of later religious beliefs?" An amused smile hovered over Aleena's lips as if she was testing the intelligence of this young god. "Your fall from the Elysian Paradise into the cauldron of suffering on this earth surely makes you the archetype of the fall and expulsion from paradise?"

"Not even close in this mundane plethora of delusions!" Hephaestus permitted himself the luxury of mirth. "My fall is only for a moment. By the law and virtue of my being the son of God, I am swiftly reconciled with my father in heaven to enjoy the feast of nectar and ambrosia."

"So no link to the stories of paradise lost, of fall and expulsion throughout the ages of religious belief and dissention?" Aleena's attention was shifted to her silver lyre as if she had not asked any question.

"None whatsoever!" Hephaestus began with a sudden burst of animation. "On the Mount Olympus, where gods dwell in a perpetual state of conflict and harmony, there is no danger of permanent fall or expulsion. Being the son of a Greek God, I believe that Greeks perfected the religion for mankind, and that no other religion would ever take precedence over what Greeks believed and practiced. *Fates can neither be fought, nor averted*, is that tablet of gold which offers itself as a gift to each generation in succession for the propagation of divine wisdom and divine knowledge."

"Such gifts are baubles to men of intellect who render them worthless." Ibrahim half scoffed; half grinned.

"Corrupt such intellect which knows not the worth of priceless wisdom." Aleena thought aloud, her gaze enveloping both the young god and the old philosopher. "If intellect were pure, one would see the seat of wisdom where Allah resides."

"Aleena, the wise and the adorable!" Jamshed's laughter echoed loud much like the tolling of the bells. "My intellect as well as my memory is rusted, young Hephaestus, but I do recall that you built palaces of gold for gods on Mount Olympus. Is that true?"

"A little exaggeration as far as truth is concerned, and that's the whole truth." Hephaestus winced against the sudden assault of pain as his wounds began to dry and throb. "The truth is those palaces were built of solid brass. I also fashioned tables and chair of the same metal which could move down the great halls of my father's palace on their own accord. Zeus loved the gold boots I designed for gods to travel with great speed over air or water. The most prized are the chariots. The horses' hoofs, too, are made of brass, but accomplishing the same effect as the gold shoes."

"A long time since I saw those chariots sail through the milky way." Jamshed's sigh landed in the Garden of Irem as if pumped from the bellows to light a huge furnace. "Could you fashion those boots of gold for me so that I could travel from this wilderness of Aden to the Eden of Irem?"

"What would happen if mortals wore those boots?" Ibrahim prodded abruptly.

"They would be consumed by the invisible flames of vengeance, turning to heaps of ashes." Hephaestus smirked under the spell of his own inner power of perception and clairvoyance.

"What is the swift course for Kilabah to break through the enchantment of this Garden of Irem and to be united with his beloved Chaviva?" Ibrahim asked cautiously, stealing a glance at Kilabah—the ill-fated lover, who had abandoned himself over the steps of the Hall of Sapphires.

"Now I understand!" Hephaestus exclaimed with a mingling of blithe and profundity. "Chaviva is the virgin child of youth and beauty. The bride of immortality, awaiting the epiphany of her immortal bridegroom in this palace-garden of Irem her parents dared built to reveal the Eden of heaven on earth. If she can retain this purity of spirit, she would be able to escape the enchantment. And if Kilabah could discover his own state of purity and immortality, he, too, would escape the enchantment of the Garden of Irem, ultimately united with his beloved."

"How would he discover?" Was Ibrahim's cry of despair and urgency!

"You have drunk deep from the cup of immortality, O venerable philosopher!" Hephaestus appeared to jeer and cheer. "You are skilled in the art of spells and incantations, and you can help Kilabah enter that state of awareness where he can witness the branching of his thoughts in space ethereal and limitless. He must seek that realm where thoughts are without boundaries. That's where all his doubts would be removed, along with the delusion of his being mortal, before he could journey on the sacred road to be united with his beloved."

Suddenly, dark islands of clouds, orchestrated by violent winds were blackening the face of the sky. Hephaestus was lifted off his feet and shooting for the dark heavens, gold shoes on his feet glittering. The Elysian Paradise was obliterated by the fury of the gray whirlwinds. The Garden of Irem, with its foursome occupants of mystery, and intrigue was plunged into complete darkness.

Forty nights of vigil to break another veil of illusion in forty zillion times four of light years.

Jamshed's litany of incantations was reaching the darkness of Irem. A volley of fiendish mirth was lurking somewhere in the distance. There was a mercurial flaming of fire in the west, slashing intermittently the puffed blanketing of clouds. Irem had become the heart of the dark night, frenzied and throbbing, its jewel palaces and jewel gardens fading and trembling. More voices were penetrating this ocean of violence, loud and sibilant. Yet the voice of Sophia with its sweet poetry of richness was seething inside the hollow hearts of the jewel trees and jewel flowers.

Little stars of perception twinkle and fade into darkness. Bewilderment and dazzling illusions, much like the canvas of existence with multifaceted dreams, shifting and phantasmagoric! Silence knows the evanescent. Darkness beholds the ephemeral. Yet life with its tinsel wrap of joys and sorrows keeps hopes alive and dreams dancing. Sounding the trumpet of Judgment Day!

By the sound of nature with all its fury and violence, this pitch black night was literally booming much like the Judgment Day. With the exception that no evil souls were sent howling to hell, or even a few pious ones to heavens accompanied by the blaring of the trumpets. Despite the onslaught of snarling winds and the raging, maddening sound of voices, the Garden of Irem was intact, swathed in a black shroud of peace and protection.

And He is the forgiving, the loving
Lord of the Throne of Glory
Doer of what He will
Hath there come unto thee the story of the hosts
Of Pharaoh and the tribe of Thamud
Nay, but those who disbelieve live in denial
And Allah, all unseen, surroundeth them
Nay, but it is a glorious Quran
On a guarded tablet   85: 14-22

A fresh dawn with its gold, shimmering panels was chasing away all darkness from the Garden of Irem. Ibrahim stood stroking his beard; yawning, as if he had dozed off but for a moment. Kilabah, over the steps of the Hall of Sapphires, looked opiate, yet rested as if no violence of nature had grazed his awareness. Aleena, in contrast, appeared startled and vigilant, clutching her silver lyre as if contemplating flight. Chaviva, not far from her, was rapt witnessing shimmering oceans of dusk, awed and humbled.

"Did I or didn't I hear the voice of the Lord of the Heavens and earth, the all loving, forgiving God, talking about some tablet?" Ibrahim thought aloud, addressing no one in particular. "But where is that tablet?"

"Right under your feet!" Jamshed's voice boomed through the tunnel of Lake Shisha, bright and cheerful. "But you have to dig deep under the ruins of eight towers until you find an octagonal fort. Buried in a niche under the lofty mehrab is this precious tablet to be discovered!"

"Shah Jam, you are shooting down these instructions as if you yourself are God Almighty?" Ibrahim laughed derisively, his eyes burning with the ardor of curiosity. "Even if I commence this arduous task of digging and finding that tablet of the Quran, what do I do with it since I have already memorized the entire Quran by heart?"

"You think you know it by heart, O erudite philosopher!" Jamshed's voice carried with it a whiff of sarcasm. "But in its sanctuary of innermost sanctity lies a most precious of gems you have missed seeing or exploring. And that gem represents the circle of unity which all religions are trying to find from east to west, even inside the jungles of ignorance from north to south."

"Neither of the east, nor of the west, prophesy the circle of unity yet to be discovered on the canvas of imponderables known to us as this world!" Aleena struck the strings of her lyre with an unusual violence.

"Circles of unity!" Kilabah exclaimed, though his gaze was communicating with Chaviva alone. "I have seen those circles. Dancing in the wind and consumed by the dust-gold in sunshine."

Ibrahim had turned his attention to Aleena, as if feeling for the first time the pulse of her wisdom.

"What do you know about the circles of unity, dear Aleena?" Ibrahim asked tenderly, his look profound and endearing.

"They are much like the crops of good deeds, knitted together as one solid whole." Aleena began dreamily. "They look like wreaths of love. Initially they are small, but when gathered together they form a large circle of joy and sunshine. Anyone can see them dancing as Kilabah said, even in sands and over the seas. But that happens only when people begin cultivating love, not hatred. Compassion, not cruelty! Generosity, not greed!"

"How can one accomplish such a task, so colossal and demanding?" Ibrahim began histrionically. "Considering this horde of humanity, where greed overpowers generosity and where cruelty is the spice of life and hatred feast of the kings. The kings who are always plotting to annihilate the kingdoms of each other on the pretense of oppression, political or religious. I, for one, have no spells or incantations to change this warring world into a world of love and harmony. Where does one begin?"

"Right here in this garden of enchantment, my Lord." A tinkling of sweet mirth escaped Aleena's lips on the verge of hysteria. "Love, not intrigue, is needed in this Garden of Irem. Sobriety, not enchantment! This Zodiac splendor would become an eternal curse if you can't devise the means to reunite Chaviva with Kilabah. To begin with, you can carve a way for Sophia and Jamshed to come here so that—"

"Ah, I knew your old flame of love for Shah Jam would kindle and flare!" Ibrahim exploded against a sudden fit of jealousy, his voice hoarse and choking.

"Pardon me for neglecting to add the worst of evils, envy and jealousy!" Aleena laughed with open derision, the gold stars in her eyes sparkling with the glints of mockery.

"An old wise man despised by a beloved most charming," Ibrahim sighed. He shifted his gaze toward the ill-starred lovers, their eyes locked together. "In this subterranean nightmare I am trying my best to accomplish what your heart desires, my love." He returned his attention to Aleena, his gaze gentle and pleading. "I am jealous of course, for Shah Jam loves you, but that doesn't keep me away from seeking the treasures of mysteries which would not only make this Garden accessible to all humanity, but would grant us the freedom to leave or stay, or choose our own destinies by our will or caprice." He murmured doubtfully, looking frail and decrepit all of a sudden.

"Shah Jam has many loves, and his love for wisdom takes precedence over all the rest," Aleena began kindly as if sensing the despair and sadness of the old philosopher. "I cannot reciprocate the earthly love. My love is neither for this world, nor for the heavens, but for that one and only who would claim me when I succeed in purifying my heart of all vanity, despair and bitterness."

Her gaze was straying toward Chaviva who seemed oblivious to all, only her gaze riveted to the Virgin of chased silver over the façade of the Hall of Sapphires. "Surely Sophia loves you, my lord and my master." She returned her gaze to him slowly and thoughtfully. "You should bring her here to cheer your wearied mind and heart."

"Alas, she has fallen in love with Jamshed!" Ibrahim assumed an injured expression, his mind heeding the familiar voice of cunning and chicanery. "Yet an old man must not dream of love from maidens young and beautiful. Yet, I would bring Sophia here as soon as I exhaust my search in learning about gods and heavens. So far, my opinion about the God of all gods is that He is cruel, heartless and malicious. Making us suffer the agonies of the damned in this life with a promise of the same in the life after death."

"If you do not accept God as all loving, all forgiving, all embracing and all merciful, doesn't mean that He has ceased to love even the vilest of creatures? Simply, because everything is His creation which He fashioned out of the clay of goodness!" Aleena intoned with a sudden vehemence. "Mankind, on the contrary, strives toward molding and remolding that clay of goodness to suit their gluttony for lust, greed and hypocrisy."

"God fashioned mankind out of ash trees, if you only knew." One thunder of strident mirth escaped Ibrahim's lips. Wild, roaring and uncontrollable!

"But you don't even believe in God! So who fashioned who, who knows?" Jamshed's boisterous mirth, mingling with Sophia's was invading the Garden of Irem.

Olympus, where, they say, the gods' eternal mansion stands unmoved, never rocked by gale-winds, never drenched by rains. Nor do the drifting snows assail it, nor the clear air stretch away without a cloud. And a great radiance plays across that world where the blithe gods live all their days in bliss!   Homer, The Odyssey

The Garden of Irem was rocked by gusts inclement. The rain in torrents was drenching the Zodiac Halls in haze and mists.

"Almeena, the mother of my sorrows, why did you feast in the palace of Irem?" Chaviva's painful lament was lost inside the heart of violence and whirlwinds.

"Beloved, how may I comfort you?" Kilabah's prayer of a plea too was consumed by the flood of tears in nature's heart and eyes.

THE SACRED GARDEN

A musical instrument
In which when Pan played
His divine and seductive music
The sun on the hill forgot to die
And the lilies revived, and the dragon-fly
Came back to dream on the river
    Elizabeth Barrett Browning

The air was fresh and fragrant in the small town of Arcadia in Greece. Sophia could feel the gentle caresses of the breeze, even in the wilderness of Aden, which had become hers and Jamshed's haven and prison. Though Jamshed was longing to escape this prison, Sophia had no intention of leaving, lest she be torn away from her beloved and go wandering like Psyche afflicted with madness. Takhti-Jamshed was their home and palace, but this particular evening they were seated by Lake Shisha. Sophia, after witnessing the unveiling of Arcadia through Lake Shisha, had abandoned herself at Jamshed's feet, her head resting in his lap, though he seemed oblivious of her wild abandonment. He was immersed deep in admiring the fertile groves and the meadows, richly adorned with flowers and flowering trees. In the semblance of a paradise, those groves and meadows were boasting of tranquil streams and song-birds of diverse warble and plumage.

"A beautiful city and a quaint garden, Jamshed, but why does Arcadia hold special interest for you?" Sophia said, more so to engage him in conversation than to know his preference.

"Because this is the only city on earth, dear Sophia, chosen by god as his earthly home." Jamshed replied, his gaze searching this earthly paradise. "Besides, I am getting wearied of watching gods on Mount Olympus, which has become a part of the Garden of Irem under the spells and incantations of Ibrahim. After watching those cataclysmic events conjured by Ibrahim, which he can neither avoid nor control; it is quite pleasant to watch another abode of some strange gods, less predictable and more enchanting."

"Which god has sanctified this place as his home, pray tell me, I have forgotten?" Sophia affected ignorance, her heart longing to declare its love.

"God Pan, surely you have not forgotten!" Was Jamshed's involuntary response, his thoughts racing after Aleena in the jewel-garden of Irem.

"Oh, that ugly god of the shepherds." Sophia couldn't control her mirth, her veil of affection torn to shreds. "Horns on his head, and his legs similar to that of goats!" He might as well be a devil!"

"Here comes my god and your devil!" Jamshed's eyes were lit up with agog as he watched Pan hobble close to the bower of roses.

Sophia sat up, squealing with delight as she watched Pan wearing nothing but his ugliness, absorbed most besottedly in arranging his reed pipes.

"Even the ghosts and goblins would flee in sheer fright at his nakedness, not to mention his ugliness, if they were to visit his Arcadian Paradise." Sophia sang hilariously.

"Despite his ugliness, dear Sophia, he has no difficulty seducing the beautiful nymphs," Jamshed intoned rather reverently. "I wish I can persuade him to seduce the three nymphs guarding the Garden of Hesperides."

"A strange wish, I must say. Why?" Sophia's blue eyes were twinkling agog.

"Just for the sake of discouraging Ibrahim from inviting more paradises into the Garden of Irem." Jamshed's gaze was sucking in the breath of paradise within a paradise. "If you have not noticed yet, your old philosopher has conjured up the Garden of

Hesperides right across from the Hall of Opals? He is becoming senile I am afraid, and—"

A symphony of divine music from reed pipes was permeating the heart of nature and cosmos, sweet and intoxicating. Pan was a part of this symphony as if his very soul was the divine instrument of song and poetry. The Arcadian heaven, with its bucolic landscape, appeared to be under some spell of awe and silence. Even Sophia sat still in one spot, rapt and listening. A gentle easterly breeze had entered the wilderness of Aden, wafting forth a scent most exquisite and encompassing. Jamshed was inhaling deeply, drinking more and more of this scent and getting drunk. So bewitching were the music and the fragrance that neither Sophia nor Jamshed had noticed the absence of Pan, until the crackling of reeds from regions remote was setting ablaze the fire of sunset into a conflagration.

Aden was burning, it seemed, but it was merely suspended against the flaming streaks of dusk, slashing the sky in color of the rainbows. Colors were bleeding into colors, even coloring the crimson sands into shades of ochre and violet. The sun in the west had turned to a mirror of gold, beckoning Sophia to behold its majesty in the waters of Lake Shisha indirectly, lest she be blinded.

Jamshed was already witnessing the dazzling ocean of sunset inside the waters of Lake Shisha. The sunset was fading slowly, revealing through the tunnel of water the subterranean glitter of palaces and gardens. A Scale of pure gold, embossed over the front esplanade of the Hall of Opals, was catching the mood-swing of the gems, solid gold at one moment and sparkling like the molten sunset the next, creating an illusion of the see-saw in abeyance. Across from this opaline wonder could be seen the splendid Garden of the Hesperides, guarded by a fierce dragon. Ibrahim was trying to extinguish the scorching breath of the dragon with his incantations so that he could enter the Garden he had succeeded in conjuring with all its aspects of beauty and terror, awful and awesome. Towering over this Garden, almost between ether and sky, was a giant Titan balancing the sky over his head and shoulders.

"No mortal can enter the Garden of Hesperides unless he is blessed with supernatural powers to kill my dragon Ladon," The Titan gurgled mockery, glaring at Ibrahim with utmost contempt.

"Who are you?" Ibrahim looked up as if just becoming aware of this Titan.

"How ignorant! I am Atlas, don't you know?" Atlas roared like the thundering of drums.

"Of course, you are still carrying the sky over your head!" Ibrahim's eyes were lighting up with the stars of recollections. "Heracles tricked you, I have forgotten the story."

"You would learn the story afresh since you have dared bring the Garden of Hesperides in your Garden of Irem." Atlas' anger was replaced by weariness, his look glazed. "The whole scenario would be re-enacted as it was eons ago."

"Aside from refreshing my memory, I am in search of truth! Longing for some knowledge, sacred or profane, that could animate the womb of death and blow out the candle of life in death!" Ibrahim's voice was carried over the mountains by a sudden violence of gusts, and blown to bits much like the splintering, crackling sounds of firecrackers.

Zodiac Halls were shuddering amidst the jewel-dance of their own fire and color, sparkling and dazzling. The air was sprinkled with gold-dust, creating waves and whirlwinds. Chaviva was riding the rollercoaster of whirling clouds, childlike and wide-eyed. Kilabah, above the balcony of opals, was swaying and struggling to keep his balance, tracing with his fingers over the golden mists some hieroglyphic designs. Aleena was suspended in ether on a prayer-rug between Venus and a Crescent.

There is after death a day of doom and reparation, and there will be no more of favor shown of me on that day than of any man. Therefore, if I have struck any man among you an unrequited blow, let him strike me now. If I have offended any man, let him do as much to me. If I have taken away man's goods, let him now receive them again. Make me clean of guilt, so that I may come before God guiltless to man.

"Who speaks?" Was Kilabah's tremulous exclamation!

"Prophet." Chaviva was swinging down the rollercoaster of clouds, her face radiant and glowing. "This was Prophet's last sermon before his death." She alighted under the tree of light, opposite which stood dragon Ladon guarding the Garden of Hesperides.

A volley of flames were shooting out of the mouth of Ladon, flaring into a myriad of stars, not dying but creating one lace of a canopy, golden and shimmering. Atlas had begun to roar, his anger rising and falling like the serpentine tongues of lightning. The spluttering of his anger was directed at Heracles who had just landed at the gates of the Garden of Hesperides.

"Who is this young man and why is he visiting this awful garden?" Sophia's dreamy voice was reaching the subterranean abode of magical brilliance, both awful and awesome.

"A goddess who recognizes not the gardens of gods and goddesses must take a trip to Mount Olympus to reclaim her share of sweet remembrance!" Jamshed's laughter was mingling with the astonishing, shimmering encounter of Atlas with Heracles. "The garden, which your old philosopher has conjured up this time, is the garden of Hesperides, as you must have figured out by now. Much like the Garden of Eden this garden has a tree of knowledge. In this case, a tree with golden apples! And a dragon instead of the serpent! The serpent, not a beguiler, but a guardian most fierce and intimidating! No wonder the fruit of temptation for Eve was named—"

A babel of sounds, whipped by a strange hurricane, was rising to a crescendo amidst the sprinkling of gold-dust from Aden to Eden from the horizon. Aleena's sing-song voice interspersed with tinkling of mirth was barely audible. Her prayer-rug was diving down the crest of Venus and settling over the heap of gold-dust between Zodiac Halls and the garden of Hesperides.

"A time has come once again, Atlas, that your sacred tree would be despoiled of its gold. When would you learn who could be the trickster and who the one to be tricked?" Aleena was laughing. Her whole being was bathed in gold-dust as if she was the goddess of gold.

Time and time again history repeats itself and it would keep on repeating till eternity. No lesson ever learnt, no call for wisdom ever heeded. No miracle new, no tragedy fresh, all compassion processed, all cruelty recycled.

A gentle breeze with silvery notes was whispering secrets sacred and profane. A rippling of voices, both tender and distant was mingling with other voices. White mythical heroes of the past ages were coming alive to reenact their part of valor, deceit or transformation.

"Impudent wretch that you are, how dare you come near the garden of Hesperides?" Atlas thundered.

Heracles, smitten by the beauty of the three nymphs, didn't seem to hear Atlas. His heart was jumping with the rhythm of a drum-beat and his mind waving the banners of revolt, outraged and admonishing.

Stay focused. Remember your goal why you came here and what you wish to achieve! Let me hold your hand and take you back to the insanity of your youth and passion. Remember this garden is a wedding present to goddess Hera when she married your father Zeus. How could you forget that Hera was the one who drove you mad with her intrigues and jealousies with no other reason than that your father was god Zeus. In your madness you killed your children and your brother's children. But when awareness dawned upon you, you felt overwhelmed by grief. Then you sought the oracle of Apollo to atone for your sin and to mitigate the burden of your torment insufferable. You have followed the oracle of

Apollo to the hilt so far; ten acts of penance out of the way and now eleventh one demanding your attention. Shake yourself free from this trance and hold on to the promise of your reward after the twelfth penance. You would be able to return to Thebes and marry your beloved Deinira.

Heracles stood there rapt and gazing. Vaguely aware of the inner journey in his head which was becoming belligerent and demanding!

Look at you, even the love of Deinira is not moving you to action. Do you want to recall the first act of your penance so that you could be jolted out of your enchantment?

Granted you killed the lion of Nemea most swiftly, but that was sheer luck in your first act of penance. When you went after the nine-headed Hydra, you encountered an avalanche of difficulties. Every wound that you inflicted and every head that you severed resulted in growth of two more heads to cover the wounds. Finally you succeeded in burning eight heads and burying deep the immortal Hydra under a large rock. Funny how you ran after the Ceryneian Hind for months to perform your third act of penance before you captured her and killed her. I won't grudge you praise for killing the boar of Erymanthus, for you killed it most skillfully. But don't tell me you succeeded in cleaning the Augean stables of king Augeas, for you merely diverted the course of a nearby river to wash away the muck. Killing the carnivorous birds of Stymphilis was no great task, though capturing the wild bull of Crete was a major accomplishment. Yes, I do hear you, you did catch the man-eating mares of Diomedes, but stealing the girdle of Hippolyta — the queen of Amazons was a difficult task with added burden of guilt and heartache. You succeeded in completing your tenth act of penance by capturing the oxen of Geryon and now —

"I have come to seek your favor, Atlas." Heracles humbled by the inner journey in his head requested most courteously. "May I pluck a few golden apples from your garden to heal my ailing friend Eurystheus?"

"Do you see that dragon Ladon over there spitting fire?" Atlas' anger was dissolving against the sudden spark of inspiration in his head to gain freedom. "He would swallow you whole if you dared but take another step! How do you know my name?" He asked suddenly, almost drunk by the soma of his inspiration, neglecting to ask the name of this young intruder.

"Everyone knows your name." Heracles tone was sad and flattering. "Even the lowly human beings know how Zeus dethroned your father and subjected you to the punishment of carrying the heavens on your shoulders." His thoughts were erecting a fence of defenses to conceal his identity if Atlas deigned to inquire. "May I enter your garden; a few golden apples would save the life of Eurystheus."

"You cannot enter the garden of Hesperides," Atlas began with an imperious tone of authority, his ego literally inflated as big as the sky. "Even if I subjected Ladon to obedience, my lovely daughters won't let anyone enter but me." His ego and cunning were colliding and somersaulting. "The only way you can get the apples is to hold this sky on your shoulders while I go and pluck some."

"I would be immensely grateful." Heracles inched closer, his own mind weaving a web of cunning and ingenuity. "I am ready. I would do anything."

The weight of the sky was shifted over the shoulders of Heracles, while Atlas bounded off with the alacrity of a young man to fetch apples. Chaviva, under the tree of light, appeared to be turned into a statue of marble, smooth and incandescent. She was watching with disbelief the transformation of Ladon from a fiery dragon to that of a devoted disciple. Even Ibrahim was astounded, shaking his conical beard, while witnessing the miracle as Ladon curtsied and groveled. Aleena, suspended between ether and sky, had better view of the whole scenario, her gaze following Atlas in his newly found joy of relief and freedom. Kilabah, too, on his balcony of opals, stood rapt and inert as if breath had been sucked out of him, his demeanor more frightened than incredulous. Aleena, apart from all observers, was neither frightened nor incredulous, but fascinated by the agility of Atlas, plucking apples under some spell of carefree abandon.

"My heart is filled with love and generosity today!" Exclaimed Atlas, flaunting the gift of apples in his possession! "I myself would take them to Eurystheus." He was gloating inwardly that he had tricked this young man into carrying the sky over his shoulders forever.

"Much obliged. You have spared me the pain of offering this precious gift to Eurystheus, for I must confess I despise him, but I am honor-bound and promised him to render this service." Heracles affected cheerfulness, pumping out a mock sigh of relief. "But since you would be long gone, could you hold the sky for a moment? I need to scratch my neck so that I could feel comfortable and pay my debt to you with great devotion and diligence."

"The least I could do since you are honest and steadfast." Atlas, drunk by the sudden stroke of luck in gaining his freedom, agreed readily.

As soon as the weight of sky was shifted over the shoulders of Atlas, and apples in firm possession of Heracles, he fled with the speed of Pegasus. He dared not look back, lest he be really tricked, his senses turning the volley of curses from the lips of Atlas into the music of exhilaration, sweet and intoxicating.

"The god is tricked by the son of god!" Sophia's laughter shook the subterranean heavens which were already shuddering against the onslaught of gusts sudden and inclement. "Just like the fruit of temptation for Eve, these apples would return to the garden of Hesperides somehow. Heracles would succeed in bringing three-headed dog Cerberus out of Hades to the surface of this world, and then he would be able to marry his beloved Deinira."

"Her beloved Hercules would be poisoned to death, succumbing to the fate of all lovers, past or present!" Jamshed's laughter was adding fresh tremors to the subterranean abode on the verge of whirling and disintegrating. "As prophesied, Heracles would reach Thebes, also marrying Deinira! But he wouldn't become a hero if everything were easy for him and his beloved. As fate would have it, before marrying Deinira, Heracles would foil the attempt of centaur Nessus in abducting his bride-to-be, shooting him dead with a poisoned arrow. But before his death, Nessus was able to plead with Deinira to save his blood in a vial as it would preserve Heracles' love for her always. Later, when Deinira suspected that Heracles was in love with Iole, she sent him a garment sprinkled with the blood of Nessus. Not in the least suspecting any ill will from his wife, Heracles donned the garment and was poisoned. He was taken to Olympus as the rumor goes, and then granted immortality —"

A great cry of agony ripped through the sky, chilling both the worlds. Atlas had turned to stone. Trees upon trees were sprouting from his hair until his statue-like body was transformed into a mountain, populated by a dense forest. This giant mountain, along with its forested rocks, was rising up as if it was an island of clouds. This mountain was acquiring the sheen of the emeralds, shooting down fiery beams into the Garden of Irem where there was nothing left of the garden of Hesperides.

"What's the use of amassing heavens, when, though heavy as the mountains, they can't stay rooted to the ground, vanishing like a puff of smoke!" Chaviva exclaimed suddenly, her dark eyes glittering.

"The use, my child, is to explore the purity of intellect where Allah resides." Ibrahim murmured patiently, his gaze sweeping over his Garden of Irem with a sigh of relief.

None of the violence inside the garden of Hesperides had touched Ibrahim's garden of enchantment, which he had built with the life-blood of his incantations profound and countless. His gaze was wandering from Chaviva to Aleena, to Kilabah whose lips were trying to shape words, his eyes burning.

"Did you find that seat of purity, Ibrahim, where Allah resides?" Kilabah's lips were trembling, his gaze already reaching out to Chaviva.

"For sure I got as close as possible right here in this Garden of Irem," Ibrahim murmured as if to his own self. "I saw Perseus on his way home after killing Medusa. No one heard him, but I did as he pleaded with god Atlas to let him rest in his garden of Hesperides before he resumed his journey. But god Atlas would not let him stay, for Goddess Themis had warned him that a son of Zeus would come to steal golden apples from his garden. Perseus was not only offended but enraged, taking his revenge by unveiling before Atlas the severed head of Medusa. The rest you just witnessed as Atlas was turned to stone, growing into the size of a mountain with forest as thick as the roots of countless trees under earth."

"Atlas is not god, but a Titan." Aleena's liquid gold eyes were lit up with scorn. "That's insignificant, though. Prison and paradise are both the same as far as I am concerned. I didn't choose any, yet I got both, and I have grown indifferent. The mystery of not knowing and knowing too little in great chunks of time doesn't appeal to me anymore. And yet, I have grown fond of Chaviva and Kilabah. Are you planning to send them to the eternal darkness of Hades, my Lord, or hurl them into one of your paradises, not ever caring if they attain bliss or damnation?"

"My beautiful rebel of a child, as always." Ibrahim shook his beard in utter denial of something only his evil heart could see or contain. "Warmth and sweetness of spirit is upon the lovers, they feel the love of God and the bliss of unity. Soon they would reach the one and the only paradise in the seventh heaven."

"If that be the truth, may heaven always guide you in the way of truth, my Lord." Aleena laughed. "Knowing you, your heaven would be guarded by a legion of liars and sycophants."

"You blaspheme, my wayward child! My beauty and my all!" Ibrahim chided; his voice rather low and maudlin.

Sibilant cries were heard from the very lips of the opals, it seemed. The Garden of Irem was being enveloped in the opaline glow of dusk and sadness.

Scent is the food of the soul. Soul is the vehicle of the faculties of man.

Who speaks?

Prophet, of course.

Of course, why?

Can't you inhale the fragrance? The gentle breeze caressing all. These are the gentle waves of love, peace and harmony.

Paradise is an illusion just like the Garden of Irem, or any walled Eastern garden. Even the gardens of Persia, or of Moghul India, illusions all, Grand Illusion!

Dewdrop mists were descending upon the Garden of Irem. A rainfall of asters much like the snowflakes were settling over the garden of enchantment.

Olives swollen with olive oil are for you to pick and gather.

Whose oil will well night glow forth.

Sweet sound of trumpets from above was lulling all to sleep.

Allah is the light of the heavens and the earth
The similitude of His light is as a lustrous niche
Wherein is the lamp, the lamp in a glass
The glass as if it were a glittering star
It is lit by a blessed tree—an olive
Neither of the east nor of the west
Whose oil will well nigh glow forth
Though fire toucheth it not

The odor of sea salt was stinging Sophia's senses as she straggled away from the briny banks, flustered and dreamlike. The sapphirine brilliance of her blue eyes was accentuated by her poppy-red lips, bright and vibrant. She could see the forested landscape not far from her, her gaze reaching beyond the groves of cedar and poplar toward white cypress with awe and fright.

"Where I am? Where is Jamshed?" Sophia's voice sounded like a lone cry amidst the vast arena of wilderness.

"You are in the remote island of Ogygia in the middle of the sea. Keep walking, dear Sophia, in the direction of the lush groves and you would come upon the Garden of Calypso, a paradise on earth." Jamshed's kingly voice was penetrating each fiber of the wilderness.

"Jamshed! Alas, I can't see you!" A cry of agony ripped through Sophia's lips, as she started running through the woods like Psyche gone mad with grief. "Of course, you have your Jam-e-Jam." Why was I cast away from you?" Her feet were coming to a stumbling halt by the watercourse of four springs edged with violets.

"Don't you remember, my dear Sophia, you didn't heed my commands!" Ibrahim's crisp voice was landing upon Sophia like a bolt of lightning. "I summoned you to the Garden of Irem, but you obstinately refused. So I had no choice but to hurl you down to the Isle of Calypso, because without you I couldn't summon this paradise to the Garden of Irem."

"And what makes you think, my crafty Lord, that you could persuade me now to come to your Garden of Irem?" Sophia laughed hysterically, her gaze riveted to the giant owl perched absolutely still over the cross-section of four springs.

"You have no option, dear Sophia!" Ibrahim's voice was descending upon the wilderness like claps of thunder. "If you don't agree, you would become a prisoner in this Isle of Calypso, not ever to leave this isle of enchantment."

A family of falcons overhead and the sea-crows roosting in the groves were jolting Sophia to the awareness of fresh grief and agony. Suddenly, the sky had turned pewter. The islands of clouds were enveloping the wilderness in a thin veil of golden dusk, gossamer and shimmering. Sophia seemed to be enveloped in a mantle of despair and mourning, her feet guiding her over the velvety path of watercourse swiftly and steadily. She was drifting toward another grove of trees. On either side of this grove were vines of red and green grapes, most vibrant like the gems all pure and precious. Sophia's feet were coming to another stumbling halt before the mouth of a cave spangled with garden vines, emerald-bright and sparkling. She advanced cautiously, wild parsley under her feet wafting some sort of exotic scent which was making her giddy and somnambulant. Her senses were in abeyance as she entered the cave, and then stood there transfixed as if galvanized.

Sophia recognized the goddess Calypso on a couch dripping with velvets, gold and crimson. As far as Sophia could remember, Calypso had become more divine than ever, a paragon of grace and beauty. A goddess of eternal youth and stunning charm in Sophia's mind was now transformed to an enchantress most seductive and nonpareil. Her auburn hair sliding over the round pillow was falling to the floor in silken ringlets. She lay on the couch in perfect immobility, appareled in a robe of gold, diaphanous and shimmering. She seemed oblivious of her surroundings splashed with rich rugs and golden vessels. Her white face, suffused with the reflection of pale gold from her robe, had the quality of marble, smooth and glowing.

The pomegranate-red upon the lips of Calypso had the sheen of rubies, but the most awesome of her features were her beautiful eyes, as if holding cups of sherry wine, sparkling and intoxicating. Her dreamboat eyes, with long lashes, were glittering. Her lips pouring forth nectar of a song most dulcet and dolorous. The rivers of pain and longing were gushing forth from her throat, pleading with Odysseus.

Sophia gasped for breath, noticing for the first time Odysseus standing by the hearth. He was wearing a white toga, its loose end tossed over his left shoulder. He turned abruptly, raising his muscular arms and yawning. A saddest pair of eyes Sophia had not ever seen before appeared to be contemplating her before settling on Calypso. Sophia's mouth was left open, one frightful scream stuck inside her throat. Her thoughts were urging her to flee, but her feet were not obeying.

"You were brave, dear Sophia, and now if you could look at yourself." Ibrahim's voice shuddering with mirth and bitterness was drumming Sophia's awareness. "Don't be afraid, dearly beloved. They can't see or hear you. My voice too is for your ears alone. Would you heed? You don't want to witness the amorous coupling of a mortal man with an immortal goddess, do you? If you agree to come to the Garden of Irem, I would transport you right now?"

"I won't agree until you give me a good reason," Sophia muttered, watching Odysseus kiss the hands of Calypso with all reverence. "Besides, handsome Odysseus is no ordinary mortal! He is favored by Zeus. Why did you call me, dearly beloved?" She asked capriciously without waiting for an answer. "I am not in Hades, am I? If I am in Hades, where is my consort? Like Hermes for Calypso, and Odysseus for Persephone?"

"You are not in Hades, dear Sophia, but in the paradisiacal garden and cave-palace of Calypso, and you would be shunted down into Hades if you remain obstinate." Ibrahim's tone was weary and indulgent. "Your love is inconstant, changing like the seasons, much too quickly. Your heart favors me no more, and now it has abandoned Jamshed in favor of handsome Odysseus." He laughed; his laughter dry and strident.

"How very strange! The accuser is the accused, forgetting Sophia and falling in love with Aleena," Sophia began with mock cheerfulness. "I have not abandoned Jamshed, my cunning friend! I am longing to be back in the wilderness of Aden." She couldn't take her gaze away from the amorous embrace of the divine couple amidst the height of their passion.

"I have no power to send you back to the wilderness of Aden, dear Sophia, you must come to the Garden of Irem." Ibrahim's stern tone was on the verge of breaking into gentle pleas.

"Why was I separated from Jamshed?" Was Sophia's hopeless plea!

"So that you could fulfill the prophecy of union with the beloved inside the Garden of Irem! We would all benefit from that, lovers with the beloveds, and I finally wedded to the bride of death." Ibrahim's voice sounded weak and doleful.

"Would Jamshed be a part of these bridal events?" Sophia's interest was fading in this parlance. Her attention was riveted to the art of love-making she was certain she had forgotten.

"He would be if you take Aleena with you from the Garden of Irem to the wilderness of Aden."

A cry of ecstasy from the lips of Calypso made Sophia shudder with the sense of awe and bewilderment. She closed her eyes, feeling as light as a feather. Gliding over the constellations, carefree and exhilarated!

"You must leave this Isle of Calypso, Sophia; otherwise, this paradise would devour you alive." Ibrahim's urgent tones were penetrating Sophia's awareness.

Sophia was outside the cave, surrounded by woods, watching one raven circle over the cypress before swooping down to peck at the bald head of a giant owl. A hawk was circling above, and white cloudlets were appearing on the horizon as if dancing and swirling. Sophia had begun to run again, wild and distraught. She was entering a sacred garden, the garden of roses—the ultimate paradise of Calypso. The scent of roses was sweet as intoxicating. She was swaying toward a marble bench, utterly exhausted. Flinging herself over its smooth surface, she lay there, panting.

"Odysseus is ready to leave on his newly built boat to Ithaca, Sophia, and you would become the prisoner of Calypso if you don't agree to come to the Garden of Irem." Ibrahim's voice with its dithering urgency was hammering over Sophia's confusion and self-surrender.

"Why did you want the Isle of Calypso in the Garden of Irem anyway?" Was Sophia's opiate inquiry, her senses overwhelmed by some scent sweet and nameless.

"Because love is more potent in the realm of water!" Ibrahim's wearied tones were penetrating Sophia's half alert, half dulled senses. "Oceans of water surround the Isle of Calypso, and sacred trees grow in profusion here to enhance the sanctity of life in loving and surrendering."

"Love in what respect?" Sophia could barely speak, her head abandoned against the trellis and her eyes closing.

"Love is a rite of passage in life and the sacred journey toward death." Ibrahim's voice was sounding shrill and crackling. "Stay awake, Sophia, you must. Open your mind, heart and soul to this intention of reaching the Garden of Irem, and you would be released from the enchantment of the sacred garden of Calypso."

"Where is Jamshed? If he could convince me—" Sophia's thoughts were trailing off, though she was managing to sit straight.

"Dear Sophia, you are already the victim of enchantment and soon would be falling into deep slumber, and slumbering for centuries?" Jamshed's soothing tone was splintering Sophia's drowsiness. "Do as Ibrahim suggests, and make a quick escape into the Garden of Irem!"

"How?" Sophia leaped to her feet as if stung. The scenery before her transformed to utter repose and pulchritude!

"I have transported you to the peace and quiet of the woods, dear Sophia." Ibrahim's voice was clear and assertive. "Snip some of that grapevine and wrap it around your head as if wearing a tiara."

"Why?" Sophia was obeying somnambulantly.

"Because this signifies the blood of the earth!" Ibrahim's voice was sharp, cutting and stabbing. "Symbolic of the life-blood of sacrifice and of menstruation! The bloodshed without a wound, thus divine life-blood as a gift most sacred for harmony and fecundity."

With the swiftness of an automaton, Sophia was obeying each instruction of Ibrahim, oblivious to the fact that she had consented to visiting the Garden of Irem. She was decking her arms and throat with wreaths of violets.

Violets represent your hopes and fears. They are also the symbol of Aphrodite—the goddess of sexual love and lust.

Sophia was sticking a cedar branch at her waist.

Cedar drives the demons away. It is a sacred tree, holding in its sap the revelations of the oracles of heaven and earth.

Sophia was busy twining the leaves of a poplar into one garland to tie below her waist.

Poplar is the Tree of Life. Look how its dark green foliage turn toward the heaven, and pale green under the surface facing the earth.

Sophia was making a bundle of leaves from the white cypress in the semblance of a bouquet.

"Though white cypress is the symbol of the Underworld, it connotes a new cycle of life." Ibrahim's voice was loud and imperious inside the Hall of Topaz where Sophia stood facing him. "Bridegroom waiting for the bride, and bride united with bridegroom. Do you see that hawk, dear Sophia? You are to ride on its back. It would carry you into the heart of the Garden of Irem. Hawk is god-ferryman, taming the waters of river Styx, and journeying toward the isle of rebirth and resurrection.

"Isle of Calypso was my paradise where my memory of Jamshed was fading!" Was Sophia's feverish exclamation as she inched closer to the gilded chair of multifaceted jewels upon which was seated Ibrahim in a state of quiet contemplation. "Now I am in Hades!" She cried in horror, watching the jeweled Scorpions peering down from the vaulted ceiling of this Hall of Topaz. "There is no Garden of Irem out there, but a prison—your subterranean underworld designed for your pleasure of black magic and necromancy." Her gaze was lured to the floor under her feet, of all opals, absorbing fantastic designs from the blaze of jeweled Scorpions on the ceiling.

"You are the goddess of wisdom, Sophia, and you are acting like a school girl." Ibrahim stroked his white beard, holding Sophia prisoner in his philosophic gaze. "Paradise is the state of bliss and repose in one's heart, physical and spiritual! Once we were in paradise together, because I was in love with you and you couldn't stay away from me, but you probably don't remember. Something happened then, you went away, and I got enamored, well, I am forgetting now. Centuries are between us and we have lost touch with life—with living. Why don't you go out and explore the Garden of Irem and its Zodiac splendor? Make friends with

Chaviva, Kilabah and even with Aleena. Or sit by the pool and talk to Jamshed through the tunnel of Lake Shisha."

"Just to get away from you and from these silly Scorpions with flaming jewels, I would even choose Hades as my everlasting abode." Sophia whirled away, cantering out of the Hall of Topaz.

The cool night air appeared to be lulling the Zodiac splendor to sleep as Sophia emerged into the subterranean enchantment, fiery and flustered. The Garden of Irem was glittering like a jewel under the moonlit night. Her gaze was reaching beyond the sky and the stars. She couldn't take her gaze away from Pluto, which had turned from a dot of mud into a globe pale and luminescent. Shuddering from head to toe, she was realizing that her former powers of youth were restored since she could see Pluto without even entering the planetary bazaar of constellations.

Is it true? Are my senses in abeyance? Is it all an illusion?

A light breeze had begun to whistle through the leaves of the poplars, accompanied by notes of music, vibrant and rippling. Sophia was startled by the sound of this heavenly music, her gaze wandering from the sparkling halls of Zodiac down to the crystal-clear rivulets, bordered by moss with a sprinkling of calendula. She stirred to her feet, tracing the music to its source. Silvery streams on the way in their sinuous course were beckoning her onward. Yet, she was pausing here and there to admire the rose-tinted fish, or fondle the intertwining branches of fruit trees blessed with the floral wealth of Eden. An emerald grove was luring her, beyond which could be seen a depression, its marble floor glistening under moonlight. Her feet were coming to a sudden halt by the posts capped with globes of burnished gold and studded with gems precious and flawless. Motionless she stood, humbled and bewildered.

Sophia was walking again, great tides of sadness welling inside her, swollen and turbulent. Her feet were arrested once again by one sparkling basin brimming with water tinted azure, as if imported from Elysian Garden to reveal its charm of bliss and beauty. In fact this basin was rendered charming by the presence of Gothic princess. Mantled in her own grace and loveliness, Aleena was evoking the loveliest of tunes on her silver lyre, not even aware of the close scrutiny of the goddess.

Through the eyes of Jam-e-Jam her beauty is deceptive, but now I can see how beautiful she is, her beauty mysterious and sparkling.

Sophia was thinking, her heart bleeding by the shafts of rage, disbelief and jealousy! She could not untangle her gaze from the swath of Aleena's glorious hair, her very soul awakening to the pangs of violence and admiration. Aleena, most probably, feeling the intensity of Sophia's gaze, lifted her eyes, the music stopped.

"So, you are the great goddess of wisdom, I have been told." Aleena's liquid-gold eyes were sparkling. "I knew you were coming." A subtle smile was hovering over her beautiful lips, her eyes lit up with the stars of curiosity.

"With your shimmering, glittering demeanor, you could very well outshine any goddess of wisdom or beauty!" Sophia confessed, trying her best to dispel the pain of her jealousy. "I wish I was the goddess of love." She lowered herself over the first tier of the marble basin, at once enamored by the star-doffed swarms of finny tribes, floating in perfect harmony with the rhythm of the moon-tides.

"Now that you have finally met each other face-to-face, may I intrude?" Jamshed's voice rippled through the waters much like the sound of bugle, disrupting the harmony of the starry fish.

"Jamshed, is that you?" Sophia's heart was leaping toward the wilderness of Aden, her blue eyes sparkling all of a sudden.

"Yes, dear Sophia. I have been watching you both." Jamshed's tone was measured and thoughtful. "I am glad you reached here safely. You would bring Aleena to me, I am sure. Won't you?"

"Yes." Sophia murmured. One cry of agony stifled within her.

"My Jam-e-Jam needs polishing. Lake Shisha alone cannot project my reflection down the azure waters of this basin. I will work on polishing my Jam-e-Jam." Jamshed's voice sounded dry and distant. "Well, get acquainted. I will get in touch with you soon."

"You are no ordinary mortal, Aleena, you could be a goddess." Sophia turned to Aleena, pretending indifference to Jamshed's solicitude. "Do you remember your parents?" Her heart was constricting and clamoring.

"No!" Aleena murmured. Her gaze was gliding past the emerald grove toward the Zodiac halls which glittered and shuddered like a myriad of suns in one galaxy.

"So sad. You could never be sure if you are a princess or a goddess?" Sophia followed Aleena's gaze. Her eyes were squinting disbelief at the grandeur of the alabaster palace yonder, trimmed with gold and onyx. It was studded with precious gems, its Zodiac halls facing the divine garden.

"All I can remember is King Habuz who destroyed our palace and the entire army of our kingdom." Aleena reminisced without a trace of bitterness. "I had lost consciousness, I don't know how and when. I do remember, though, that I became a prisoner of King Habuz and then of Ibrahim."

"Ah, my venerable philosopher, old and cunning!" Sophia exclaimed suddenly. She was watching Chaviva and Kilabah over the balcony of the Hall of Topaz. Standing there like the ill-starred lovers. "What is to become of them?" Her gaze was shifting to the jeweled Scorpion over the parapet, bright and blazing.

"They are drunk by the nectar of love, and learning the art of grace and wisdom," Aleena commented disinterestedly.

"Love and deliverance as I understand it, or did one time, now I don't," Sophia demurred aloud. "What are Chaviva and Kilabah really learning? If they are, would that be of any benefit?"

"They had to learn from the passion of Calypso, Ibrahim said, the concept of love and betrayal?" Aleena claimed her silver lyre, fondling its strings tenderly.

"The beauty of Aleena has a soothing affect even on you, my Sophia." Ibrahim emerged forth from the emerald grove like an apparition, inching closer, reluctantly.

"Yet, her beauty fails to soothe your temperament or inclinations." Sophia bristled with a quick surge of anger. "Meddling with sacred gardens of the earth, so that you could bring them to the Garden of Irem, time and time again, for what?"

"For the sake of merging this Garden of Irem with the Eden of the heavens, from which it has been severed since eons," Ibrahim muttered profoundly. He stood facing them across from the marble basin, his gaze searching. "Lovers need to be united without the taint of impurities in this world and in the world hereafter. The baptismal waters of holiness are to be sprinkled over each shrine on the face of this earth before saints and sages could dissolve the eternal pang of separation between the worlds both mortal and immortal."

"When would Jamshed be coming here to fit in this scheme of lovers?" Sophia was probing her own thundering heart than pleading with the mad philosopher.

"You sound like a frightened child, my dear Sophia." Ibrahim indulged, shaking his beard as if it were a broom. "As I told you before, Jamshed can't come here; you have to take Aleena up there when the time is appropriate."

"What if Aleena doesn't want to go?" Sophia asked with a mingling of hope and hopelessness.

"Aleena, my dear Sophia, is the emblem of beauty supreme, beyond petty decisions and inclinations." Ibrahim's voice was so tender that it didn't seem to belong to him. "She reigns like a queen wherever she lives, and her will is honored." The rivers of sadness in his eyes were turning to Aleena. "Would you mind going to the wilderness of Aden, my dear Aleena? Replacing this dotard with a young charge, not that you need one." A little tremor in his voice was making him look weak and vulnerable.

"No." A subtle smile kindled Aleena's eyes to burnished gold. "No, I don't mind leaving this subterranean world as long as I am getting closer to finding my parents."

"He doesn't mean it that way —" Sophia's voice was swallowed by the crackling sound of the moon bursting in twain. The sky was lit by the swords of lightning shooting from the very heart of the horizon.

Chaviva had vanished from the balcony, screaming. Kilabah's arms held out to comfort her were hugging emptiness. He had turned to a statue of ice, not even knowing that Chaviva was gone. The jeweled Scorpions over the parapet had come alive, laughing and twittering! Gusts of zephyr were spraying white mists over the Garden of Irem, but the sky had turned black. Ibrahim was swaying toward his palace of Zodiac splendor. Sophia had abandoned herself by the basin, peering through mists at the azure waters in hope of catching a glimpse of Jamshed. Aleena was the only brave one, watching the fireworks in the sky and the swirling of mists with utter fascination.

The bright and glorious goddess Calypso in all her blossoming fertility and vibrant beauty is revealing her dark shadow, though nurturing life.

Jamshed's voice was clear and crisp. Enveloped in mists a great hush had fallen over the Garden of Irem.

No new fashion of hardship, none unexpected rises to confront me, all have I anticipated. All have I traversed in my mind.   Virgil

The Garden of Irem, this particular evening, had turned to a turquoise city, for only the Palace of Turquoise in the Zodiac Avenue was lit to refulgence. It was lit by a myriad of lamps and candles, accentuating a jeweled Archer on the parapet. Abundance of turquoise embedded on the body of the Archer appeared to be polished to the sheen of the oceans and sunlight, alive and glittering. *The reason for lamps and candles,* as Ibrahim had proudly announced, *was that this night is the night of Shab-i-Barat.*

Ibrahim, after eons of philosophic retreat, had looked joyful while talking about the night of Shab-i-Barat.

It is the night of atonement, or of forgiveness and anticipation. He had expounded to all who heeded, of which there were many, for he had invited the Buddhist Paradise packed with inhabitants of the earth into the Garden of Irem. *It is also believed that on this night God writes the destinies of the human beings for the coming year by taking into account the deeds committed by them in the past year. Some believe that this is the night of good fortune, while others believe that their deceased relatives or ancestors visit them this particular night. Another belief is that this night the Prophet visits each home to relieve the pain of the suffering humanity.*

Actually, this strange scene, with Ibrahim's cheerful intonations, was alighting in Sophia's mind as she stood under the Tree of Awakening, thinking about Jamshed. This Tree of Awakening was a part of the Buddhist Paradise, so fathomlessly tall and gigantic that all the inhabitants of any paradise could see it, regardless of any direction or remoteness of the place where they were interned. A gossamer net of gold was woven over all the branches of this tree laden with jewels. Besides jewels, this tree was hosting garlands upon garlands of flowers, colorful and fragrant. Sophia's senses were drunk by the scent of those flowers and she heard herself speak aloud to Jamshed.

"We are one hundred thousand million Buddha fields away from each other, and getting further apart every minute. Can you hear me, Jamshed? Where are you?"

"I am closer to you than your heartbeat, dear Sophia." Jamshed's voice was touching the hem of Sophia's awareness.

"Jamshed, is that you? Where are you?" Sophia's gaze was cutting through the shimmering folds of gold netting, and beholding a glimpse of distant paradise she had not noticed before.

"I am with you if I may repeat." Jamshed's laughter trickled down like the tinkling of bells.

This Tree of Awakening, in fact, was adorned with silvery bells. They had begun tinkling with joy in some rite of jubilations, their sound dulcet and ineffable.

"You can see me through your Jam-e-Jam, but I can't see you!" Sophia lamented without bitterness. "How can you hear me? Most of all, how come I can hear you?" Her gaze was exploring one golden pond edged by pearls and sapphires with its inner border of mother-of-pearl.

"You are standing under the Tree of Awakening, dear Sophia, you should know the answer to each why and how," Jamshed began cheerfully. "Whoever stands under this tree is touched by *light*, becoming a channel of understanding between mind and senses. This is the best thing that Ibrahim has done in centuries by inviting the Buddhist Paradise into his Garden of Irem. By its mere presence all hearts are touched, even Aleena's, she is not averse to talking with me. If only the old crone could keep this paradise in his Garden, we all would be together, living happily Everafter!"

"What kind of tree it is?" Sophia asked, noticing with a pang of astonishment that all the venom of her jealousy was drained. "I have never seen the likes of it! I heard Chaviva exclaim that this tree is the sacred fig. But I think Ibrahim is right that this tree is similar, not exactly, to Bodhi tree—the tree of enlightenment for Buddha under which he resisted the temptations of the king of Mira and obtained enlightenment."

"Believe it or not, dear Sophia, in reality there is no Bodhi tree. Yet this name has become synonymous with bliss as is obvious in this quatrain." Jamshed paused before reciting.

"This body is the Bodhi tree
The mind a mirror bright
Take care to wipe them clean
Lest dust on them alight."

"You must have visited that cave where this quatrain is inscribed," Sophia chirped with a sudden flash of recollection. "So vivid is that memory in my own mind of that evening when I straggled into a cave. I was more impressed by the quatrain inscribed under it than the one you just recited.

There is no Bodhi tree
Nor any mirror bright
Since nothing at the root exists
On what should what dust alight."

"Your preference meets my approval, dear Sophia!" Jamshed intoned genially. "Actually, that was not a cave, but an old, dilapidated monastery. I had witnessed the inscription of both the quatrains at the time when they were inscribed. A senior monk had inscribed the first quatrain. His disciple and a younger monk, after reading that quatrain of his master, took the liberty of inscribing his own at the bottom; obviously, of much superior quality. Talking of superior, Sophia, I fear the quality of my Jam-e-Jam is depleted, rather corrupted. I can't see Aleena. Do you know where she is?"

"So you need me to find your beloved!" Sophia laughed. She was seized by a wave of astonishment, once again, that not a trace of jealousy was left in her heart. "The last time I saw her she was sitting close to Ibrahim in his philosophic retreat inside the Palace of Turquoise. She was playing her silver lyre, accompanied by sweetest of smiles I had not ever seen before."

"Pincers of jealousy are constricting my heart, dear Sophia," Jamshed lamented as if suddenly stabbed with the knife of pain. "To assuage this pain I need diversion. Would you do me the kindness of walking with me in this Buddhist Paradise? With your eyes and through this Jam-e-Jam, maybe, the bliss of this paradise would reach me, too, absolving my pain and torment."

"So vast this paradise, I have explored but little!" Sophia gathered her silvery skirt before taking a step toward palm and banana trees circling this paradise. "Countless inhabitants in utter bliss, attended by youths of grace and by nymphs most beautiful." She had left the trees behind and was approaching close to the railing of gold and silver. Carved in designs of vines and flowers, this railing was studded with crystals and emeralds, exquisite and sparkling.

The pure land of bliss as Buddhist paradise was envisioned was unfolding before Sophia's sight like a dream within a dream. She could feel the presence of Jamshed with her, though he didn't say a word and she herself couldn't voice her thoughts. Awed and humbled, she was drifting along, her gaze alone speaking volumes.

This is the Buddha Field, Sophia's psyche was murmuring. *Total absence of evil and suffering in this Field makes it the Field of absolute bliss and happiness.* Wild birds of bright plumage were chirping. Music was in the air, some nameless tunes of love, peace and harmony, sweet and soothing. Her heart was filled with an astonishing sense of peace and she was becoming aware that music was actually coming from cottony clouds, swelling and constricting with the rhythm of nature's own cosmic surrender.

A light drizzle had begun to descend over the Buddha Field, but it was nothing like rain. Instead, a gentle shower of flowers was bathing the Buddha Field with sweet fragrance. Sophia was in a daze, drifting along will-less, and caressed at each step by the light of love and beauty. Rivers of paradise were within her sight, shimmering against the radiance of the jeweled lotus flowers, floating serenely and beautifully. Music was following her from the lapping of the waves, though she was entering a grove of jeweled trees with colors all fiery and dazzling.

The grove was teeming with occupants of all ages, all friendly and cheerful. It was also furnished with crystal-clear ponds and fruit trees of variegated varieties. There were fountains also, spilling ruby-red wine, and welcoming all to fill their goblets. At the edge of one large pool were many crystal flagons, brimming with pale, amber wine, luring the denizens of this paradise to drink and rejoice! Some were bathing in the fragrant pools, while others sipping wine, and talking and laughing. Scattered in small groups, some were dancing to the dulcet notes of the nature's own musical instruments. Young lovers could be seen strolling in the garden redolent with flowers and flowering trees. Palaces decked with gems precious and priceless were coming into view against the sprawling lawns with the sheen of emeralds.

Sophia could feel and touch the love of the companions of this paradise, her heart gathering joy, peace and harmony. She didn't know if her feet were guiding her, or the silent thoughts of Jamshed in obedience to the will of Ibrahim. A festive bazaar was coming into view, white parasols of the ladies held high or aslant to reveal their loveliness. Buddhist men in robes of ochre were fluttering from one stall to the other, purchasing items for their homes or families. A great variety of wares were on display, from rugs to vases, from goblets of gold and silver to birds carved in jade and alabaster. Further down the bazaar, over a low hill, was another colony of palaces with large verandahs, flaunting jeweled vines and motifs of flowers exquisitely carved!

The facades of the palaces were aglitter with jewels, sifting colors into the verandahs so very opulently furnished. Reclining upon velvety couches could be seen men or women, some appeared to be indulging in the art of story-telling, and others simply luxuriating in the idle pleasure of watching the antics of their children. A great feast was being served on the front lawn of one palace under a crimson marquee. The platters of gold and silver were heaped with food, no matter how much was being consumed by old and young alike, their appetites too large and unslaked. Some sat drinking from their gold goblets, already drunk by the scent of the flowers, and drinking more from the music of the distant cataracts.

Strange that the platters of food remain forever full, and the gold goblets brimming with wine—Sophia was thinking.

"You are in the land of Bliss, dear Sophia, if you have forgotten." Jamshed's voice was like music in the void inside Sophia's psyche. "Everyone here stays in a state of absolute bliss, receiving spiritual feast or spiritual entertainment, whenever they want or whatever they desire."

"How come the platters stay heaped with steaming delicacies?" Sophia murmured, her whole being luminescent and in abeyance.

"Spiritual feast, dear Sophia, as I said before." Jamshed's voice sounded hollow, bouncing off the jeweled palaces, radiating thoughts than words. "When they are hungry, all they have to do is to think about food and it appears before them. They don't have to eat it, yet they enjoy and relish its taste through desire. While they are in such a state, the food is already consumed by their bodies. The same with everything else; if they want to hear music, if they prefer silence, whatever they want they get. Bathing is another of their spiritual pleasures, the temperature of water changing in rapport with their thoughts, individually or collectively."

"So, I can wish and desire you to be here with me, and you would appear suddenly," Sophia intoned wistfully.

"Not so quick, my dear Sophia, no! That cannot be." Jamshed's voice sounded sad and remote. "You are in Buddha Field, but you are not part of it. And I am cursed not to enter any paradise, but the paradise of my own making, if I have the mind and the skill to construct one like the Garden of Irem."

"You should cultivate hope, king Jam!" Ibrahim's voice had the echo of a gong, heavy and strident. "Soon my Garden of Irem will be obliterated, and you should construct a replica of this paradise. You will have the freedom of staying a prisoner to Aleena's beauty, or choosing self-imprisonment in your own paradise."

"I hope, but I don't have faith—in you, my revered philosopher," Jamshed began caustically. "What fools we men are, thinking, that we can alter the course of our destiny. I hear a storm. First and foremost, your Buddhist Paradise is going to vanish."

The prophecy of Jamshed was promptly fulfilled, the fragrant breeze changing to bitter gusts. The jewel trees, jewel flowers and jewel palaces were shattered to bits. Ponds as well as rivers were engulfed by billowing mists, rising and swelling. In a flash, the entire Buddha Field was gone like a puff of smoke. The Garden of Irem was coming alive as if through the labor pains of a new birth. The Zodiac Avenue was groaning under the burden of jeweled palaces. Amongst those was the Turquoise Palace throbbing with life, its Archer blazing with the pulse of light as if ready to jump out of its jeweled armor.

"What purpose did Buddhist Paradise serve here, my sagacious Lord?" Sophia protested, her heart seething with rage and bitterness. "Only to be blown away like a dream, leaving no trace of its bliss in reality?" She was trying her utmost to stay calm and indifferent.

"A goddess who doesn't understand the purpose of divine interventions is not fit to claim the gift of immortality," Ibrahim bristled forth impatiently. The hazel gleam in his eyes was cutting open the heart of the Garden of Irem. "Buddhist Paradise was here to lend a boost to the rite of passage for Chaviva and Kilabah in their sacred journey toward home, where they will attain everlasting bliss in union." He was walking ahead of Sophia in his haste to reach his own Garden of Eden.

"Now that the Buddha Field is no more; would their progress on the sacred journey be diminished?" Sophia's feet came to an abrupt halt by the white gate, beyond which lay the Garden of Irem, sparkling and dazzling.

Ibrahim halted, too, turning to face Sophia, the gravel as the mixture of pearls and rubies under his feet crunching. His back was toward the Garden of Irem as he hobbled close to Sophia, cursing himself inwardly for forgetting his staff. Not quite reaching her, he stopped again, his gaze reaching out to Chaviva and Kilabah. They were standing on the balcony of the Turquoise Palace with their backs toward each other, individually lost in their vacuum of silent contemplation. A zillion stars scattered over the rim of the sky and a countless zillion more clustered inside the rotunda of the horizon appeared to reach down to ruffle the solitude of the silent lovers.

"Realization of truth manifests itself but rarely, and touches only a rare few," Ibrahim began pontifically. "The Buddha Field has left behind a lamp of understanding for these two lovers. They are challenged by a divine power to dive deep into the ocean of knowledge individually, before they attempt to understand each other. Touched by the grace of love as they are, they need not express their love in words."

"They seem to be touched by grief, not love!" Sophia stood oblivious to the aura of enchantment enveloping her from above and beyond. She could only feel the pulse of her heart, which had turned to a cauldron of grief and sadness. "They look estranged."

"The poison of estrangement leads to the nectar of reconciliation." Ibrahim stood watching the soft, white profile of Sophia with much longing and concentration. "They are on the verge of touching the essence of true bliss, their hearts not ever to be corrupted by fear or doubt. Soon their purity of heart would blend with the purity in cosmos. They would be leaving the Garden of Irem and entering the abode of everlasting joy in love and union."

"Sounds terribly romantic and frightfully mysterious." Sophia turned her head, realizing with a sudden jolt of awareness that Ibrahim was ogling her with desire and tenderness. She had seen that light in his eyes before when they were lovers, and she had succeeded occasionally in deflecting it before it could turn into a conflagration of passion mad and uncontrollable, but now this light was filling her heart with loathing. "Where is Aleena?" She could barely murmur.

"I am glad you didn't hear her howling when the Buddhist Paradise was lifted off this subterranean enchantment."

"What would happen after Chaviva and Kilabah leave?" Sophia asked, placating her heart with promises false and daring.

"You would take Aleena to the wilderness of Aden, I am hoping." Ibrahim dared not look at her, his old heart awakening to the pangs of passion he had not experienced in centuries, not even with Aleena, so beautiful and adorable. "Lovers are destined to be united in the scheme of cosmic balance."

"You would be left alone, the sole occupant and guardian of the Garden of Irem! Would you keep it as it is?" Sophia was shifting her attention to the balcony. She was keeping her heart in check while it was opening its gates to the briars of misery and hopelessness.

"Let's put it this way, the Garden of Irem would stay intact. Alluring and enchanting as long as I stay here, hoping and praying that you would come back," Ibrahim responded. He was hoping beyond hope that she would fall in love with him this second time around. "We would be the last of the lovers to be purified and sanctified. I better not disclose more—"

"Do as your philosophic friend says, dear Sophia. He is wise and all-cognizant." Jamshed's voice trickled down with a sense of appeal and urgency. "Ibrahim, my friend, would you kindly go and comfort Aleena? She has been crying her heart out, and is now evoking the saddest of tunes on her lyre. I would keep Sophia entertained, and would try to convince her to agree with you as long as your intention stays purely selfless."

"My intention is always pure, king Jam, don't you doubt that!" Ibrahim protested, infusing warmth of tenderness in his voice and darting a quick glance at Sophia before turning to leave.

"Are you not jealous of Ibrahim that he might cast a spell over Aleena, making her fall in love with him?" Sophia asked as if Jamshed was leaning over her shoulders. Her gaze was following Ibrahim down the marble path edged with fountains.

"He wouldn't try!" Jamshed's voice boomed high since he could see Ibrahim vanishing into the Turquoise Palace. "His spells, such as tampering with the lives of others, have lost their efficacy, and he knows it. Any attempt at such a spell might have a dangerous affect on him as well as on the recipient. Besides, he is feeling more like David, finding comfort in the company of Aleena, as David did with Abishag—the Shunammite. Look Sophia, how Chaviva and Kilabah are smiling into the eyes of each other, so very adorable."

"They are fortunate indeed," Sophia hissed, her thoughts bleak and turbulent.

"You look so sad and frightened, dear Sophia, why?" Jamshed's voice was falling like a caress over Sophia's shoulders.

"I wish Buddhist Paradise was here," Sophia intoned evasively. Her thoughts were in utter chaos, working toward concealing her love for one man and her loathing for the other, the latter of course, Ibrahim. "That experience was awesome for me, and devastating."

"You need cheering, Sophia. I would take you to a paradise you have never seen before," Jamshed promised generously.

"Would you, dear Jamshed?" A spark of hope escaped Sophia's lips.

"Well, in imagination right now, but in reality when you bring Aleena here. We would all go together." Jamshed bristled with excitement, his heart already holding Aleena in its ardent embrace.

"Where is this paradise?" Sophia's curiosity was awakened with a mingling of hope and intrigue.

"West to Spain, it is almost hidden by the sloping hills in the country of Colaygne," Jamshed began with a renewed surge of animation. "Imagine, dear Sophia, rivers of wine instead of water. Palaces made of cake and barley-sugar. Streets paved with pastry, and buttered larks fall from the sky like manna."

"Surely, you jest, dear Jamshed." Peals upon peals of laughter were escaping Sophia's lips, tears glittering in her eyes like blue diamonds.

"I dispelled your sadness, I am glad!" Jamshed quipped merrily. "That paradise is a reality though, held in poetry in the Year 1305 by an English poet. A lovely poem if you would care to hear it?"

"Might as well, I don't want my feet sticking in pastry as a test of reality." Sophia couldn't stop laughing. The diamond-tears in her eyes matching the stars in the heavens, bright and glittering.

"Sit down, dear Sophia. Take a deep breath. You might be choked by the slippery wit of this poem." He left a great pause before reciting.

"Far out to the sea to the west of Spain
There is a land that is called Colaygne
Paradise, true, may be merry and bright

But the land of Colaygne is a fairer sight
Geese that have been roasted on a spit
Fly to the abbey — I swear by God
Crying out loud: Geese, all hot, all hot"

Sophia swayed against the surge of her own laughter and
giddiness. She was holding on to the pillar of jasper, but the wind
was suddenly picking speed. It was changing to violent gusts and
thrashing all around, and Sophia could see herself falling flat over
the gravel of pearls and rubies. Heaven and earth were thundering
mirth, it seemed, and more mirth was escaping the balcony of
Turquoise Palace where Chaviva and Kilabah were enveloped in
volleys of laughter.

They were both gazing at the sky, lowering red, hot bolts of
lightning. Those stark bolts were swirling and cutting open the
very heart of the sky and revealing a blazing hearth with stars
gathered at the rim. An ominous cloud of fire, as vast as a
continent, was lighting up the horizon from east to west. Eve was
materializing at that hearth, praying fervently. Adam was
appearing on the scene, agitated and restless. His son, Seth, was
following him, trying to catch his attention. Suddenly, father and
son were confronting each other. Adam's gaze as well as his lips
pouring forth a litany of confession!

I tell you, Seth, Michael the archangel, a messenger of God came to
me. And I saw a chariot like the wind, and its wheels were fiery. And I
was caught up into the Paradise of righteousness. And I saw the Lord
sitting, and His face was a burning fire that no man could endure.

PARADISE IN THE SKY

The Zodiac Avenue, this particular morning, was bathed in the golden light of the sun. Its Garnet Palace was the abode of Ibrahim since the night before last. Emblazoned with a white, pearly Goat over its balcony studded with garnets, this Zodiac marvel of a palace appeared to be sparkling! In fact, it seemed to be burning, yet no wild fires with sparkling tongues of flames could ever consume the beauty of this glorious wonder amongst wonders. Sophia had been distraught all morning, wandering in the Garden of Irem like a spirit alien and restless. Now she was seated by the crystal pool edged by trees bearing jeweled fruit. She was hoping to get a glimpse of Jamshed in the reflection of its clear waters. Her very heart and soul was pleading with Jamshed to sit by Lake Shisha as was his wont when engaged with her in jests and parlance. The doleful tunes from Aleena's lyre were penetrating Sophia's awareness. Sophia turned her head to watch Aleena where she sat leaning against a palm tree, surrounded by a tapestry of wild flowers. Her silvery gown, with sparkling jewels, was lending her the semblance of a beautiful flower, her fingers working magic on the silver lyre. She seemed oblivious to her surroundings, though her gaze was fixed to the fields of saffron which shone much like patches of sunshine.

"Is that the door to the heavens, Kilabah?" Chaviva's voice rang loud against the morning hush, serene and ethereal.

They had just appeared on the balcony of the Garnet Palace, holding hands for the first time since they have been together in the Garden of Irem. Against the gold-dust of sunshine, a door to heavens was thrown open, revealing a splendid throne. A firework of lightning was commencing in front of the throne, followed by peals of thunder. Then, suddenly and astonishingly, all were quiet as if morning hush was not ever broken. Chaviva's dark hair, falling to her waist against her silvery dress, was silken and gleaming, her eyes fixed to the epiphany shuddering behind the gates of the heavens. Kilabah's ruddy complexion was turned to opalescent pale, his dark eyes piercing the globe of the heavens. His lips were trembling, his hands caressing absently the edge of his white robe tossed over his left shoulder.

"All I see is the ocean of glass, more like crystal." Kilabah squeezed Chaviva's hand, feeling the warmth of her fingers course through his body like the fever of longing.

"Don't you see the throne of jasper and carnelian? And the one seated on it light upon light, moonbeams dancing in his eyes and sunbeams weaving a crown of gold over his head?" Chaviva couldn't tear her gaze away from this divine vision of glory and majesty."

"I see a rainbow," Kilabah replied heedlessly. "Colors of nature, so vibrant and illusive!" His eyes were lit up with awe and astonishment. "No, it's not a rainbow, more like streaks of emeralds suspended over the ocean of glass. Oh, yes, now I see it, dear Chaviva! How could our mortal sight endure such vision of divine light and divine beauty? We should not look, lest we be blinded."

"Don't worry, dear Kilabah! That vision is zillions of light years away from us. No harm will come to us," Chaviva responded sweetly.

"Veils upon veils of light, dear Chaviva, do you see those?" Kilabah exclaimed. His heart was clinging to Chaviva; fearing, lest she be torn away from him and be sucked into that light.

"Look through those veils, dear Kilabah, more thrones are coming into view!" Chaviva exclaimed under some spell of awe and ecstasy. "Each throne hosting a man in a white robe, and each man wearing a gold crown."

"Wonder of wonders, twenty-four thrones altogether!" Kilabah blinked away his disbelief. "Who are those radiant ones?"

"They are called elders. Their sole pleasure is to sing praises to the All Highest." Jamshed's voice boomed through the tunnel of Lake Shisha.

Sophia shuddered, smiling into the reflection of Jamshed's eyes inside the crystal pool. The music from Aleena's lyre suddenly stopped. Her gaze was reaching up to the heavenly vision, shimmering in the blue bowl of a sky turning crimson. Chaviva and Kilabah were clinging to each other, awed and speechless.

"Four rabbis, for sure!" Aleena began profoundly. "Four visiting six times in a row, and appearing to be twenty-four," Her gaze appeared to be cutting open the sky beyond light and illusion.

"How do you know, fair Aleena?" Jamshed was puzzled by the luminosity of her gaze than by the profundity of her expression.

"Ah, king of Jam speaks fairly, or dissimulates." Aleena didn't shift her gaze away from the shimmering veils. "Anyone born in a Jewish home knows the story of the four rabbis and the precepts of Merkabah mysticism. As the story goes, four rabbis decided to enter the Divine Garden without any concept of proper etiquettes in honoring the sacred Garden. The first rabbi, by the name of Ben Azzai, stepped on holy ground by avoiding the path of pure marble, mistaking it as a crystal-clear lake and dying immediately. Ben Zoma, witnessing the sudden death of his rabbi friend, went mad with grief. The third rabbi, Aber, thunderstruck by the tragedy of loss and madness of his friends, abandoned his faith and managed to escape the Divine Garden. The forth rabbi, Akiba, by the virtue of his faith alone, remained unscathed, and was granted the privilege of seeing the All Highest."

"Are we all not privileged to see the All Highest?" Jamshed said aloud. "We have done so without any gift of virtue or without the intervention of divine guidance. You, dear Aleena, have had the glimpse of All Highest, Sophia, too, and Chaviva and Kilabah, though sinners all of us if I presume to say so." Jamshed's reflection inside the pool was shuddering as if someone had just dropped a pebble in its sparkling depths. "Maybe only the old astrologer is the pure one, hiding himself in the Garnet Palace, and deigning not to come out to see the glory of the Lord."

"From the glory of the Lord I must hide for I have transgressed. And that, too, many countless times in my ignorance to learn spells and incantations than to surrender to the light of the All Highest." Ibrahim appeared on the balcony like some prophet, ancient and formidable. "The final journey of Chaviva and Kilabah is almost at hand, but the last rite of the first beginning must be witnessed before they embark on a journey toward unity and everlasting bliss. Since I can't snatch the Jewish Paradise from the sky and bring it here, I have succeeded in bringing Adam and Eve along with their burden of disobedience, expulsion and repentance." He waved his arms toward the gates of the Garden of Irem. A great body of water gushed out of the very gates, snaking its way through groves and orchards and expanding into a river at the base of the Zodiac palaces.

"That's the river Tigris!" Jamshed's cry of incredulity was swallowed by the roaring of a waterfall, foaming and frothing.

The awesome glory of the heavens was forgotten since all eyes were turning to the sudden appearance of a waterfall over the waters of Tigris. Even Sophia had abandoned the shuddering reflection of Jamshed in favor of the tragic scene spurting forth amidst the whirlpools of water, whipping and swirling.

Eve was standing on a boulder with water high up to her neck, her wet hair clinging to her waist like black yarn, gnarled and twisted. She seemed oblivious to the roaring violence of the waters. Her eyes were closed.

"Look at Adam standing in the middle of the river Jordan!" Ibrahim's voice sounded urgent and imperious.

River Jordan, indeed, had materialized right across from the River Tigris. It was creating ravines and gorges down the groves of palms, and vanishing beyond the orchards of fruit trees. Upon a giant rock, polished by the lapping of waves, stood Adam, water rising up to his neck, much like the level of water in which Eve was immersed. Both were facing each other, Eve's eyes still closed, while Adam's were feverish and restless.

"After their expulsion from Paradise, Adam and Eve had nothing to eat but grass, since there was no food around." Ibrahim was commenting with the authority of a proud scholar. "Eve, suffering the pangs of hunger, had pleaded with Adam to kill her, but Adam had suggested that they should do penance, and God would have mercy on them. Their self-inflicted mode of penance was to embark on a forty day fast. They would stand still, she in river Tigris and he in river Jordan, so that they don't tempt each other, or be tempted to cut short their mode of penance. Only three days are left until their penance is—"

The glass ocean in the sky was crackling and breaking into smithereens. Bolts of lightning were piercing the River Tigris, but sparing the River Jordan, as if aiming straight for the boulder where Eve stood, numb with exhaustion.

"Eve! All Highest has accepted your penance." Lucifer, attired in armor of silver, hovered over the waters, wearing a charming smile and a golden crown. "Come out on the shore and partake of good food as your reward of endurance." He held out his arms to snatch her up from the whirlpools of water.

Eve's eyes shot open, her look glazed and startled. She murmured her assent, her naked body falling limp into the arms of handsome Lucifer. He carried her swiftly out of Tigris into the orchard of jeweled trees, abandoning her there without a word. She collapsed on the gravel of pearls, blue from cold and hunger, groaning and wailing. Lucifer flew over to the river Jordan with the intention of tempting Adam, but Adam's attention was riveted to the lumpish form of Eve in great throes of anguish and bitterness.

"What use your grief and wailing, my Eve?" Adam's eyes were flashing anger and rebuke. "You have twice fallen victim to Lucifer, first in the form of a serpent, and now to his Lucifer-charm in person."

"Don't rebuke her harshly, Adam!" Lucifer hovered above him, flapping his slivery wings and laughing. "She was neither tempted by the serpent, nor did she tempt you. Both of you ate of the forbidden fruit with your own free will."

"Accursed you are till the end of the world, Lucifer!" Adam bristled forth with ire and chagrin. "You have lost your power to tempt me."

"I am not here to tempt you, but to make you aware of your ridiculous act of penance." A volley of laughter escaped the lips of Lucifer. "Don't you think God already knew of your disobedience in advance, planning it that way since the beginning?"

"You lie like the cicadas!" Adam's eyes were flashing fire and disdain. "Can't you hear all the living creatures of this river grieving and lamenting just because your evil presence is casting a shadow of fear over them?" He, himself, was stricken with fear as the waters began to recede, leaving his naked body raw with blotches of red and blue, his private parts shriveled.

A volcanic ocean of laughter was exploding forth from the lips of Lucifer, followed by dark, billowing islands of storm-clouds. Bolts upon bolts of lightning were lowered from the menacing sky, sucking dry the river Tigris and river Jordan. No trace of Adam and Eve or of Lucifer was left behind, but the dewdrop silence, while the storm-clouds were vanishing and the sky clearing.

"Silence most sacred from the realm of spiritual light to the physical light of the heavens and the earth!" Ibrahim exclaimed, his arms shooting up toward the heavens histrionically. "Yes, my children, the time has come for you lovers to taste the bliss of union and joy everlasting." He rested his hands over the shoulders of Chaviva and Kilabah.

Against the veil of silence, the former hush of the morning had returned to the Garden of Irem. Chaviva and Kilabah were stricken mute by the unfolding of another scene in the mirror of the sky. A panorama of mountains streaked with the colors of the rainbows was rising high, lofty and majestic. Sophia and Aleena were captivated by the glorious play of light and shadow they had not ever seen before. Even Jamshed had abandoned his seat by Lake Shisha, fascinated by the astonishing beauty of those sky mountains. To have a closer look, he was resorting to peek through his Jam-e-Jam. Instantly, he was rewarded with a breathtaking view of flowers growing out of lichen rocks, amongst them narcissi and carnation the loveliest. Another vista was opened at the foot of the mountains, replicating the beauty of the heavenly paradise.

"Do you see the awesome view of those seven mountains?" Ibrahim was resuming his tone of authority, though his voice was heavy with the burden of fatigue and urgency.

"Splendid! Marvelous!" Chaviva and Kilabah were murmuring amongst themselves, half heeding the words of Ibrahim, half dreaming.

"The tree sprouting from the bed of flowers at the foot of the mountains is the Tree of Life." Ibrahim appeared to be reciting from the book of knowledge. "Its leaves are of precious emeralds, but its fruit shaped like the stars is heavenly delicious. Only a few chosen by the Eternal King are permitted to taste this fruit and attain immortality."

"Is that a chariot?" Chaviva was pointing at the sky with the enthusiasm of a school girl, brimming with joy and curiosity. "Garnet wheels and spokes of pearls, their rims sparkling with the fire of rubies."

"The chariot of Ezekiel! Is he the one driving?" Kilabah's voice was quivering with the anticipation of bliss everlasting.

"No, he is Enoch, the descendant of Adam's third son, Seth," Ibrahim chanted with a fresh burst of animation. "He is holding a wand of light. Watch it flaring into golden sparks. Hold out your arms in unison, and the golden light would lift you up into the jeweled chariot for your sacred journey into the Land of Bliss."

A gossamer web of gold was lowered from the sky down to the balcony of Garnet Palace. Its shimmering length of a magic carpet was cradling both Chaviva and Kilabah, and sailing back to the sky with the happy lovers locked in an eager embrace. They were welcomed into the sparkling arms of the divine chariot, which itself was lost in a tunnel of light, leaving behind a volcanic eruption. The sky was painted in luminous streaks of the wildfires, amber and yellow flames licking up the crater of fire and polishing it to a mirror bright and dazzling.

"The songs of the Sabbath sacrifice, can you hear them?" Ibrahim appeared to commune with the winds, standing there like a corpse, his face ashen and his eyes glazed. "The God of the gods of the chiefs of the heights, and King of the kings of all the eternal councils!" He turned to his right, leaning over the balcony, his beard conical and scraggly. "Can't you hear the songs, dear Aleena?" His eyes were suddenly glittering.

"No, my Lord, I hear only silence." Aleena's sing-song voice carried along with it a dint of laughter, an enigmatic smile hovering over her beautiful lips.

"Do *you* hear the songs, dear Sophia?" Ibrahim appealed, his pallor heightened against the feverish gleam in his eyes.

"I hear nothing but the voice of doom!" Sophia's eyes were attaining the sparkle of the blue oceans.

"What a pity, no one can hear the songs of life and celebration," Ibrahim sighed .

"Don't be disheartened, old philosopher, I do hear the songs!" Jamshed's voice rang out clear from the tunnel of Lake Shisha. "Have you sent the lovers to Shoel or to Paradise?"

Sophia caught the reflection of Jamshed's smiling face in the crystal pool and shuddered. She was feeling numb and listless. The only part in her body alive was her heart, thundering and pleading. It was longing for the nearness of Jamshed. She was trying to snatch each word of parlance between Jamshed and Ibrahim, but her gaze was following the luminous trail of Chaviva and Kilabah, and her heart throbbing with a rent of grief over their absence.

Sophia's very soul was carving a ravine of sorrow. The canker of jealousy inside her was throbbing, pounding to pulp Jamshed's love for Aleena before turning into a splinter of dread for her own captivity in the Garden of Irem if she didn't comply with the wishes of Ibrahim. She couldn't think beyond that, closing her eyes and letting her thoughts wander aimlessly from the Garden of Irem to the wilderness of Aden.

Everyone has to go to Shoel, good or bad, before the privileged few amongst them are permitted to enter Paradise." Ibrahim permitted himself one sliver of a smile, his pallor replaced by a sudden flush. "But be assured, king Jam, Chaviva and Kilabah are in the Land of Bliss, blessed by the bounties of abundance in whatever they desire."

"Does that mean Aleena and I have to visit Shoel? That land of gloom, teeming with ghosts, all whispering and conniving?" Jamshed protested rather cheerfully. "I would rather we shoot straight for Paradise."

"You would, king Jam, you would—to Paradise, I mean!" Ibrahim stretched his arms over his shoulders. He could feel the rush of energy entering his old veins, lending him the warmth of tingling delight. "Just like Chaviva and Kilabah, they didn't have to go to Shoel."

"Shoel is a place where even God is forgotten," Sophia commented; her eyes still closed. "If all went to Shoel, who then would offer praises to God? For in Shoel, all memory is blotted and remembrance is known as oblivion."

"Dear Sophia," Jamshed said without turning his gaze away from Ibrahim. "How soon could Sophia bring Aleena to me, now that Chaviva and Kilabah have attained the station of everlasting bliss in love and union?"

"I feel I have become one of those shadowy creatures in Shoel, since you are talking about me as if I am not here." Aleena stabbed the strings of her silver lyre with anger on the verge of violence. "Isn't it arrogant and presumptuous of you men to choose for me as to where I should live, not even having the courtesy to ask what is my preference as to the mode of my living?"

"Forgive me, Aleena," Jamshed pleaded most tenderly. "You have forgotten all, and you don't have—"

"Then I am in Shoel for sure, and not in the Garden of Irem!" Aleena interrupted, her eyes flashing.

"Dear Princess!" Ibrahim interceded with a painful gesture of his arm. "It's just that you don't remember your past. You seem so content—rather indifferent. Not talking much, nor showing any inclination of preference or revulsion. You don't even remember anything about your parents."

"I am remembering, slowly and painfully," Aleena confessed, striking doleful tunes on her silvery lyre. "And when I am convinced that I know for sure, I would let the heavens and the earth know in my own way I know how."

All were quiet as if the entire Garden of Irem had held its breath, listening. Music had died since Aleena had abandoned her silver lyre, and was now seated in a prayerful posture with her hands clasped. Ibrahim was standing still as if fallen into a state of deep meditation. Absolute stillness was pervading the palaces and gardens, too, though the gems were sparkling. The gold-dust from sunshine seemed to be hovering in midair like a sheet of gauze, silken and shimmering. Sophia was holding and beholding Jamshed's reflection in the crystal pool with bated breath, her heart screaming and somersaulting.

"Forgive me, dear Sophia, I am needy of your forgiveness the most." Jamshed was pleading most humbly and earnestly. "It was so much fun when you were here. We spent beautiful moments together, but I didn't get to know you. Then you were gone. I missed you, but hope is my talisman that you would bring my Aleena back to me. And, that you would be happy with Ibrahim. But now, well, it's strange! It might be my imagination, you don't look happy. What's wrong?"

"Nothing, dear Jamshed." Sophia summoned a smile. "I am not so sure, with Ibrahim, I mean. It has been so long, and he is not the same person I used to know." She was guarding her love for Jamshed, and trying her best to find the right expression. "Would you be happy with Aleena?"

"Surely!" Jamshed intoned brightly. "She has forgotten everything, but I am sure I would win her love back. Don't be afraid, dear Sophia, you would be happy with Ibrahim. We, as a trio of lovers would meet in the Isle of the Blessed. Chaviva and Kilabah are already there. Aleena and I are next, then you and Ibrahim."

"It sounds so simple." A dry, bitter trilling of mirth escaped Sophia's lips.

"Isn't it so, Sophia?" Jamshed challenged brightly.

"I am not so sure, dear Jamshed." Sophia's heart stung by jealousy was clamoring for compassion. "It would be difficult for Ibrahim to let go of his Garden of Irem."

"He would let go of countless such gardens for your beauty alone, dear Sophia." Jamshed laughed.

"Wish it was for my wisdom alone!" Sophia resorted to dry humor. "Would you abandon your Jam-e-Jam and Takhti-Jamshed for Aleena?"

"Without a doubt, yes, a million times, yes!" Jamshed was drunk by the power of his passion, blind to the pain and jealousy of Sophia. "Aleena is to me as Beatrice was to Dante."

"Then she would chide you most certainly, king of Jam." Sophia feigned cheerfulness. "For Beatrice was angry with Dante for looking at her. Saying, *Why does my face so fill you with love that you do not look rather to the fair Garden which blossoms beneath the rays of Christ? Here is the Rose wherein the Divine Word became flesh. Here are the sweet smelling lilies who took the right path.*"

"That Rose, my dear, is the Virgin Mary. The lilies are the blessed heaven. The Garden is heaven itself. Another rose, the last one in Dante's poem is symbolic of love and praise," Jamshed began reminiscently. "*Into the yellow of the eternal rose which rises in ranks and expands and breathes forth a scent of praise to the sun that makes perpetual spring.* Beatrice says something about that too, but I can't recall. Since you know Beatrice well, do you remember what she said?"

"Then you don't know your Aleena either," Sophia teased, stifling one anguished sigh within her. "*Behold how great the assembly of the white robes! See our city, how wide is its circuit! See our seats so filled that there is no room for only a few more souls. Rose is the light of Paradise!*"

A voice from within the Garden of Irem rose high, sprinkling gold mist perfumed with the scent of roses. Gold mist was settling swiftly over the subterranean paradise as if the whole sky was emptying its rotunda of wealth. Even the crystal pool was transformed into a mirror of gold, and Sophia seated by it had become a goddess sculpted in gold. The breeze was scented too, frolicking and singing some alien hymnals. A familiar voice from deep within the Garden was rising again, joyful and comforting.

> *Allah is the light of the heavens and the earth*
> *The similitude of His light is as a lustrous niche*
> *Wherein is the lamp, the lamp is in a glass*
> *The glass as if it were a glittering star*
> *It is lit by a blessed tree—an olive*

Irem of the Crimson Desert

Neither of the east nor of the west
Whose oil will well nigh glow forth
Though fire toucheth it not
Light upon light
Allah guides to His light whomsoever He wills

Once out of nature I shall never take
My bodily form from any natural thing
But such a form as Grecian goldsmiths make
Of hammered gold and gold enameling
To keep a drowsy emperor awake
Or set upon a golden bough to sing
To lords and ladies of Byzantium
Of what is past, or passing, or to come   Yeats

The wilderness of Aden was glowing from the molten gold of a sunset as Jamshed, seated on his Takhti-Jamshed, was lost in the worlds of his own youth he had long forgotten. Now he was visiting those worlds through his Jam-e-Jam as if renewing his contact with the life of ancient myths and remote continents. His gaze this particular moment was sweeping the Elysian Fields in one passionate embrace.

The scene upon which his gaze was lingering was one of serenity and pulchritude. Golden sands welcoming the lapping of waves, all soft and gleaming. Overlooking the sea were orchards, beyond which wild flowers had woven a carpet of silk and gold so exquisite that it appeared to throb with life and vivacity. The orchards themselves were a tapestry of colors, laden with delicate blooms of pear, apple and pomegranate. Fig and olives were already ripe for the picking.

Jamshed gasped for breath, his eyes suddenly shining with awe and wonder. His Jam-e-Jam was revealing another breathtaking scene with sunlit meadows, flaunting tapestries of flowers and thorn-less roses as big as dinner plates. A garden manicured to perfection was emerging forth with flowers in hues of rainbows. In the center of the garden was a Tree of Life, watered by four streams. Jam-e-Jam had captured this tree, like a canvas receiving brushstrokes of some artist, in this case the *divine artists*. The Christ figure was growing out of this tree with his hands stretched out in the formation of a Cross. His left hand was grasping one branch, of which there were seven. In his right hand he was holding a royal orb with the sun on one side and the moon on the other.

"Ah, what is this Christian Paradise doing in the Garden of Irem?" Jamshed exclaimed suddenly, noticing Zodiac splendor in the background.

Amethystine Palace, embellished with amethysts in designs of bridal creepers and violets, was throbbing like a purple wound within wounds, gathering sparkle and glitter from the jeweled palaces in Zodiac colonnade. A Water Carrier molded in gold and studded with amethysts was suspended over the façade of the palace by a pair of ladders encrusted with multicolored gems and crystals. On the balcony of this palace, seated over a carpet of rosettes was Aleena, leaning over one velvety pillow. She appeared to be drowning inside the flood of music she was evoking through the magic of her silver lyre.

"A beloved incarnate," Jamshed sighed to himself.

He had completely missed noticing Sophia who was standing not far from Aleena. She was gazing down at the Christian Paradise which seemed to vie with the Garden of Irem, awesome and challenging.

A garden enclosed is my sister, my spouse, a spring shut up, a fountain sealed. Thy plants are an orchard of pomegranates, with pleasant fruits, camphor with spikenard, spikenard and saffron; calamus and cinnamon, with all trees of frankincense; myrrh and aloes, with all the chief spices. A fountain of gardens, a well of living waters and streams from Lebanon.

Jam-e-Jam almost slipped out of Jamshed's hands as he tried to trace the voice to its source, which belonged to no other than

Ibrahim himself. The old philosopher was leaning against the crenellated wall of the Christian Paradise, his gaze reaching out over the balcony of the Amethystine Palace. He appeared to be studying the jeweled features of the Water Carrier, but in fact, was watching Sophia, his gaze piercing as if entering the very fabric of her soul. Jamshed's own gaze was now following Ibrahim's and resting on Sophia, but his thoughts were clinging to the words of the song Ibrahim had chanted.

"Never in all my lifetimes, would I have ever imagined that you would be the one lending voice to the Song of the Solomon." Jamshed's voice was drumming Ibrahim's ears, half amused, half incredulous.

"So presumptuous of you, king Jam, to think that I would not deem Song of the Solomon worthy of expression." Ibrahim tossed his response to the winds, a shadow of annoyance crossing his features. "Song of the Solomon is my talisman against any evil which may strike me, since I have dared bring Christian Paradise into the Garden of Irem."

"What has the Song of the Solomon to do with the Christian Paradise?" Jamshed asked mirthfully.

"Is it possible that a king could be so naïve?" Ibrahim scoffed. "Song of the Solomon sings of God's love for its people in rapport with the Christian Paradise. It is an enclosed Garden, representing virginity of a Christian soul, a clear conscience."

"You really don't believe that, Ibrahim, do you?" Jamshed's mirth was penetrating the silence of the Christian Paradise. "Song of the Solomon is just a simple song addressed to a girl whose virginal state is expressed in three metaphors."

"You would be losing the love of your life from your previous lives, king Jam, if you keep indulging in inanities," Ibrahim warned. He was strolling toward the gate of the Paradise, also studded with amethysts. "Now that Chaviva and Kilabah are happy together in the Isle of Bliss, I have to convince Sophia to escort Aleena to your wilderness of Aden." He had left the jeweled gate behind, and was now approaching close to the Tree of Life.

Ibrahim's feet were coming to a slow halt before the Tree of Life, under which were flowing four rivers of Paradise. Jamshed was tilting his Jam-e-Jam to have a better view, for what he thought were streams, were in fact rivers. At a closer look, even the Christ crucified on this tree had a kingly demeanor, fully attired, his silk robe matching the purple wounds on his feet and hands.

"If truth could be judged as the kernel of inanities, then I am already doomed," Jamshed murmured profoundly. "You don't have to convince Sophia to bring Aleena to me. She would be delighted to undertake this journey. As to her returning to the Garden of Irem, I am not so sure. She is the mistress of her own will and decision."

"That's what I am afraid of." Ibrahim lowered himself on the marble bench under the bower of roses. "That's why I have dared bring this Paradise into my paradise. These four sacred rivers are here for a purpose. Sophia has to bathe in each one of them to cleanse herself of passions corrupt and formidable. This river Pishon here, as you see, would dispel her own river of envy. All her anger would be drained into the waters of this river by the name of Gihon. River Tigris would dissolve her passion of jealousy. And River Euphrates would wipe her heart clean of any kind of bitterness."

"An onerous task, considering Sophia's own rivers of knowledge and skepticism flowing inside her, eternally fresh and bottomless," Jamshed commented sadly, stealing a glance at Sophia and Aleena, and then focusing his attention on the rivers. "Sophia's memory for old names is tarnished by forgetfulness, though she would recognize the names of the Tigris and the Euphrates. The other names of the rivers familiar to her would be Nile and Ganges."

"If her memory is like the Rivers Tigris and Euphrates, the one of forgetfulness and the other of remembrance, along with the qualities of purging and soothing, she might as well forget about the Nile and the Ganges, too." Ibrahim arched his bushy eyebrows, his gaze slashing the tree of forbidden fruit, almost concealed by a barrier of haze on the verge of darkness. "Look, king Jam, can you see Adam at the foot of the other tree. Look closely and you would see a serpent coiled around that tree. Eve is standing to the right, naked and unashamed. Pilgrims are gathering around the tree, rapt and spellbound. Eve is snatching the apple right out of the mouth of the serpent and offering it to the pilgrims. To the left of the tree is standing the second Eve—Mary in her blue dress, offering apples to the worshipers who are kneeling at her feet." His voice was truncated abruptly.

"And if you look closely right through the abundance of foliage, you would see the figure of Christ nailed on the Cross in the middle of the trunk." Jamshed's voice was a trickle of amusement and indulgence. "You didn't notice it, did you, Ibrahim?"

"I was just testing you, king Jam, to see if you were paying any attention." Ibrahim allowed himself a chuckle, the hazel gleam in his eyes twinkling. "Christ is a second Adam, if you didn't know."

"Every man is the Adam of his own soul, I know that much," Jamshed declared with a dint of impatience. "Though Christ is not like Adam. Adam brought ruin upon mankind, while Christ brought blessings. The door of the paradise was shut after Adam was expelled, but Christ opened the door of paradise for mankind."

"If we believe in what has been said, or conjectured, then we must believe in this, too, that Christ is a second Moses since he brought a new kind of law." Ibrahim waved his bony arms, the sleeves of his blue robe hanging loose. "A second David, too, since he came as a king." He was shielding his beard with his hands against the sudden gust of wind which was picking speed.

Attested by those who brought near. Lo, the righteous verily are in delight on couches gazing. Thou wilt know in their faces radiance of delight. They are given to drink of a pure wine, sealed, whose seal is musk. For this let all those who strive, strive for bliss.   83:21-26

"Who speaks?" Ibrahim stood darting fierce glances at every tree and plant his gaze encountered.

"A goddess of wisdom and your humble slave," Sophia chanted beamishly.

She had stolen behind Ibrahim, and now stood facing him, her blue eyes flashing. The gusts of wind were replaced by gentle breeze, but Sophia shuddered, drawing her star-studded shawl closer.

"A queen of beauty and wisdom to rule over all!" Ibrahim smiled winsomely. "You can be slave to none, dear Sophia, not even gods can command you."

"If I have to do your bidding, my Lord, then I am your slave." Sophia stood smoothing her silvery skirt. Her gaze was slipping down the valley of crisscross rivers as if searching for something.

"Anything you do, dear Sophia, has to come from deep within you. I can entreat, but not ever command," Ibrahim replied humbly. "Rare it is to have the privilege of your company, but may I ask what prompted you to venture into this paradise?"

"The prerogative of a goddess!" A tinkling of mirth lit up Sophia's eyes. "I thought I heard the voice of king Jam, so coasted down here to make sure. Were you talking with Jamshed?" She drifted toward the river Tigris, lowering herself over its banks, and dipping her hands in its crystal-clear waters.

"He is the one who initiated the conversation," Ibrahim intoned cautiously, his gaze piercing. "I can't see him, and neither would you, even through the tunnel of Lake Shisha. If he wishes to join us in our parlance, he would, but I can't reach him."

"What were you talking about?" Sophia splashed the waters with her hands, her gaze still diving down the river.

"You have registered each word of our conversation in your heart, dear Sophia, I am sure, so why pretend?" Ibrahim challenged. He began to pace between the Tree of Life and the Tree of Forbidden Fruit.

"I have not ever been accused of pretense, my Lord, not until now," Sophia protested. "Surely, I recognized the voice, but no words were decipherable. I can guess the drift of your conversation, though. If I am to take Aleena to Aden, am I not right in assuming that you were talking about that? If so, what I am supposed to do, really?" She asked genially, concealing her pain and bitterness within her.

"There is Holy of holies within this Paradise, and you are the only one who can find it, on a condition that you must search it with all the love in your heart and soul," Ibrahim demurred aloud, utterly absorbed in his pacing. "Once you find it, truth would be illumined by the light of your love. It would be as if you were holding a lamp of revelations. With this sacred, eternally luminescent lamp in your right hand, and your left hand clasping the hand of Aleena, you would be whisked through voids, landing safely in the wilderness of Aden."

"Would Aleena be willing to come with me?" Sophia asked feebly, her heart sinking with dread and longing.

He had a dream in which he saw a stairway resting on the earth, with its top reaching to heaven, and the angels of God were ascending and descending on it. Genesis 28:12

"Jamshed, is that you? Where are you?" Exclaimed Sophia, her face lifted up, eager and frightened.

"Not really, dear Sophia. I merely captured the voice, and you heard only the echo." Jamshed's voice was heavy with the burden of awe and astonishment. "I am watching Aleena. She, at this precise moment, is witnessing the unfolding of a unique heaven. It is suspended in void, hosting a host of angels, circling a throne of dazzling colors, and singing ecstatically. Aleena's eyes have become my mirror of observation. She has abandoned her silver lyre for the first time in the past few centuries, and it seems to have become a relic on the balcony of the Amethystine Palace."

"Rub al Khali!" Ibrahim declared, his feet coming to a stumbling halt over the bank of Tigris across from where Sophia sat immersed, deep in her flood of misery and hopelessness.

"What did you say, Ibrahim?" Jamshed's voice rang out loud, rather demanding.

"Rub al Khali, it is the sacred door to the Void," Ibrahim repeated, as if to himself. "Rub al Khali served to protect caravans traveling the frankincense route from the groves of gum trees throughout the land of Ad into the Rub al Khali."

"You mean, the gate to death?" Jamshed's voice sounded distant and subdued. "A gate with a silver key which would unlock the successive doors, which bar our free march down the ravines of space and time to the very gorge under wilderness where no man alive has set foot?"

"Some have, only to be annihilated soon after," Ibrahim intoned, his gaze reaching out to Sophia. "The tribes of Aad in the south, and of Thamud in the north. Also the tribes of Tasm and Tadis in the center of the peninsula! None to tell the tales of glory and the splendor. Only the tongues of tragedy weaving the tapestry of doom and devastation!"

"There are powers divine and awful. Powers much higher than the powers of us base mortals." Aleena's voice was penetrating the walls of the Christian Paradise with an echo, mysterious and frightful.

Aleena was sailing in through the Amethyst Gate like a wraith of light, her gown of stars and crescents throbbing with life of its own, vibrant and sparkling. She was wearing her silvery lyre with a cord around her neck, which was suspended down to her waist. The liquid gold in her eyes was aflame with some inner fire of love grand and love ineffable. She looked angelic and ethereal, her black hair braided around her head and secured with a tiara of diamonds. Her steps were small and measured, yet she appeared to float over the lush green carpet of grass. She appeared to be studying the face of Ibrahim before lowering herself beside Sophia.

"Nemesis of Flame. Have you ever heard about that?" Aleena seemed to be questioning the waters of the four rivers than Sophia or Ibrahim. "Nemesis of Flame is a factual story told by an old man from Yemen, who escaped alive from the Crimson Desert after having the privilege of visiting the City of Pillars. He even explored the subterranean shrines of Nug and Yeb, writing about them after returning to Yemen. To him, the city of Irem existed for the sole delight of mankind, who could honor it with songs of love and beauty. He could not even think that this city would ever fall prey to the trumpets of surcease and annihilation." A slight tremor grazed her red lips. Against the pallor of her face, her lips were glistening like a wound, raw and bloody.

"Aleena dear, I haven't heard you talk like this since eons." Jamshed's voice was literally dancing upon waves of joy and astonishment. "That means you would remember—hope is alive! I am still alive in this Crimson Desert. We would escape together. Would you come?"

"I don't know," Aleena said, becoming aware of Sophia's pallor, stark and throbbing. "Sophia told me. I trust Sophia." Her confusion was replaced by a spasm of fear as she looked at Ibrahim.

Ibrahim stood there, quiet and contemplative, under the tree of Forbidden Fruit, brushing his conical beard with his long fingers. He looked frail and vulnerable, but there was a gleam of strange light in his eyes which looked evil and ominous.

"Don't be afraid, dear Aleena." Ibrahim summoned a quick smile. "I am greatly pleased by the improvement of your talent in decoding ancient knowledge and in the art of remembrance. You hardly spoke for centuries, and now you are willing to talk, longing to unleash the knots of precious knowledge without prodding. Trust your own instincts, dear child, and you would be released from the Garden of Irem." His gaze was embracing both Sophia and Aleena in the fire of hope, beyond which lurked the soot of premonition.

"You mean, my Lord, I have been a prisoner all this time, and still am?" Aleena's eyes widened with chagrin and disbelief.

"No, my dear child." Ibrahim infused cheerfulness into his tone, both indulgent and patronizing. "On the contrary, I have been your prisoner. Whenever I tried to talk with you, you struck the strings of your lyre, making me drowsy. There, I would lay at your feet, sleeping for hours, if not for months. Perhaps, half dreaming, half slumbering—" He was caught in his own cesspool of lies while trying desperately to escape. "Well, it's a long story. We would get to it, by and by—" His brief pause was snatched by Jamshed, whose voice appeared to be foundering amidst the waves of sanity and sane reasoning.

"The short of it, wise philosopher, is that you are sending Aleena to Aden, chaperoned by Sophia." A dint of suspicion and impatience was surfacing in Jamshed's urgent tones. "How you are going to manage it is becoming nebulous, if not ambivalent. Paradise upon paradise, very puzzling. I hope this is the last paradise on earth in your Garden of Irem!"

"The last if all goes well." Ibrahim appeared to shrink, but his voice was imperious and challenging. "Look at the gate of the Garden of Irem, king Jam. There you would discover a pair of hands which are destined to clasp each other under the shadow of love, peace and harmony. A bright star and a gleaming Crescent are suspended right below the hands, and a Cross right across from the Crescent. When the hand of Yahweh would claim the silver key, unlocking the door to paradise, then this age-old enchantment over the Garden of Irem would dissolve. Lovers would be united with the beloveds, and age of bliss would descend from heavenly isles to the isles of earth."

"All this I know, and all this I have seen." Jamshed's voice was becoming remote and strained. "The hands would meet twain, and the Cross and the Crescent would merge. Peace on earth and peace in—"

A host of flames from under the earth was swallowing the Christian Paradise. A curtain of darkness was being lowered from the sky, and all sounds were licked dry by a bonfire of flames meeting halfway down the curtain.

> *Adam was heedless*
> *For the crafty thief*
> *Suddenly entered*
> *Leaving aside the fruit*
> *Which most men would covet*
> *He stole instead*
> *The Garden's inhabitant*
> *Adam's Lord came out to seek him*
> *He entered Shoel and found him there*
> *Then led and brought him out*
> *To set him once more in Paradise   Ephraim*

JEWEL OF ARABIA

When the event befalleth
There is no denying that it will befall
Abasing some, exalting others
When the earth is shaken with a shock
And the hills are ground to powder
So that they become a scattered dust
And ye will be three kinds
First those on the right hand
What of those on the right hand
And then those on the left hand
What of those on the left hand
And the foremost in the race, the foremost in the race
They are they who will be brought nigh
In gardens of delight
A multitude of those old
And few of those of later time
On lined couches
Reclining therein face to face
There wait on them immortal youths
With bowls and ewers and a cup from a pure spring
Wherefrom they get no aching of the head or any madness
And fruit they prefer
And flesh and fowls they desire
And there are fair ones with wide, lovely eyes
Like unto hidden pearls
Reward for what they used to do
There they hear no vain speaking, nor recrimination
Naught but the saying: peace, and again peace   56:1-26

The Garden of Irem, this particular evening, was radiant and shimmering, since all the Zodiac halls and palaces were lit to full refulgence. The Hall of Bloodstone—the last of the Zodiac splendor, was emulating the rest of the eleven, its jewels throbbing with a splash of color and vivacity. A large Fish studded with bloodstones was affixed over the railing of the balcony of this palace.

Jamshed, in his wilderness of Aden, was anxious and restless. Since morning, his heart had been a cauldron of fears and doubts, his thoughts simmering with the steam of hope and anticipation. He was pacing, oblivious to the onslaught of evening shadows, intent only in chasing his thoughts to the very gates of hopes fulfilled and joys countless. Though his heart was drumming presage, sounding warnings that Aleena would not reach here as promised by Ibrahim. The Crimson Desert before his sight was attaining the semblance of a hoary furnace, but he could feel the gentle touch of cool breeze massaging his neck and shoulders. He was seeking the comfort of his Takhti-Jamshed, but his feet were guiding him toward Lake Shisha.

Lake Shisha was reflecting the crimson of the desert as Jamshed settled himself at its rim, rubbing his hands against the gold of his Jam-e-Jam as if for warmth. Tempted as he was to look into his Jam-e-Jam, or peek through the tunnel of Lake Shisha, he was stifling this wild impulse, rather forcing his thoughts to discipline and stillness. Many times during the day he had studied the Islamic Paradise installed into the Garden of Irem by Ibrahim, searching for the enchanted steed promised by Ibrahim, which was to carry Sophia and Aleena to Aden, and then carry Sophia back to the Garden of Irem. And yet, he had been unable to find such a steed, feeling dejected and lonesome. Even now, an overwhelming sense of loss and grief was constricting Jamshed's heart, and he closed his eyes, trying to force his thoughts toward the rungs of joy and sunshine. With the tenderness of a lover, he slipped his Jam-e-

Jam into the pouch of his purple robe, intending to rest, but his eyes were shot open by a sound most shrill and chilling. Some sort of primordial scream from deep within Lake Shisha had jolted him to awareness, his gaze shooting down the tunnel and witnessing once again the Islamic Paradise.

The Garden of Irem, with its firmament illumined by sun, moon and diamond stars was no match to the dazzling Paradise, rising high and shimmering. It seemed to encompass lovely dawns, glorious sunsets and rainbows slashed with colors vibrant and throbbing. Tides upon tides of color were swirling and dancing the dance of love, beauty and harmony. A stairway to heaven, it seemed, was spiraling up and up as far as the sight could reach. Its gold steps and silver railings were adorned with pearls, tracing a path in the sky, glittering all the way up to the heavens until there was nothing left but a silver lining.

The grand stairway in the Garden was leading to a pearly gate, hosting seven heavens. The Tree of Knowledge of Good and Evil was in the middle of the heavens, watered by a cistern divided into four quarters as rivers. One magnificent tree, its foliage the color of emeralds, was bearing ruby-red fruit of pomegranates. Not a creature was seen in any of the heavens, yet the murmur of distant cataracts was pouring music into this heavenly abode of peace and serenity.

Jamshed inhaled deeply. The scent of roses from subterranean heavens was reaching him in waves upon waves of memories he could neither forget, nor decipher. He was feeling sad, rather giddy, his gaze intent on visiting all seven heavens. Garden of Majesty—the first heaven was the handiwork of some jeweler divine. This garden with its moss-laden paths was walled by sheets of soft, round pearls, glowing like a myriad of globes, white and incandescent. It shone like a jewel-garden with roses as big as sun-disks, and the ponds shimmering, edged by a mosaic of violets.

The second heaven above it was the Abode of Peace, adorned with sapphires. Its Peruvian blue lakes were laden with lotus flowers in shades of pristine white and royal purple.

A Garden of Refuge was the third heaven with trees of gold, bearing flowers of pure chrysolite.

The fourth heaven was the Garden of Eternity, embellished with yellow corals. Multicolored blooms of some exquisite variety were blooming in abundance, inhabited by butterflies.

Garden of Bliss was the fifth heaven, silvery and ethereal. It seemed to float in ether, gathering more mists in lace-patterns.

The sixth heaven was the Garden of Firdows, veiled in red-gold haze of peaceful dusk, sublime and shimmering.

The Garden of Eden on top of all heavens was the seventh heaven, a jewel adorned with gems most precious. In the center of this garden was the Tree of Knowledge of Good and Evil.

Jamshed couldn't take his gaze away from this tree, devouring its fruit with his gaze alone, rather peeling it open to separate the seeds of evil from good. His attention was claimed abruptly by a voice most imperious and commanding.

You, who brought to earth this image of Paradise, may the peace of God stay with you eternally.

Jamshed's honed senses were tracing this voice to the Hall of Bloodstone, his hands reaching down for his Jam-e-Jam. His crown, studded with amethysts, was catching a shaft of gold from the very heart of the dying sun and sparkling like the swirling of countless flames with purple tongues. A bonfire of fear and longing was kindled inside his heart, too, as his Jam-e-Jam arrested the inner sanctum of the Hall of Bloodstone.

This sumptuous hall of marble and gemstones was spangled with hangings of silk and damask. A magnificent davenport, upon which Aleena sat lolling against a velvety pillow, was ablaze with the fire of jewels leaping up from its base and headrest. Her eyes were closed, her black hair woven in pearls and her gown of stars and crescents lending her the semblance of an angel in a state of eternal repose. Across from her was a canopy of glowing silks, the likes of which could only be seen in the palaces of Ispahan.

Sophia was seated on a rich carpet of rosettes and medallions, her lips moving, but Jamshed couldn't hear what she was saying. His attention was shifted to Ibrahim, seated opposite her on an oriental couch, looking frail and more haggard than before. He was making a desperate gesture with his hands, the swollen veins on them as blue as his robe. Voices were penetrating Jamshed's awareness now, and he listened most intently.

"You voiced that injunction, my Lord, didn't you, to lend yourself the aura of holiness?" Sophia was saying, her gaze swaying and shuddering over the silver and crystal lamps lit to full effulgence on either side of Ibrahim.

"My lips didn't move. You were watching me closely, dear Sophia, were you not when that divine voice trickled down the rotunda? Didn't you see all the jewels blazing and shuddering?" Ibrahim intoned gently, his gaze feverish and thoughtful. "Besides, I don't have to pretend to have the aura of holiness; I am all holy, mentally and physically. Didn't you will my death when the Christian Paradise departed from the Garden of Irem, and no harm came to me? This proves the state of my holiness that no power on earth can injure me as long as my intentions stay pure and incorruptible."

"You are talking like the rabbis now," Sophia scoffed. "If you are that holy, my Lord, why do you need to surround yourself with paradises along with your incantations evil and dangerous?" Her heart was vacillating between obeying the wishes of Ibrahim, or surrendering to the will of her mind.

"If you had not forsworn your promise of taking Aleena to Aden, I had no need to summon the Islamic Paradise," Ibrahim replied patiently. He was trying his best not to offend the goddess, lest she disobeys once again, bringing doom on continents upon continents.

"I am getting weary of this blame-game since the inception of time," Sophia began under some spell of utter despair. "Adam blaming Eve for being tempted and tempting." She was becoming conscious of her inward resolve not ever to take Aleena to Aden. "If you were not sending me in a chariot of fire, I would have gone," She declared belligerently, her heart longing for the nearness of Jamshed.

"That's why I have chosen Pegasus for your journey to Aden and back." Ibrahim sat combing his white beard, aimed at his heart like an arrow. "Although, the fear of fire was not your prime concern for refusing, but I do not wish to dwell on that. As for Eve being tempted and the temptress, that doesn't sit well in Islamic Paradise. Does it not say in the Quran that Adam and Eve ate of the fruit together?"

"Yes, and much more," Sophia bristled forth under some strange spell of misery and giddiness. "There is no mention in the Quran that Eve was created from the rib of Adam. According to the Quran, both were created from a single soul. Why am I explaining this?" Her blue eyes were sparkling with anger. "Where is Jamshed? Why is he not saying anything?"

"You can't see him. And his voice can't pass the barrier of Islamic Paradise until you succeed in delivering Aleena to him and returning as swiftly as reaching the wilderness of Aden," Ibrahim expounded reluctantly, stealing a look at Aleena who looked like the incarnation of Sleeping Beauty.

"What do I need to do?" Sophia's voice was more of a lament than her willingness to comply.

"Since you missed the Holy of holies in Christian Paradise, you need to observe the Journey of the Soul in Islamic Paradise," Ibrahim intoned enigmatically.

"How do I do it?" Sophia appeared keen and calm, but her thoughts were gathering storm-clouds of death and devastation.

"Very simple, dear Sophia," Ibrahim encouraged tenderly. "You fly from one heaven to the other until you reach the seventh, the Eden. That's where truth would be revealed to you, and you would witness the marriage of the souls."

"I am not a bird that I can easily fly, my Lord!" Sophia protested deliriously. "What appears simple to you is even beyond the powers of a goddess."

"You would be like the Simurgh—the mythical bird of Paradise. Feathers of your imagination would lend you wings, guiding you on the sacred road to journey home." Ibrahim was feeling exhilarated as if guiding his wayward child on the path to love sublime and love supreme. "The first valley is the Valley of Quest, the second the Valley of Love. The third is the Valley of Understanding, and the fourth the Valley of Detachment. The fifth is the Valley of Pure Unity, and the sixth the Valley of Astonishment. The seventh is the great Valley of Poverty and Nothingness, beyond which you would go no further."

"In that state of nothingness, how do I escort Aleena to Aden?" Sophia was gloating inwardly of her own resolve of self-immolation and destruction.

"In that state you would witness the marriage of the souls in Eden. Lovers in pairs enjoying the delights of the Garden. In the center of that Garden you would discover a sacred pool, much like Lake Shisha. A Pegasus of kingly bearing would be watching his reflection in the pool, waiting for your command to carry Aleena to Aden."

"A pagan horse inside the Eden of Islamic Paradise! What a farce!" Sophia began to laugh, her hysterical mirth swallowed by the sudden thundering of a song from the heavenly vaults.

May these vows and this marriage be blessed
May it be sweet milk
This marriage like wine and halva
May this marriage offer fruit and shade
Like the date palm
May this marriage be full of laughter
Our every day a day of Paradise
May this marriage be a sign of compassion
A seal of happiness, here and hereafter
May this marriage has a fair face and a good name
An omen as welcome as the moon in a clear blue sky
I am out of words to describe how spirit mingles
In this marriage.   *Rumi*

"Annihilation of truth," Aleena's sing-song voice echoed like a gong inside the Hall of Bloodstone.

She was jolted to awakening on her davenport, dripping with lace and velvets. Fear sparkling in the liquid gold of her eyes was stark and shuddering. Her hands were fumbling to retrieve the round pillow behind her to lean against. She was staring at the ottomans of gold brocade as if trying to snatch truth out of the caskets of lies and glitter. Her rose-petal lips were trembling, trying to form words, but no sound was escaping her lips.

"The song you just heard, Aleena, was about marriage and blessings." Sophia was the first one coaxing her to speak, her eyes flashing. "And you are talking about the annihilation of truth, why?"

"I see the worlds spinning and the heavens shattering." Aleena's voice was barely audible, her eyes glazed and unseeing. "I see the disappearance of Kaaba and the evaporation of all words from the pages of the Scripture."

"You are having a nightmare, dear Aleena. Wake up and look at me," Ibrahim commanded. "You are safe and comfortable here, surrounded by objects precious and beautiful. Inhale deeply; a subtle perfume is in the air to delight your senses. Can't you catch the whiff of roses from the perfumed baths in this hall?"

Ibrahim stole a glance at Sophia; his heart shuddering as if it had just received a bolt of lightning! Sophia was looking at Aleena, hatred shining in her eyes, stark and formidable. Paradoxically and astonishingly, Ibrahim had not seen the naked dagger of hatred in anyone's eyes for the past few centuries, and now suddenly encountering it, he was feeling ill, on the verge of physical nausea. But he mastered this feeling as swiftly as Sophia replacing the daggers of hatred in her eyes with the shafts of concern and solicitude. Aleena was wide-eyed and frightened, noticing nothing but her own fear and weakness.

"Where is Jamshed?" Aleena's voice was low and tremulous. Her fingers were absently fondling the silver lyre at her breast.

"So, we are back in the memory lane of love and union." Ibrahim heaved a sigh of relief. "Are you ready for your journey to Aden? Sophia would accompany you."

"Yes, I can't wait," Aleena murmured, shifting her gaze to Sophia.

"Are you ready, dear Sophia?" Ibrahim asked tenderly.

"Can't wait." Sophia mimicked Aleena. Her heart was gloating with the challenge of pain and betrayal.

Allah knows all things full well

A heavenly chorus trumped down the jeweled rotunda, jolting all to their feet. Sophia was the exception, easing herself up slowly and gracefully.

"Well, this injunction is the heavenly consent to commence your journey on the sacred road, where your heart's desires are fulfilled." Ibrahim waved his arms, chanting a litany of incantations.

The Garden of Irem was enveloped in golden mists. Ibrahim was whirled out of the Hall of Bloodstone, and tossed outside the pearly gates of the Islamic Paradise. He was physically unscathed, but mentally bruised, madness rising within him like fever and delirium. The pearly gates of the Eden were barred shut to his face after Sophia and Aleena were whisked inside the sanctuary of the heavens. Shaken like reeds, they were shuffled from one heaven to the other until they found themselves inside the seventh heaven, the Eden of bliss and tranquility. Ibrahim could not enter the heavens, raving outside like a madman, his beard strewn with pearly tears. Sophia and Aleena were seated by the cistern in Eden, lulled to ease and warmth of serendipity by the Tree of Knowledge of Evil and Good.

All was not as tranquil as it seemed, for Sophia's mind was awakening to the pangs of longing and hopelessness. She was becoming aware of the white steed with moonbeam eyes and gossamer wings, waiting for her command to take her to Aden. Something inside her was breaking and splintering. She couldn't bear to take Aleena with her. The cry of agony within her was pleading with Jamshed. Her gaze was cleaving down the crystal-clear waters of the cistern, searching for a glimpse of Jamshed. A gasp of astonishment filled her lungs with fear as she noticed that she and Aleena were not alone in this heavenly abode of silence and serenity. The clear waters of the cistern were parading all kinds of birds hovering above, and hosting more from the Tree of Knowledge of Evil and Good. Soon, the rim of the cistern was crowded with birds, all appeared to be dancing or prancing. Sophia stole a glance at Aleena, who seemed to be utterly at home with the birds as if she was accustomed to their company. The birds had begun to introduce themselves most eloquently, and Sophia almost swooned with shock and delight that she could understand their language.

I am Hoopoe from the kingdom of Sheba, and a guide to King Solomon.

All know me as Wagtail. I resemble Moses on Mount Sinai, but I am here to celebrate the true knowledge of God.

I am Parrot as you can tell, with my collar of fire and my robe of beautiful colors.

You are looking at a proud Partridge here. See how graciously I walk, but I can fly over the mountains and talk with God.

No one can help but notice the royal Falcon. I have a piercing sight, but I have renounced my violent nature. Ready I am for the cavern of unity, where I am expecting the company of Prophet Muhammad.

I am the spirit of love in the body of Quail, and through me the spirit of God reaches mankind.

Garden of love is my abode; and lovers know me as Nightingale. I lament like David from the purity of my heart for God.

I am no ordinary Peacock, but a friend of the Friend. I was expelled from Eden by a seven-headed serpent, but Adam brought me back.

All befriend me, saying: Pheasant, you have dispelled darkness from your heart, and have found the ocean of light to reach the throne of God.

I am Turtle-dove, aspiring to reach the summit of moon.

The favorite of Khidr, I am known as Pigeon, seeking the way of understanding with an offering of seven plates of pearls for my holy guide.

I am mighty Hawk, who has kissed the hand of Alexander.

The light of God is my salvation, though I am lowly Goldfinch, surrendering all and knowing the secrets of God.

The waters in the cistern were singing, *Seek knowledge as far as China.*

Gentle waves were rising to the surface from the turbulence down below. Jamshed's face, flushed and glistening, was reflected inside each wave and wavelet.

"Hurry, Sophia, number thirteen! Thirteen wise birds and thirteen verses sublime from the chapter Dawn in the glorious, living Quran. Hurry, before the Simurgh joins these birds. Pegasus is waiting. Make Aleena sit in front of you, and ride swiftly, otherwise all would be lost."

"Jamshed!" Sophia groaned, leaping to her feet.

"Jamshed!" A cry of delight escaped Aleena's lips.

"Jamshed!" Pegasus whinnied.

Sophia stood by Aleena, clutching her hand, her lips moving, but no words issuing forth. The birds had flown back behind the Tree of Knowledge of Evil and Good. Only Pegasus stood still, wide-eyed, shedding moonbeams.

"Dear Sophia, hurry," pleaded Jamshed!

"I can't!" One agonized lament broke through the lips of the goddess.

"Why, dear heart?" Was Jamshed's hopeless plea!

"Because I love you more than my life, and can't bear to—" Sophia jumped into the holy cistern, taking along with her the frightened princess.

The earth shuddered and the darkness gaped open the tunnel of torment, where Sophia and Aleena were sinking deeper and deeper into the vaults of oblivion.

"Had you told me before you loved me, dear Sophia, I would have never sought the delights of heavenly paradise!" A cry of agony from Jamshed's lips ripped open the heavens. "I would have become the king of love sublime and love immortal. Alas, now I have lost all! The earthly beloved, the heavenly beloved, and the paradise promised to the ones who spurn not the gift of faith and longing." His Jam-e-Jam was shattered to pieces, and the moon up yonder was rent in twain.

The paradise was lost, and the Garden was swallowed by the cup of immortality. Nothing could be felt but the pulse of a universal mystery, where the signet-ring of time had lost its luster of prophecy. Down amidst the ruins of the Garden of Irem, Ibrahim was whirling and screaming. Feverish and demented, he was plucking out his white beard, and spluttering down poetic inspiration from the pages of the Quran!

Irem of the Crimson Desert

Allah is the light of the heavens and the earth
The similitude of his light is as a lustrous niche
Wherein is the lamp, the lamp is in a glass
The glass as if it were a glittering star
It is lit by a blessed tree—an olive
Neither of the east nor of the west
Whose oil will well nigh glow forth
Though fire toucheth it not
Light upon light
Allah guides to His light whomsoever he wills
Allah sets forth parables to men
Allah knows all things full well.   24:35

Ibrahim was laughing hoarsely, singing the songs of illusion, where the gossamer mists were cutting the veils of knowledge, and waters of enchantment were swallowing continents. His soul had suddenly abandoned his body, and all were silence. An ocean of nothingness, glittering and dazzling! This ocean of awesome silence was broken by a song from the sand-dunes of memories.

Now this religion happens to prevail until by that one it is overthrown
Because men dare not live with men alone
But always with another fairytale.   Abu al-Alasa al-Maarri

About the Author

Farzana Moon writes Sufi poetry, historical, biographical Moghul sagas and plays based on the stories from religion and folklore. Published works in the series of her Moghul sagas are: *Babur, The First Moghul In India; The Moghul Exile; Divine Akbar and Holy India; The Moghul Hedonist: Glorious Taj and Beloved Immortal. Answers from Mount Hira*—biography of Prophet Muhammad is published by Dreamcatcher Books. *Holocaust of the East* is published by Cambridge Scholars Publishing. Born and educated in Pakistan, now she is a US citizen.